mother

Hannah Begbie studied Art History at Cambridge University. She went on to become a talent agent, representing BAFTA and Edinburgh Comedy Award-winning writers and comedians for fifteen years until her youngest son was diagnosed with cystic fibrosis.

In 2015 she joined the board of The Cystic Fibrosis Trust, to raise awareness and advocate for the CF community. She also enrolled in The Novel Studio course at City University, winning that year's new writing prize. The book she developed there became her debut novel, *Mother,* which later went on to win the Joan Hessayon Award for New Writers from the RNA. The TV rights were snapped up by Clerkenwell Films.

She lives in north London with her husband, a screenwriter, and their two sons.

@hannahbegbie

mother

HANNAH BEGBIE

HarperCollins*Publishers*

HarperCollins*Publishers*
1 London Bridge Street
London SE1 9GF

www.harpercollins.co.uk

Published by HarperCollins*Publishers* 2018
2

A catalogue record for this book
is available from the British Library

ISBN: 978-0-00-828323-0

This novel is entirely a work of fiction.
The names, characters and incidents portrayed in it are
the work of the author's imagination. Any resemblance to
actual persons, living or dead, events or localities is
entirely coincidental.

Set in Sabon by Palimpsest Book Production Limited,
Falkirk, Stirlingshire

Printed and bound by CPI Group (UK) Ltd, Croydon CR0 4YY

MIX
Paper from
responsible sources
FSC™ C007454

This book is produced from independently certified FSC™ paper
to ensure responsible forest management.

For more information visit: www.harpercollins.co.uk/green

For Tom, my North Star

PROLOGUE

We were a normal family for exactly twenty-five days.

On the second day we brought her home from the hospital in a car seat. We put it down on the black-and-white weave of the living room rug and Dave said, 'I feel like I can breathe again.' Because for most of the pregnancy it was like we had held our breaths.

'Dave, come on. She's almost asleep.' My smile was fading but his was wide and bright like a row of circus bulbs and part of me thought, let him just enjoy it.

'BABY!'

His volume made me flinch. 'Dave, please stop.'

'What? Come on! Mia is here!'

Mia. Found on page 89 of *The Great Big Book of Baby Names* and circled like a bingo number. He kissed me on the forehead and I smiled for him. I kissed Mia and there we were, connected in a Russian doll of kisses. *What a lovely family*, someone looking on might have said.

'It's all right,' he whispered. 'Nothing's going to get us now.'

And I believed him. I really think I did.

1

*   *   *

It was the kind of summer where everyone knew it was going to be a good one, right from the first days of the end of spring. The week she was born, the doorbell rang twice a day with deliveries of fresh-baked muffins, wrapped packages of soft toys, and cards printed with storks, peppered with sequins.

Mum, my sister Caroline, Dave's mum. Our house seemed constantly full of people making the tea, padding in and out of the living room in their socks holding plates of cake, burbling their news. I would look up occasionally, to make a show of listening, but she was always there, cradled in my arms – a tiny person wrapped warm and safe in blankets, peacefully living out her first days in soft, new skin that shone like crushed diamonds.

I am *lucky*, I thought, in the mornings, as Mum emptied the dishwasher and waxed lyrical about the church pews being cleaned with an alternative furniture polish that had given Sarah-from-six-doors-down a terrible thigh rash.

I am so *fortunate*, I thought in the afternoons, as Dave and I walked – no, strolled – in the local park, gripping pram handle and coffee cup, like all the other parents.

A hood and a hat for the blinding sunlight.

Balled socks and folded babygros in neat stacks.

Floral fabric conditioner and frying onions lacing the air and warm, sweet milk everywhere. Bubbling away in me. Poured over the porridge that would feed me, so that I could make yet more milk to feed her. I never felt like an animal, not in the way of feeling hunted or preyed upon, but I also didn't feel any more complicated than an animal. It was hard to explain exactly. Grazing and feeding her. Sun up, sun down.

There were plenty of times when, despite how happy I was, how honestly happy I was, I would start to think about the past. But I could always stop myself, because the important thing was that she was here.

Dave and I had spent ten years together already, looking at each other – across kitchen and restaurant table. Staring and blinking and watching and glancing in bed, meeting rooms, waiting rooms and at parties. De-coding the hidden messages in each other's eyes. We knew every wrinkle, line and tic in each other: the single eyelash that ran counter to the rest. How the face contorted with laughter and tears.

The right time, then, to greet something new, a new version of ourselves with her barely there hair and tense red fists wrapped in a cellular blanket – cellular, like the mathematics paper marked with its complicated workings and rubbings out.

And there were other times, more than I care to remember, when Mia writhed and bobbed and made her warning siren sounds with a rounded mouth. And I worried. Like any mother would. I would pull her away from a feed, the sweat that had once sealed us now escaping, tickling and itching, all the while thinking: She is in pain. Something is hurting her.

'She needs a new nappy, that's all,' Dave would say. 'You're just worried about things going wrong.' That smile again.

Didn't he know that after ten years together you can tell a genuine smile from a fake smile?

Why didn't he say what he meant? *Don't spoil this for us, Cath.*

On the early evening of the twenty-fifth day I drew the curtains against the setting sun and answered a phone call.

'Is this the mother of Baby Freeland?'

Her mother. Hers.

Yes, I belonged to her.

'Mia Freeland is her name now.'

I wanted her tone to change, to lilt into a floral exclamation of how *lovely* a name, but she was hesitant. She told me that her name was Kirsty and she was a health visitor, based at our local GP practice in Terrence Avenue.

'There were some results from the blood test, the heel-prick test,' she said.

I got hold of a flap of skin on the edge of my thumbnail and sucked through my teeth as it tore. *Test.* My four-letter word. Dave and I had failed so many tests already, each time more stinging than the last. But Mia was here now. Our final pass.

'Are you still there?' said Kirsty.

The heel-prick test, yes. They had taken a spot of blood

from Mia's heel when she was only a few days old, like they did with every newborn in the country. I had flinched when the thing like a staple gun had punctured her snow-white skin, so much worse than if it were piercing my own. A card was pressed to this tiny new wound and then lifted away to reveal a roundel of red. Now there were results. They hadn't told me to expect results.

'Yes, I'm here. Do you phone everyone with their results?'

'Not unless there's something, you know, *definite* to say. In Mia's case they are *inconclusive*, which means we need to do more tests. Can you come to Atherton General tomorrow morning at eleven?'

'The hospital?'

'Yes, Atherton General, a bit past Clyde Hill . . . Fourth floor, paediatric outpatients' reception. They'll know to expect you.'

'But what are the tests for?' My stomach twisted and complained.

'Her levels look a bit abnormal.' There was a pause and paper shuffle. 'For cystic fibrosis. I'm putting you on hold for a moment.'

The soft thump of blood drummed its quick new tune in my ears as I googled:

Cystic fibrosis – A genetic disease in which the lungs and digestive system become clogged with thick and sticky mucus . . .

Stomach pain . . .

Trouble breathing . . .

Must be managed with a time-consuming, daily regimen of medication and physiotherapy . . .

Over the years, the lungs become increasingly damaged and eventually stop working properly . . .

Debbie Carfax, twenty-three, was diagnosed with cystic fibrosis at the age of two and has been told she has less than . . .

Catching the common cold could kill this young man with cystic fibrosis as he waits for a life-saving lung transplant . . .

End-stage cystic fibrosis and how to manage the final days . . .

One in every 2,500 babies born in the UK has cystic fibrosis . . .

Average age of death . . .

Like drowning . . .

Just breathe.

A piece of hold music droned on, vanilla and classical, chosen to calm interminable situations.

I could feel the adrenalin rise inside me. Everything sharpening, narrowing, ready for flight as I stared at that single question.

Her levels looked abnormal.

I understood that there was a level to everything.

Under the right level, you drowned.

Above the right level, you overflowed.

Finally, a new crackle as the hold music was killed.

'Yvonne says it'll be something called a sweat test. You'll need to bring lots of blankets for the baby to make her sweat. Do remember that. Blankets. And maybe some snacks and mags to pass the time?' I had no time to reply before she said, 'And make sure that your husband is with you. Have you got the address? Paediatric outpatients . . .'

'Yes. Thank you.'

'Best of luck.' And with that, Kirsty was gone.

I hung up, the appointment details scribbled on the back of a tea-bag box with a free T-shirt promotion.

Make sure your husband is with you is the same thing as saying: *Are you sitting down?* It's what a person says before they give you the news that will knock you to the floor and turn out the lights.

The consultant with a blunt fringe took a deep breath before she said, 'I am sorry to have to tell you . . .'

The hospital, God, just the smell of the place – the mashed potatoes and disinfectant and newly opened bandages – the only way to have kept that air from crawling into my cells would have been to stop breathing altogether.

I threw up when she told us, but I made it to the sink. Still holding Mia, there was no time to pass her to anyone.

Everything emptied.

Chapter 1

Late one afternoon, on a day that was hot and thick and had been promising a storm for too long, I boarded a red London bus. Three passengers on the top deck, dotted far from each other, heads bowed to their phones. Windows closed, greenhouse conditions. I pushed hard at my nearest window pane and was the only one to flinch when it opened with a bang, like something being fired.

I sat, felt the scratching nylon pile beneath my fingertips and resented the electric blue and fluorescent orange chosen to cheer the commuter. *Don't tell me how to feel with your upbeat seat fabric! I will make my own decisions about how I feel.*

And I felt fine, actually. Probably better than in the three weeks and six days since diagnosis because now I was on my way to *do* something. I was on my way to meet people who shared my new language, to ask them: *What is this island we have been exiled to? How long have you been waiting for the boats and how do we bring them here quicker?*

Mum would be pleased because the kind of thing she

might have said if it hadn't sounded so harsh in the circumstances was, *You're a mother now! Take responsibility!* Then I could say to her, *But that's exactly what I'm doing! Taking responsibility for my family. And my feelings.*

Because the truth was that no one else – no husband, doctor, sister or friend – was actually *doing* anything to change the fundamental facts of it and so it was up to me. That was how I felt.

The bus sped through the paint-splatted, urine-stained, poster-torn mess of a city with its crammed stacks and storeys, its ripped holes and soldered joints. If it were up to me, I'd wipe the whole lot away with a bulldozer and start again.

Learn to clean up your own mess, Mum used to say when I was growing up.

I'm doing it, I'm doing it. Once I've finished, can I go out?

I was dealing with the mess. I was taking action.

The consultant with the blunt fringe had said: *Delta F508 is the name of the mutated gene that you both carry. Mia has taken a copy from each of you.*

Then I had said, *She didn't take them. We gave them to her.*

She'd said something nice like we mustn't blame ourselves. But who else was there?

I had plugged Mia into my own life source and helped her build her heart and lungs and organs using my blood and my oxygen and my energy.

I was her mother. I had given her life.
I was her mother. I had given her a death sentence.
Those were the fundamental facts of it.

I rested my head against the bus window, trying to stop my stomach from swimming and heaving, studying the tiny greased honeycomb prints of other people's skin on the glass. I watched the sunlight thin under gathering clouds and reached for my belly, longing for the solid, reassuring curve of pregnancy and life – instead feeling fabric and loose, scooped-out flesh. Evidence of that life released into the world, my genie out of her bottle. And now I wished and wished and wished.

The panicky stuff had started small – the hours lost to finding my phone (in the fridge) and my keys (in the door). Those things might have been fine, the kind of thing a person does when they aren't sleeping enough, but in the back of my mind I recognized the pattern in it all – the way my thoughts splintered and the tears came and any light in me felt dimmed by a choking smoke. But I couldn't dwell too much on patterns and pasts because there was too much going on, what with the nappies and the feeds and trying to quell Mia's tears and my tears and the anxieties of other people when they said to me *How can we help?* as I forced a smile and struggled to find an answer for them.

I got more frustrated and panicked as the words people

spoke (mother, mother-in-law, sister, friends and other in-laws) rang hollow, fell flat, downright collapsed on the road to meet me.

Pavlova and lasagne? How lovely! It was kind of them, honestly it was, to think that they could change things with a meringue and a béchamel. They weren't to know that, along with so much else, taste had been blunted in me.

The letters people wrote were sending me into a tailspin. The last time I'd even got a letter, in proper ink on paper, had been after Dad's funeral. After someone had died, for God's sake.

One of them started, 'Of all the people for this to happen to . . .' It made me think of a film I once saw, 'Of all the gin joints, in all the towns, in all the world . . .' People were amazed by the news. Privately relieved, some of them, I think . . . because statistics had to happen to someone. That's the nature of the beast. My misfortune kept them safer. At least some good was coming of this.

But none of them did anything. None of them changed anything.

I wanted to throw up on the deck of that bus, like it was the only way I would rid myself of that grinding, persistent angst.

Fat drops of rain had started to fall and I was glad of it. I would be able to wash my face in them. Feel their chill on my skin.

As my stop approached I made my way to the top-deck

stairs. The driver braked suddenly, before the lights and before the stop, and if I hadn't been holding on so tight I would have fallen headfirst. *A double tragedy*, people would have said of our family. And then, when Mia was old enough, they would have said stupid things about chance and randomness and accidents – things they thought would reassure her. Leaving her equipped to deal with her mother's death-by-bus-stairs.

A ridiculous balancing of deaths, one stupid but fast, the other lifelong, grinding and airless.

I had thought about running away, every single day since diagnosis. I had a credit card and phone – all that I needed to set up life elsewhere.

She loved you, they would tell her. *She just couldn't . . . some people simply don't know how . . .*

It must happen all the time: leaving it for someone else to deal with, telling yourself that someone else will be better equipped to meet the needs of the child. Believing it too, maybe.

Would you teach yourself to forget their face? Would that be the key to it?

My feet made hollow, violent hammering sounds as I ran down the stairs, unable to disembark quick enough into the rain, people on the lower deck looking alarmed and suspicious as I banged at the closed sliding doors with flat palms; *Get me off this fucking bus!* I couldn't breathe. I was going to be sick.

Chapter 2

All the windows were opened wide in the main meeting room of Cystic Fibrosis Now's HQ. It smelt of cleaning product and the kind of damp and mossy earthiness that emerges from old walls with the onset of rain. The lighting was stripped and white, headache-bright. Chairs were arranged in a circle, ten or twelve in total perhaps, and the carpet was office-block blue-grey. The few people who had arrived before me stood in pairs. Were they officials who knew what was what, or were they new parents like me? I twisted a button round on my raincoat, as far as it would go, wondering when the threads that anchored it might snap, considering what would happen if I didn't have the strength and the words for the strangers in that room, if I left that room a few hours later with nothing changed.

I searched the room. A tea urn on a trestle table. Everyone congregated around tea. It gave you something to do while you found the words. Make the tea, drink the tea or beat the walls and chew your fingers. I went to the table and began to make tea I didn't want.

Teaspoons knocked on the sides of mugs and biscuit wrappers crackled. Conversation was at a constant low murmur, as if a church service was about to begin.

'Can you pass the sugar, please?' A woman leaned across the trestle table and touched me on the sleeve. She was petite and she carried a plastic mac dripping rainwater in the crook of her arm. 'I know I shouldn't, I'm trying to lose a bit,' she said. I felt my shoulders drop as she smiled and the thin skin beneath her eyes crinkled to reveal pale, unblended smears of make-up – the kind applied to cover dark shadows. 'But I can't do tea without it now.'

Sugary tea is what they brought me after I was sick in that hospital clinic. They let me finish the tea, and then the lessons began. Administer this, administer that, was about the shape of it. Administer medicine to help her absorb nutrients because her digestive organs are clogged with mucus. Administer physiotherapy to get rid of the mucus on her lungs. Administer antibiotics to protect her from the ravages of environmental bacteria that might stick in the lungs and cause damage. By the end Dave had taken copious notes, even drawing a bar chart at one stage. He was strong when it came to administrative tasks so I suppose it made a kind of sense for him to pretend his daughter was a problem that might be solved methodically.

I passed the sugar bowl and smiled. 'Are you a . . . ?' I tried, faltered because even memories of numbness lodged in my throat like tickling kapok.

'Parent, yes. I've got a one-year-old boy.' She smiled. 'With CF, obviously. You?'

'Two-month-old girl. Just diagnosed.'

She put down her cup after dropping in two lumps. 'Amazing you're here. I was still weeping in my pyjamas at your stage. My little bugger didn't sleep at all, which made things ten times worse.'

'How is your little boy? If you don't mind me asking?' I asked her the question before I realized I didn't want to hear the answer, at least not if it was about hospitals, or worse.

'Doing very well. Started walking the other week and it's adorable: he looks like a penguin. Kind of tips side to side.' She put her arms on her side and moved her neck, and we both smiled.

'What about his medicines?' I said, emboldened.

'Oh, spits them out, hates them, but you find a way to get them in. My husband covers that kind of stuff. Amazing how creative you can be. It's a shame he's not here tonight, but he's got a rotten cough and nobody needs that from us. He hates missing things like this. What's your partner like? Is he doing OK?'

'Endlessly practical, my Dave.' I smiled weakly. 'He's got a list for medicines, a list for before breakfast, one for after breakfast. A list to keep track of his socks. He loves making lists.'

'Sounds useful to have around the house.'

'Yes, he is. Tonight he's at home training his mum to look after Mia . . .'

'Wow.'

'It's so he can go to football. He didn't want to come here. Says he'd rather talk to his friends than a bunch of strangers.' She raised her eyebrows and I worried then, about being disloyal. 'Don't get me wrong . . . I don't want to be unfair. Being so practical is the way he's always been and it definitely has its uses. His ability to categorize and look at, you know, what really matters, took the stress out of organizing our wedding. I don't always agree with . . . anyway, the real thing here is that he wants to take Mia swimming at some point. It's on one of his lists.'

'Oh, that's good,' she said, dunking her biscuit. Her face was soft and kind and calm and being like that seemed such an impossible achievement in the circumstances that she was god-like to me. 'It took me and my husband ages to work out what we were doing.'

My fingers traced a seam inside my pocket, feeling its ridge, searching for another thread to unpick as I fought the urge to grasp her arm and say, *I'm so glad you said it takes a long time because I'm still waiting, I am.* But I held back because I wasn't sure whether by 'doing' she meant the practical stuff or the emotional stuff you 'work out' together as a couple.

To talk about being a couple with someone I had only known for a minute might be too much, too intense, but

I wanted her to say more so I said, 'Sometimes I'm not sure how much my husband gets it . . . I mean, at the moment, you know. As we work out . . . what we're doing.'

Dave was the one who, in that clinic, holding his full cup of sugary tea, had said, *How do you cure it?* And I'd felt so sad to watch the penny drop. He wasn't one for in-depth research at the best of times and after we'd got the call, he'd been the one to say, *It's probably nothing.* And I'd tried to believe him. Then, in that room, I'd wanted to hold his hand when his eyes filled with alarmed tears as the consultant said, 'There is no cure.' But his gaze was fixed, watching the moment of impact when they said our daughter would have a record with them for life.

And then he asked for a pen so he could take some notes.

I put my mug down on the table. 'When the consultant – you know, the consultant at . . .'

'The hospital?'

'Yes, the one at the hospital, but the one specifically at . . .'

'Diagnosis?' She looked up at me, hands curled around her cup, chewing her biscuit thoughtfully as I spoke.

'She told us to get rid of our fish tank because the pump aerosolizes bacteria from its stagnant water. She told us to get rid of it at the same time as saying we should make sure Mia avoids mud and wet sand and lakes and ponds and rivers. I mean, it felt like she was saying avoid life. Avoid fun.'

'It's all a balance.'

'Dave said maybe we could hide the tank in the roof. Practical, I guess. But when bacteria is out there, I mean, when something is out there, it's out there and it can do damage. Isn't that right?' I unbuttoned my raincoat from round my neck to make space for breath, for words. 'So I said, *Dave, let's throw the fucking fish away*. I thought, you've just been told your daughter will live a half-life and most of what she wants to do will be off-limits and all you can think about is where we house the fish?'

'Hey, hey,' said the woman, laying down her mug and grasping my arm. My eyes stung and my cheeks tickled where they were damp. 'That's men. Isn't it? Not to be a feminist or anything, but they do tend to take their time, you know, processing things. That's how they are.'

A hand held at last.

The rest of the words I wanted to say were desperate to get out of the airless place they had been living inside me, but I kept my mouth shut, sealed it all in, all the reckless damage those words wanted to do to me.

'You should help yourself to a couple of those biccies,' she said. 'The sugar will do you good. But come and find a seat first.' She led me to a chair at the circle. 'They're about to start.' I looked round, to smile and thank her for her kindness, but her attention was already turned to her phone and to finding her own seat.

I rubbed at my tired eyes and wiped where mascara had run with the pads of my fingers, remembering why I hadn't worn make-up in weeks.

Another woman walked into the room at the kind of speed that suggested her day had a momentum that could not be broken. She waved a greeting at someone and settled down in the circle with a clipboard. I laid my coat on the back of my chair and smoothed down my T-shirt, canary yellow – too bright, too try-hard in a room of people shaking off navy rain macs, brushing down grey trousers, adjusting khaki suede boots and pulling out black pens from dark bags.

'Welcome to our biannual new parents' meeting,' said the clipboard woman loudly and abruptly. 'My name's Joanna and I'd like to thank you all for coming, both those for whom the experience is still very new, and those who have lived with cystic fibrosis for a long time and are here to show their support tonight. We do appreciate you taking the time to help newly diagnosed families find a path through what can be a very challenging period.'

I looked over at the woman I had cried in front of and she gave me a thin smile before gazing out at the rain still hammering the window panes.

Joanna swiped at her ponytail. 'A bit of health and safety first. Our cross-infection policy is very strict. For the benefit of newer parents I'll quickly go over it. The longer you have cystic fibrosis, the more likely it is that your lungs will become colonized with disease-causing bacteria, some of which can become resistant to antibiotics and get harder to treat. We don't want those infections passing from one patient to another. That's why people with CF can't mix.' She adjusted the position of her biro at the helm of the clipboard. 'It's very important to understand that indirect transmission is a possibility too because certain bacteria can survive for hours, sometimes even days, on clothes and skin and surfaces. So I know it sounds rude, but we encourage you *not* to shake hands with fellow parents because you may be the unknowing vehicle for some nasty bugs. Use the antibacterial gel provided when you leave the event. I don't want to sound grim but we think it's crucial that we get this bit right.'

Everyone adjusted themselves for comfort and checked their phones one last time.

'Onwards! I want the agenda to be driven by you. Let's start by discovering what your main concerns are.' She motioned to a man in khaki cargo pants and a black T-shirt. 'Mark, perhaps you could expand on what you were saying to me the other day about diagnosis being a steep learning curve?'

Mark looked to be in his mid-thirties and losing his hair. He cleared his throat and sat forward on his chair, scratching his forehead, talking to his lumpy leather boots. 'There seems to be so much to get your head around. What I'd like to know is how you tell a normal cough from the kind of cough that might signal an infection?' He caught the eye of a few people around the circle, waiting for an answer. 'I don't know . . . that's it, I suppose.' I could see the bright but shy flicker of hope in his eyes as he voiced a concern that until then had probably circled his head like a bat at night with the relentless pit-pat flapping of wings.

'Yes, I worry about that too,' said a woman hiding in an oversized cardigan, 'but the other thing . . . the thing that keeps me up? Like makes me insomniac, and I've never been a great sleeper and now I'm like the world's worst ever sleeper, it pisses my bloke off no end because I'm tossing and turning . . . The thing for me is the antibiotics? Everyone's always going on about taking less of them, right? Because, like, you don't really need them most of the time, right? You go to the doc and they're like *It's a virus* and they leave it because they don't want everyone on antibiotics and making it so that none of them work. But what about our kids?' She shuffled on her seat. 'If our kids are on them a whole lifetime, to treat and protect them . . . well, they say it in the news all the time. What happens when the antibiotics stop working, like what Joanna said before about the bugs getting resistant. That's proper bad news for our kids, isn't it?'

The charity worker nodded her head. 'Yes, it's a serious issue.' She stood up, pen in hand, and wrote BACTERIAL RESISTANCE and COUGHS on the whiteboard in cramped letters. 'We'll cover this. Any other questions to get on to the board?'

'Does the physiotherapy hurt them?' said a man quickly, the white-skinned bones of his knees jutting through torn jeans. 'All that bashing at their chest to loosen the mucus in their lungs. You never know with a tiny baby. They cry all the time anyway. Our eldest saw me do it the other day and he started crying because he thought I was hurting his little sister. And then his little sister started crying. It was chaos.'

'I think it's so sad.' A woman with a thick fringe and a broad Scottish accent spoke. 'How are these kids with CF going to find a community to support each other when this risk of them cross-infecting each other stops them from meeting? I know we've got the internet, but it's not the same as face-to-face. Seeing the whites of a person's eyes, right? It's lonely for them. Can we at least get them Skyping or something?'

CHEST PERCUSSION – HURTS?

The squeak of pen on whiteboard.

COMMUNITY/SUPPORT. The charity worker turned to consult her notes and I looked at those faces, wide and afraid, all their fears out there, swimming around trying to find which way up the surface was.

I understood it, I did, and yet most of their questions were practical and could be worked out by asking doctors and looking at the internet. I knew; I'd spent hours researching that kind of thing.

In the days after diagnosis Dave often found me in the dark parts of night gazing at the shining bright of my computer screen as if it were an open casket of jewels. The talk boards, news sites and pharmaceuticals headlines that kept me enchanted, appalled and gripped, an infinite reel of possibilities and answers and endings.

Cystic fibrosis sufferer Stacey marries her childhood sweetheart only days before her death . . .

One in three die waiting for a lung transplant . . .

The first time Dave found me like that, he sat with me and cried and said, *Well, this feels like old times.* The second time he found me, he kissed me on the head and cleared up the research papers at my feet. The third time he stood at the doorway and offered to make me tea. The fourth time he said he should cut off the broadband, like I was a teenager that needed to be told a thing or two. Then I wasn't just sad, I was angry. *But we have to do something*, I'd said, gripping the duvet or my jumper sleeve or the skin on my arm. That's when he said something like all we could do was try and keep her healthy, day to day, and that we should do something useful like enrol her in swimming lessons until the doctors told us to try something new.

After that, things mostly ended with me crying and him saying he'd put the kettle on and that we should talk again when I'd calmed down.

But we never did, and soon enough all the times I cried and he put the kettle on became one big blur and he'd pick a phrase to console me, one plucked from a carousel of options that turned and turned:

Are you all right?
I don't know what you mean.
There's no magic wand.
You should get an early night.
Did you speak to your sister yet?
Things will seem better in the morning.
I won't be out late.

'I feel lonely,' I said to the empty floor at the centre of the circle. The words took me by surprise. 'And I feel breathless, all the time, like I can't keep up with everything that has to happen to keep my daughter healthy. It's only been a few weeks – God, she's only two months old, but already it feels like a lifetime. I feel like I'll never get to where I hope I'm going because that place doesn't exist yet. There's no end in sight. This is our life now. Constant medication and physiotherapy and protecting her from endless threats hidden in normal places. And then the waiting . . . waiting for the day it gets worse and worse.'

On another day I might have stopped there because I saw the faces of the people around me and one person looked away from me, like she was embarrassed, but I didn't, I couldn't. 'I . . . I don't know if I can live like that. And so my question is, if I don't know how to live with this illness, well . . . how am I supposed to teach my child to live with it?'

A crow cawed outside. Maybe it had been there a while, but we all heard it now in the silence I had made. The charity worker crossed her arms as she mused on how to translate my sentences into a single penned and capitalized word. Several throats cleared and for a moment I wondered if what I'd said would be passed over. Too awkward, too ruined. I felt bad and exposed and a failure for not having the right words to share with these strangers.

'That's easy,' said a man in a blue suit sitting opposite me. His voice was clear and deep, he was clean-shaven, broad-shouldered and slim, his shirt white and his tie orange. He held a pen and pad and nothing else. He looked so tidy, so unencumbered by his life.

'Teach your child not to be an arsehole,' he said. There was an amused 'Ha!' from somewhere inside the circle. 'That matters. And then work to cure CF. That way you'll raise a healthy adult with half-decent manners.'

A relieved ripple of amusement travelled the room and everyone looked gratefully in his direction. But my heart crumpled into disappointment at his flippancy.

'And while you're waiting for their adulthood and the arrival of their manners and the cure,' he said, seemingly emboldened by everyone's laughter. 'While you're waiting for all that, I suggest you drink vodka and dance to Phil Collins.'

More laughter filled the room. Joanna uncrossed her arms as if she was enjoying herself too, and meantime I was even more annoyed.

'And what are you supposed to do . . .' I said over the laughter. 'What are you supposed to do,' I said, louder now, 'if mixing a bottle of antibiotics feels like quantum physics because your brain is exhausted from being up all night worrying? I dream about flowers on her funeral casket.' My words were piling out at speed again, and they were getting louder, so that by the end I was almost shouting, as if this was my last chance to ever be heard.

The Scotswoman nodded gently. 'It's all right, pet, we get it,' she said.

The man smiled and then his brow creased. 'Sorry, I didn't mean to be crass. I'm not denying it's hard. It's very hard. All I'm saying is, there is light. You can experience being a normal parent.'

'But how? How are we supposed to dance around knowing how badly all this is going to end? I don't see it.' I slid forward on my seat, confronting him in a way I had never confronted anyone before. I wanted to know how and why his smile was so full and so very alive.

Everyone in the room seemed to hold their breaths in one collective lung-filling exercise.

'I dance to Phil Collins in the knowledge that all my friends and family are going to die. All of us. Life is short and Phil is a gift.' There was more laughter as the man looked to me for a response and, perhaps seeing something in my face, changed tack. 'You need to remember that it's different to the way it was even five years ago. There's a lot of hope now. There are so many new treatments coming out of America and they will be game-changing for the CF community. Your kid's going to be OK.'

'Yes, thank you, that's useful,' said the charity worker, cutting him off when I wish she hadn't, but she'd picked an opportunity to slash through a conversation that was awkward at best and threatened to derail her whiteboard bullet points at worst. 'There is indeed a wonderful pipeline of drugs in development. Let's talk through some of the more practical things you've all raised, like physio and antibiotics and psychological support, and then we can end with the treatments on the horizon. I think we have a nice full agenda.'

PIPELINE OF NEW DRUGS.

The man in the navy suit and citric orange tie pressed the pen hard to the page of his notebook and wrote quickly, as if the words were too important to lose. I would have craned my neck to read them, had I been sitting closer.

As the event drew to a close everyone gathered back at the trestle table but I buttoned up my raincoat to leave. To return to Mia. To cuddle her.

I turned towards the door but the man in the suit and orange tie stopped me, holding out his hand to shake. 'My name's Richard.'

'Ah, Flippant Richard.' I held out my hand. 'Cath. Pleased to meet you.'

He grasped mine heartily. 'I bet you're only slightly pleased to meet me, at best, but I am honestly pleased to meet you. And I'm sorry about earlier. I've been living with my daughter's CF a long time. You find a way of looking at it, of living with it. But my way doesn't suit everyone.'

'I was probably a bit . . .' I looked down, taken aback by his new humility. I saw his polished shoes and it made me wish I'd worn the red ones I'd bought while pregnant that were still wrapped in tissue paper.

'My daughter is a teenager now. Black humour has probably become my . . . Anyway, I wanted to apologize for behaving badly.'

'How's your daughter doing?'

'She's doing very well. She's healthy and . . . stroppy but happy. Her name's Rachel. But what about you? Look . . . what I wanted to say in that discussion – and I didn't, because I wasn't sure it applied to the rest of them – was that you have to believe. Believe that your daughter will be cured. Be positive. Know this can end happily and then help make it happen. I'll continue to pitch Phil Collins as a good soundtrack to that endeavour though. Some of his work, particularly with Genesis, is very emotional.'

I smiled as I turned the possibility of feeling differently about CF around in my mind, like I was examining the facets of a diamond. I looked back at him and his face was an invitation to say anything, so I told him, 'Diagnosis felt like failure to me. Perhaps because the consultant looked like my old maths teacher and I always did badly in maths. She had exactly the same fringe.' He laughed.

'They told me my baby's sweat test scores were in the nineties and eighties and the first thing I thought was, who doesn't want 87 per cent on a test? But then they said those scores actually meant her symptoms would be severe. Requiring daily pills and antibiotics and physio. High scores equals bad results. Fail.'

'Your world's been turned upside down. I get it. What's your kid's name?'

'Mia.'

'Mia will be more than fine. You,' he said, 'will also be fine.'

My eyes stung, staring at him like that: like I didn't want to miss anything about that moment. The idea that she might not . . .

I looked at his suit and how well it fit him, at his clear skin and dark eyes, at the clean and scruffy coal-black hair.

'But is that true?' I asked him.

'I don't know you well enough to bother lying to you.' He had a smile that was generous and full of china tea-cup white teeth.

I laughed and sneezed, covering my face. 'Sorry, I'm getting a cold. It's not bad but . . .' I scooped a plastic bottle of antibacterial gel out of my handbag and poured it into my palms.

'I should use some of that too. You shook my hand.'

I looked up and we locked eyes. 'Sorry, I forgot. We weren't supposed to do that because of cross infection. Sorry.'

'They're only being careful. It makes sense: as a charity, as an expert in the field of CF, it's their responsibility to give you the worst-case scenario. But just because something could happen, doesn't mean it will. Right?'

'Right.' And I smiled again because there was something about him that insisted on it.

'The research is still being done and it's not conclusively proven that bugs can transfer from patient to patient via a third party *and* survive long enough to cause symptoms. It's a bit of a stretch, in my opinion.'

I saw a loose thread at his collar and a patch of stubble he had missed.

'I've read some of the papers,' I said. 'There actually is some evidence to suggest . . .' He raised his eyebrows as I spoke and it occurred to me that though I may have read a lot, he had experienced CF for years longer than I had. Of course he knew more. 'In any event, you really don't want to take my cold back home to your daughter.'

He smiled. 'No, I do not. She'd kill me if she missed any more school.'

I poured antibacterial gel in to both our hands. I rubbed it into my palms and then around my fingertips as the CF nurses had taught me to do. My broken cuticles stung.

'I suppose people aren't used to meeting without shaking hands. Without touching,' he said. 'But it can be done. Life with CF can be done. You just have to find new ways.'

He looked at me then, like he recognized me. Perhaps

I looked like someone from his past. I had one of those faces, lots of people said it.

Joanna's voice tore through the moment. 'A few final things, folks.' She held her arms aloft and called out again to address the still chattering room, ponytail swinging obediently in her slipstream. 'Please, folks! A moment of your time before we have to lock up for the evening! Thank you all for coming. There is more advice and further tips for getting involved in fundraising on the website. And our annual conference is coming up in the last week of August. That's in only six weeks' time and we're still hoping that the parent of a newly diagnosed baby will speak. Please do give me a shout if you're interested. We want to make sure that all the research talks are balanced with the real-life stories of people actually living with the illness. Thank you, and good night!'

'I need to go,' I said, glancing at my watch face. Mia would need a feed.

'Me too.' Richard walked with me.

'Is your husband babysitting?' he said, opening the fire door for me to step through.

'Kind of. Not exactly. My mother-in-law. She's trying, I guess.'

Outside the rain had stopped, the rush-hour traffic had thinned and soon the sun would set. The air was still warm but clearer for having been washed by the rain.

'Let me get you a taxi,' he said, as he tried to hail one without an orange light.

'No, it's OK. Thank you.'

'You should think about talking at the conference. You're the kind of person they need.'

'The kind of person who rambles about how they don't understand anything any more?'

'Someone who's honest, and brave, but doesn't know all the answers.'

'But I don't know *any* of the answers.'

'Exactly my point.'

My stomach knotted. 'I have to go. It's getting late.'

He touched me lightly on the sleeve as I turned to leave. 'My daughter and I are very close. There's nothing I wouldn't do for her and CF has given me countless opportunities to fight for her. To make her proud of me. In a strange way, it's been a gift. Be brave. Go out and fight for your cub's life.'

He looked down at his feet then, overcome by emotion or else sensing that he had gone too far – I didn't know which.

But he was quick to look up, smiling, recovered. He loosened his very orange tie and undid a button and I thought, yes, he's right about going out to fight.

An answer, at last.

'Here, before I forget.' He tore a piece of paper out of his notepad. 'It's a list of Phil Collins' most upbeat ballads to cheer you up . . . and also my contact details in case you want to run that draft speech by me.' He folded the page and handed it to me.

'Thanks, but I'm thinking I might do better starting with a fundraising cake sale than standing up and talking to a whole load of people.'

'Like tonight? Tonight wasn't all bad, was it?'

'Goodbye.' I smiled.

'Let me know about that speech. Or if you just need other advice, help, whatever.'

I stood on the kerb and watched him hail another cab – a single sharp swing of his arm to command its attention, after which it cut through a lane of traffic to meet him. Its orange light flicked off and I heard him say, 'Hampstead.' A mumbled address that I didn't catch, then, 'That's right, near the running track.' He took his seat and looked out of the window at me.

I smiled, waved, then looked away first because I'd been taught never to look as desperate as you feel.

Chapter 3

I bounced on the back of my heels and glanced down the canned goods aisle for any sign of my mother. We'd arranged to meet by the custard but then I was early, much earlier than I usually was to meet a mother who was always, without fail, on time.

We'd last spoken a few weeks ago, the morning after the parents' meeting, when I'd telephoned to tell her about this *thing* that I'd met some people at and that I'd felt positive about. But I hadn't got into the details of the *thing* before she asked me who had babysat that night. I hadn't been prepared for the silence that followed when I told her it was Dave's mum. I hadn't been prepared for how bad I'd feel when the conversation ended without her knowing anything more about the *thing*.

In the end I'd been the one to break the silence by calling her after ten days and telling her that she was needed.

I pointed the trolley in the direction of the home products aisle and checked Mia was still comfortable and curled into my chest, still safe and snug in the soft hold and stretch of the sling. I held my ear close enough for it to be tickled by the soft fuzz on her head, which smelt of warm milk and clean new skin, and listened to the snuffling sounds she made before sleep. I set off at a slow pace, keen to deliver her into a heavy slumber so I could get a head start on buying the bleach.

Above me a luminescent sign waved on cold breezes – on it, a scrawl in thick black text, silently shouting:

Promotion. Buy One Get One Free.

Just buy the bloody tinned peaches.

Don't say we don't do anything for you.

And I wondered how Mum would be that afternoon.

You buy bleach like other people buy milk, she'd said to me the other week as she beheld five empty bottles of the stuff lying in the recycling box like a gang of defeated bowling pins. And she was right – we used it so much nowadays to keep an army of disease-causing bacteria in retreat: MRSA in the fruit bowl, E. coli in the toilet – but the way she'd said it had sounded like we were being hysterical.

I arrived at my aisle and began filling the trolley with soft bricks of antibacterial wipes. A long time ago, five years or more, Dave and I had taken a set of glorious supermarket shopping trips nestled within a set of equally glorious sunny days when we had filled most of a trolley with bleach and wipes and floor cleaner. Once upon a time those products had been used to clean and polish the big new house we'd found to fill and decorate with candle-holder, casserole pot wedding gifts. The same house in which we'd planned Dave's new plumbing business, discussing his dreams of one admin assistant and fifteen plumbers by the second year, laying out the budget sheets on a family-sized kitchen table. The same big house that would accommodate our shared dream of two, three, perhaps four children.

Products to buff a shining dream!

Products to bury mortal threats!

Back then we'd wiped away the ghosts of the previous occupants – eradicating their food smells and the stains of their lives with nuclear yellow floor cleaner, bars of sugar soap and piles of scouring blocks. Then, in another glorious trip, we'd filled another trolley at the DIY shop – this time with sandpaper, paint samples (cerulean, slate and rose white) and plastic-sheathed brushes. *Three children or four?* we'd asked each other.

The sky's the limit!

Then we waited in our new house. And those big spaces accumulated dust and spider legs, and the paintbrushes remained unopened.

And then I had thought: All right, maybe not four or even three children, as Dave employed his sixth plumber and thought about getting that office help.

We put down our paintbrushes and started having tests instead. Juggling the mood swings from hormone injections – too much! too little! – and the mood dips, and the terrible grinding disappointment of it all.

And, later still, when I'd lost count of the plumbers on Dave's burgeoning books, we said: *Maybe one would be enough. One child, and a spare room?*

I'd travelled back and forth to the hospital on the number 8 bus. And in between appointments there was still the matter of getting to work on time and the dentist and the things people said, oh the things they said, the work appraisals and office politics, and the nausea and the bloating, the making time for 'us' and feeding ourselves.

Up until then, we'd always taken it in turns to cook, to surprise each other at dinner with the way Camembert didn't work with chicken as expected, or how passionfruit worked better than expected with chocolate. And wine. Always too much wine! But then the tests and the waiting for results took up lots of energy. Something had to go. It's not like we stopped having dinner. We still had dinner. Dinners at home, dinners out, aborted dinners, miscarried dinners. But they were increasingly silent and, I suppose less surprising because we knew by then that chicken did not work with Camembert. The point was that we were still sitting at that table together, the point was that *in the middle of it all we hadn't forgotten about us*.

All the false starts. The recoveries. Starting all over again. No end.

Not for years.

'Cooee!' Mum called to me from the end of the aisle, waving a cauliflower in the air. 'I've been here an age.'

She was inspecting the loose potatoes like an archaeologist with a new find when I arrived at her side. 'Looked for you everywhere. We did say the custard and there you were, daydreaming by the floor mops, so I thought I'd make a head start on the fruit and veg essentials.'

She had once been tall, statuesque even. Now I spoke down to a silver-gold helmet of hair. 'Thanks for coming shopping with me. It's hard . . . with Mia. She's fussy a lot of the time so having you here, it's . . .'

'Don't be silly. It's nice to be helping somehow.' She made space in the trolley for the potatoes, nestling them between a bag of onions and a bag of apples. She had always been strategic like that. A knack for not bruising soft things.

Then she turned to me and laid her cold palms on my cheeks. 'You're always so proud. Like your bloody father, God rest his soul. It's that Scottish DNA. You think you can do it on your own but there aren't many who can do that and the sensible ones don't even try. If your father had complained a bit more then maybe he'd still be here. Oh dear.' She turned away from me to study a row of mangoes. 'Look at these. Obviously hard as rocks!'

She knew I hated it when she talked about Dad's death.

'I'm not being proud,' I said. 'And I don't want to do any of this on my own. The opposite, really, but the thing is that I'm finding people and what they say, well . . . quite hard. You know what Dad was like. He'd have found a way of laughing about it all, or at least he'd have something to say—'

'I'll tell you exactly what he'd be saying now.' I flinched and a little boy looked over from the lemons towards Mum. 'I'll tell you exactly what he'd be saying now,' she said more softly. 'From that pedestal made of cloud and bloody sunshine you have him sitting on.'

'I don't—'

Mum snapped her handbag shut, having pulled out a carefully folded tissue. 'He'd say there's no use in dwelling. That it's time to focus on the positive and the plans you can make. Work out what on earth you're doing with your life.' She found it easier to channel the things she wanted to say to me through my dead dad. 'Dear oh dear, what on earth are the grapes doing under the satsumas?'

I rescued the grapes from under the satsumas. 'I can't think about what I do next. I struggle to plan for tomorrow. I don't, I can't think about next year or the future in general, I—'

'You never could plan, and that's why time ends up passing. It slips away from you. Always has.'

Mum had never been shy voicing her opinion of my IVF treatments, coming close to blaming my failure to get pregnant naturally on my general habit of tardiness. A failure of the uterus to make up its bloody mind.

'I need to get my head around this situation. I've still got nine months of maternity leave left to decide what I do about my job and if I go back and—'

'Last time you showed any ambition was when your dad was around and as he's not here, I'm merely doing what he would have done. Encouraging you.' She dabbed under her eyes with the tissue. Air conditioning always made them water. 'But I've done a terrible job, haven't I? Nothing's moved on. You haven't so much as researched new vocations. Office management clearly doesn't suit you – your words, not mine. And so what about the inland revenue? I saw something in the supplements about them looking for heaps more tax inspectors.'

'I hate numbers, Mum. They're the main reason I don't like my existing job.'

'So useful to have a head for numbers in this world. Oh dear . . .' She balled the tissue in her hand and looked around, eyes wide with panic: it was a moment before I realized it was because she couldn't see an accessible bin. I took the tissue from her and crammed it into my own pocket.

'It's not up to you to have the answers,' I said softly.

'I feel terribly disappointed for you.'

One. Two. Three. Four. Five.

If you're disappointed tell me it's because your grand-daughter will die before she has even lived, or that you lost your husband before his time, not because I don't get on with office spreadsheet software.

Six. Seven. Eight.

Breath. Breath.

Then reply:

'You don't need to feel disappointed, Mum.'

'And you look exhausted. Though this light is very unflattering. Come on, let's get more fruit and veg into you.' She piled courgettes into the crook of one arm and hooked a bunch of bananas with her free hand.

'Thanks,' I said. 'But Dave doesn't like bananas so we don't buy them.' She laid the bananas back with a sigh. 'Although I saw some banana milk in his bag the other day, so that could have changed? We're not getting the chance to catch up on that kind of thing . . . or anything much.' Mum hadn't interrupted me so I kept going. 'I honestly don't feel like talking about anything at the moment.'

She was rolling lychees between her palms like Chinese stress balls. 'The weather doesn't help. We all feel a bit low in the rain, particularly if the sun is supposed to be out. Now come on – if he doesn't like bananas, then what? Peaches?'

I looked behind me. A mother was heaving her toddler-filled trolley toward us as if the summit of her mountain was still so far away. As she passed us she pulled a bag of something off a shelf and, tearing it open, crammed the contents into her child's mouth. Bored and hungry, her toddler needed feeding and she needed silence.

'Peaches are fine. Thanks.'

'Well, I can't reach them.' She tipped her head in the direction of a green plastic basket on the top shelf. 'Can you?'

I craned over the lychees and blueberries, holding Mia against me, and slid out a box of peaches I knew we'd never eat. 'I'm cooking when I can, Mum. I even made a stew last week. I've got some left. You could come back and maybe we could have lunch? It would be nice to talk through some of Mia's stuff. I . . . What's wrong?'

Mum's brow was furrowed and she scratched at her temple with nails she'd filed into soft-pointed triangles.

'Oh dear,' she said. I'd given her bad news, again. 'If you'd come up with that plan before . . . but I've got a church meeting and it's important that I go. Attendance hasn't been good this last month. Any other time. Or maybe you'll have dinner with me next week? Let's say Wednesday. I'll cook a chicken the way you like it, with all that artery-clogging butter. We'll do that. Seven p.m. sharp.'

'Dave's mum and dad might be coming to stay that night.'

'Oh. They're babysitting again, I suppose?'

Mum was stockpiling green peppers into the bottom of the trolley, and wouldn't meet my eye. I had no use for seven, eight, nine green peppers but I had even less use for an argument about whether they'd stay in the trolley.

'They're only coming for dinner, Mum, and if they stay the night they get to spend time with Mia first thing. It's hard for them to see her otherwise. They both work in the week. It's nice that I get to see you during the day. When you're around.'

She tried a smile. 'I suppose there's an upside to my being too old to contribute to the economy. What marvellous people Dave's parents are, fitting it all in.'

I stroked the length of Mia's spine to calm the restlessness in her and in me. 'The truth is that we don't see many people at all at the moment. I just don't feel like seeing—'

Mum came to an abrupt standstill opposite the yoghurts. 'Look at me,' she said. I looked down at Mia. 'No, look at me, Cath.' I looked at her. 'Don't think I'm not listening when you tell me repeatedly that you don't want to see anyone. Are you getting out of bed in the morning? I don't suppose you have a choice, what with the little one. Do you need pills again? At least we know which ones work. You must say something, you must ask. They did warn you, Cath. If you catch it once you can catch it again.'

'Depression isn't like getting a cold.' My fingers worried at the folds of Mia's sling, itching to pick up a pot of yoghurt and hurl it across the aisle as I screamed. Anything to shock her, to reboot her.

'I wasn't suggesting it's a cold. But depression can be passed through the genes.' She coughed into a balled fist. 'I'm not at all sure whose side you'd have got it from. I did have an aunt who—'

'I'm not depressed.'

'I'm only trying to help.'

She took a deep breath and began buttoning her coat because the freezer section was always cold. I watched her as she did it, all the way to the topmost, strangle-tight button.

'You've got a newborn baby,' she said eventually. 'And this rainy summer is very depressing for everyone.'

'It's not the weather.'

'Even people who are normally very cheerful can end up feeling at odds. I heard a programme about it on the radio. In some countries they make children sit under light bulbs or none of them can get out of bed.'

'That's Vitamin D.'

'No, I'm sure this was for depression.'

Mia squirmed angrily. I paced to keep her still, paced to walk off some of the blistering hot anger I felt at always having to soothe my mother every time she came into contact with something about me that she found difficult. As if I was a puzzle she found too frustrating to solve. Over and over. Time after time. I came to a halt at the end of the frozen aisle.

She'd followed me, a few steps behind. 'What support are you getting?' she said. I turned to see her, arms crossed tight across her chest. The cold was really coming off those freezer cabinets.

I looked at her closely and wondered when she'd decided to put fine lines of black back into her gold and silver hair, and when the skin had begun to sag off her bones like that. Like sheets draped off ladders. Because it was like seeing her again after an absence of years – as I thought, if Dad had been here, you wouldn't have had to ask about what support I was getting because it would have come from him. You'd have known that and you'd have let him get on with it.

'Well, let's see,' I said. 'The thing I tried to call you about last week, the CF parents' group? That was great actually. Everyone sat around and talked and we shared some of our experiences. I might try and do some fund-raising, or something.'

'Parents' group? What, like AA?'

'It's run by one of the charities for cystic fibrosis. It's a support group for parents of children with CF.'

'I understand. Sharing the burden.' She scanned a shelf of fish fingers. 'If it's sharing the burden you're after, you'd be better off at the church.'

I clenched my fists and adjusted something on Mia that didn't need adjusting. 'Let's not talk about me for a bit. How are you, Mum? Tell me how you are.'

'Bearing up.' She released a resigned and exhausted sigh. 'Sarah Blackwell keeps on at me about Dad's headstone. Tiresome cow. I won't be pushed on it, particularly as all she wants is symmetry in the graveyard. All that landscaping. You'd do a better job of it than her. You've got a good eye for design. Perhaps you should consider that for your next career? Get your hands into the earth sometime?'

'I can't work with damp earth. With Mia, the bacteria – did you read the email Dave sent out with all the things that are dangerous for her? Like sandpits and lakes and soil?'

'Yes, of course I remember, but you're obviously feeling over-sensitive so I'll keep my thoughts to myself. Oh look, coconuts on offer. In the frozen aisle, for no good reason.' She picked one out of its wooden box and held it against the strip lighting. 'I read that these give you a lot of energy. Something about the fats in them. You'll be as right as rain after a few of these.'

I pressed a palm against the top of my head, but it was no good. The words began erupting before I could start counting to stop them. 'Mum.' I brushed a strand of hair from my face and straightened my back.

She lowered the coconut.

'It's not my diet, or the sleep I'm not getting, or the absence of a career plan. Coconuts aren't going to relieve the burden. I've got feeding and nappy stuff to do, like everyone, but as well as that I've got nearly ten drugs a day to administer and a hundred threats to watch out for and hours of physiotherapy. And I don't know if I'm doing any of it right. Too many digestive enzymes will hurt her. Not enough and she'll get stomach cramps. I worry about walking under shop awnings when it rains in case dirty water drips off it and on to her. I cross the road when the street-cleaner vehicle is coming. Every single minute of the day I'm terrified I'll get it wrong and it'll be the start of her getting really ill. I'm so tired, Mum—'

'Yes, all right. I understand.' She flapped her hands like she was trying to disperse a cloud of tiny flies.

And I was crying again.

I'd spent a lot of time crying in the bathroom before we had IVF, and even more during IVF. Perched on the edge of the bath, overflowing with disappointment when another pregnancy test failed to produce a pale blue line. At the beginning, Dave was always there, his hand held over mine, our faces buried in each other like a couple of swans. But toward the end, after months and years had passed, he was there much less. And even if he was, I was never sure if he had heard me somewhere in the house and just decided not to come.

I wasn't sure because I never asked and I never asked because I wasn't sure if I wanted to hear the answer. But one day, after another negative test, I'd had enough. I had grown so tired of the prodding and the poking and the lacking and the not knowing that I walked into the kitchen and said to Dave: *Let's put the house on the market because, really, what's the point of this place if it's only going to be you and me? Have you ever thought that maybe this isn't happening because we – you and me – don't work? That maybe this isn't supposed to work?*

Despite all the tests, the doctors never found out what was wrong with us. There wasn't a single sperm count or hormone level that was abnormal.

Dave left the kitchen after that outburst. It was a Saturday and the football was about to start but I think he missed the match that time.

We never spoke about what I'd said and then on the

Monday he left for work with a smile, like our conversation was forgotten, like life had grown over any wound I had made. And, soon after that, an embryo grew anyway. There was life inside me and no space left for old memories of tears in bathrooms and kitchens.

Mum almost had her back to me now, like she was sheltering from the wind.

'I don't think you do understand,' I said, crying. 'No, of course you don't. Why would you? You never ask.' The last confrontation I'd had – with Richard – had felt exhilarating. But this had the contours of an old habit. Goading her. Pushing her for more than she knew how to give. 'I'm tired because when I'm awake all I think about is how to keep her alive and when I lie down to sleep all I can think about is her dying anyway. I have dreams when I bury her and I wake up and nobody can tell me it's only a bad dream.'

Come on, Mum. Tell me that you feel something. Anything.

Mum looked up and down the aisle. 'Do calm down.'

She placed her basket carefully on the floor in front of her and bowed her head, as if she were taking Communion. When she looked up again her eyes were cold and determined. 'Come to church. Next Sunday.'

I searched for a tissue in my pocket. 'Mum, you're not listening.'

'There's a noticeboard that people pin prayers on, prayers for people who are unwell or in need. If you come and look at that board you'll see exactly how much illness and sickness is around us. You're struggling, granted, but we are all tested at some point. Deborah Maccleswood posted a lovely little note about her daughter's breast cancer. Such a difficult thing for that family to be going through, but they're praying together and they're supported by all of us in the church. You might find some solace in that.'

'Why would I find solace in another family's suffering?' I pressed the tissue angrily to my cheeks. 'And if there's a God, a truly all-powerful God, then he or she or it is a fucked-up deity. Letting *children* suffer and die.'

Her face had lost all its colour. I didn't care.

'There's nothing there,' I said. 'And if there was something up there? I'd spit in its face for allowing this.'

'He gave us his only son,' she said tearfully, angrily.

'I wouldn't give Mia's life for anyone or anything. That's what a mother should be, isn't it? The person saying: No, stop, you'll have my child over my dead body. But I'll have to watch her be taken from me all the same.'

Mum turned to the cereals shelf and pulled a yellow-and-blue box off the display. 'She'll be eating porridge, soon.' I could tell from the quiet of her voice that tears were near. She turned abruptly and walked back in the direction of fruit and veg, then halted – torn between her desire to be away from me and to have the last word.

'You're impossible. As bad as your father. I always say it.' She swallowed. 'I wish he was here too, you know.' She turned her back again.

And just like that, the anger that had given me so much heat and speed was extinguished, leaving a leaden cold sadness in its place.

'Mum. Please don't go.'

And she didn't. Instead she turned and walked towards me, her cheeks red and damp with tears. 'Stop taking it out on me.'

'I'm not.' I wiped my tears away with cold fingers, my tissue now balled and crumpled up against Mum's in my pocket.

'You blame me. And you should. After all, I probably gave you the faulty gene. It won't be your father. Nothing was ever his fault.'

'It's no one's fault. It doesn't matter who gave anyone what.'

She looked so sad and desperate then, lost like a child swallowed by a crowd. And so I went to her and hugged her as close as I could with Mia in the sling between us. 'It's OK, Mum, honestly it is.'

'It doesn't matter what you say. I know that Jesus loves you,' she whispered to me. To Mia.

Chapter 4

I pushed our trolley through the supermarket car park and, as I searched for my keys, a Range Rover ploughed through a puddle so big that it showered Mia and me with muddy rainwater. My jeans were covered in it. Mia's legs were stippled with it. I looked down and her head and face were baptized by it.

Back at home I took Mia out of the sling, laid her down in the hall and patted gently at her cheeks with an antibacterial wipe – the tenth or eleventh time since leaving the car park. But what if the bacteria had made its way into her mouth? I pulled gently, as gently as I could, at the corners of her tiny mouth so it stretched like a clown's, and wiped the insides with the bitter and abrasive wipe.

I took shallow breaths that didn't fill my lungs as Mia wailed. I did the only things I could remember to reassure her – kissed her, sang to her, *I will love you love you love from the bottom of my heart* – all the while crouched on the floor by the front door, trying to think and remember and please think, think, what should I do to stop that puddle from seeding a new and corrosive sickness in her?

Still she cried and with every piercing call issued from her tiny mouth I wondered how this puzzle would ever resolve itself. How there would ever be a time when we wouldn't be lashed together like that, trapped – her helpless without me, me powerless to truly help her.

I looked up. 'Dave, where are you? I need your help. We're covered in muddy puddle water.' But there was nobody home. A pile of unopened post in a shoebox by the door. The burnt remnants of lunch in the air. The rug that had rumpled and turned as I hurried out of the door earlier, anxious not to be late for Mum. All of it, exactly as I had left it.

I lifted Mia to the ceiling and held her there, hoping that my face would cheer her up. But she wailed more, now turning crimson in her anger.

'I love you. It's going to be all right. You're going to be all right. Dave, please, are you upstairs?'

I stood up, pressing her close to me as I kicked off my shoes. Balancing her with one arm as I hooked a finger under each sock, peeling each one off in case splashes of dirty puddle water had touched their fibres.

I walked to the bottom of the steps and buried my face in Mia's neck, trying to calm her with my closeness, trying to slow my own breathing and thinking of how Mum had said: *Yes, yes, I understand*, even though she hadn't understood. About how Dad would have listened and how I would have listened to him.

I kissed Mia's cheeks over and over, tasting the salt of her tears. Kissed her brow, tasted the salt of her skin and my heart broke once more with the facts of it:

Salt.

Once so cheap and inconsequential in our lives. Pinched into soups, scattered on icy doorsteps. Swum in and washed off. Salt had once scattered and flowed round us so silently and unmemorably that we had barely noticed it.

Now salt was of consequence. Salt was the missing ingredient in Mia's life: her body's inability to hold on to it made the mucus in her lungs a thick and sticky spider's web for infection.

I thought of the waiting room we'd sat in, moments before diagnosis, as the sun tried to cut through the pollution-dusted window. How I had licked Mia's brow and tasted the sea.

Woe is the child whose brow tastes salty when kissed, for they are cursed and soon must die.

The first time a salt-doomed child was recorded in writing, back in the Middle Ages. The words rang around my head as I held on to the stair banister for balance, sad wisdom from another age, written of the babies who coughed and coughed then died before they even learned to talk.

We knew more now, but not enough.

'Dave,' I shouted. 'Please be here. You have to come here.'

Another way of looking at things, Richard had said, eyes shining.

But as the sweat gathered on my skin and my mouth dried of the right words and songs for my daughter, all I could see was life spiralling angrily and painfully towards a series of horrific endings.

Hurry, hurry.

Time is running out.

'Dave!'

I sat on the stairs and thought of the bacteria now finding a new home inside her chest. I imagined it, sly and malignant, bedding down into her lungs, twining round her like poison weed, doubling and doubling in numbers, every tick of the second hand rooting them deeper, letting them burrow where no antibiotics would ever find them.

I was late to administer her last dose of antibiotics for the day. *I'm sorry, so sorry.*

I scooped her to my chest and ran, thundering down steps, my bare feet slipping, almost losing us on the bottom step, until I reached the kitchen.

Mia screamed and screamed. I couldn't think. Maybe she was in pain, maybe she was hungry. Maybe she was dying.

Alone with the choices, alone with the syringes and the screaming, the baby screaming, I tried to remember what she needed first, what the danger signs were, where the new dangers lay, what might need to come first.

I took the antibiotics out of the fridge with hands that

shook. The cap locked as I tried to unscrew it. I pressed it down hard, tried to release the safety catch and turned again, and again, and again but still it stuck, still it resisted. It fought me, kept me from helping her. I screamed to something above me in anger, defiance and frustration. I pushed and turned through gritted teeth, pushed so hard that the bottle slipped through my grasp as the lid opened. Heavy brown glass bounced on the wooden floor leaving a trail of medicine, and for a moment I gazed at it, spreading into a glistening white fern pattern.

The pharmacy was closed now and that was the last bottle. I had nothing in stock in the cupboard.

Bad mother, bad mother. Screaming child still screaming.

'Dave!' A sound so splintered and spitting I did not recognize it as coming from me. 'Please help. I need you. I don't know what to do. Please help.'

A damp towel sat in a mocking heap by the dishwasher, reminding me that I should have put it in a boil wash that morning to kill the bacteria that would harm my baby if left to multiply. I hadn't done it, I had forgotten, and now my baby was screaming with hunger and the pseudomonas bacteria were increasing at such a rate that I wouldn't be able to touch that towel without rubber gloves in case my skin became a vehicle for their transmission.

How long, how impossible the battle when the enemy was everywhere you looked, on every surface forever.

In frustration, I raked at my arms with my fingernails. Then I remembered reading that many people, most people, unknowingly carry staph bacteria on their skin and it doesn't harm them. But it would harm Mia if it got into her lungs. And now it was surely under my fingernails because I had put it there with my panicked, silly scraping, and I would need to clean and scrub at them with anti-bacterial soap and while I was there, clean the floor that the dirty towel was on, with the bleach I had bought, then clean my skin, and her skin and maybe her mouth again.

Who would be the first to surrender? The bacteria or me? Of course defeat was coming, a horrible, inevitable defeat. It had been on its way from her first moments and there was no one to back us up when we fell.

I remembered Mum in that supermarket and how my thing wasn't big or painful enough for her to finally look me in the eyes and say, *That must be terrible for you. Not me. You, dear. You.* The kind of thing that someone who loved you might say.

The kind of thing a mother might say as part of her battle cry as she stood by her daughter's side, spear at the ready – to fight for life. To the death.

I don't remember why I emptied the cutlery drawer on to the floor. Perhaps I needed a new sound to cut against Mia's screams, or to wake me up from the screams in my head, or to tip me over.

I went to the drawer stocked with syringes and took out one box. I laid one aside because I would need it for Mia but the rest I tipped out and the plastic clattered lightly on to the floorboards. Then I stamped on them all, their plastic cases shattering under my bare feet, and I cried and screamed and shouted with the pain of it.

I opened the fridge and called out for Dave again. Was he in the house? He was in the house, of course he was, he could hear me and he'd decided not to come to me until I was calm. He was thinking about all those times I'd sat, perched on the bath, digging that lying plastic stick into my palm, and thinking: she needs to calm down first.

'Dave, if you're here, I need you. Please come.'

But he didn't come and I needed to make him hear so I reached into the fridge and took other bottles. Milk. Orange juice. Dressing. And I threw them, one by one, at the floor. And when the sight of broken glass and liquid hadn't made me feel better, I took the other medicine and I threw everything she needed on to the floor. Against the wall. On to the floor. Bang. Bang. Against the wall and on to the floor.

The ones that didn't break I emptied down the sink, one by one, like a child pouring away her angry drunk of a father's whisky bottles as his eyes glaze and he turns into someone she doesn't know.

'Go away. Get out of my house, ' I screamed – defeated and yet fighting – as I smashed anything I could find against the wall. 'Go, get out!'

Then Dave was in the kitchen and his face was twisted with alarm. 'Are you OK? Is someone here?' But all I could do was cry. 'Cath. Speak to me. Who's been here? Are you OK? Who's hurt you? Where's Mia?' He looked to Mia lying on her mat and satisfied she was OK, turned his attention back to me. 'Please, speak to me.'

'No,' I managed through tears and gasps. 'No one's here.' And I wept harder then, so much I thought I'd never stop. Part of me didn't want to stop because stopping would mean talking and there were no words. 'There is no one here.'

Dave held me tight at the wrist and a line of blood dripped over where his thumb grasped me. 'Calm down and look at me. Look at me. Are you sure no one is here? Who did this to you?'

I felt my mouth and eyes stretch wide, spaces opening to allow an overflowing dark smoke to escape.

'I did,' I said.

Pity and anxiety filled his eyes and I thought he would cry when he turned abruptly away and towards Mia. He collected her up, made comforting sounds and Mia's cries stopped right away. He glanced at me again then changed Mia's nappy, her babygro. Whispered in her ear and held her tight. Put her down on the play mat. Gave her a bottle.

By the time he was with me I was sitting silently on the kitchen floor, the anger emptied from me, drained and dripping through the floorboards along with the antibiotics.

He tore off some kitchen towel and wrapped it around my foot, around my wrist – both, bleeding. I buried my face in his sleeve. There was silence and for a fleeting moment I was soothed. Oh, to be carried and loved and rocked until you sleep.

His eyes were full of sadness as he looked around the broken mess in the kitchen. 'Why? What happened?'

I wanted to say:

I was sad.

I saw my mum but I wanted my dad.

Then we were drowned by a puddle.

I'm drowning in it all, Dave. Drowning every day.

'Where were you?' I said.

But when he saw an empty medicine bottle on the floor and the cracked syringes in a pile on the boards, he looked up at me with an expression I didn't recognize – or didn't want to recognize. 'Are they . . . they're Mia's antibiotics. What have you done?'

'I don't know,' I said, straitjacketing my arms around me.

'Have you given her the evening dose of Augmentin?'

'No, no I haven't. I dropped it on the floor. That was how it started . . .'

'How it started?' He looked at the open, gloating fridge and its empty shelves. 'All Mia's medicines are gone from the fridge. Cath? We don't have any drugs for tonight or for the middle of the night. You know that all the pharmacies are closed? There's nothing until the morning?'

Maybe it was the internet or possibly the doctors or even the leaflets that said:

The babies that do better, the ones that live a little longer, are the ones who have parents who stick to the regime. The ones who are compliant with treatment.

'Cath? Are you even listening? This is a huge problem for us. She needs her dose. She can't skip one.'

The babies that do best are the ones that avoid early chronic infection: their parents watch for any signs. They watch, they test, they assess, every day.

I curled over and laid my palms on the floorboards.

'Cath? Snap out of it now. We need to sort this out. She needs her meds and physio and a bath and bed. We need to get her sorted out first.'

The babies that die slower are the ones that keep weight on. It helps them fight off infections when they're too ill to eat. The consultants like their children to carry a little bit extra. Every meal helps. Every breastfeed.

'You can do the crazy mental stuff after we've sorted this out, but I need you back in the room now helping me clear this mess up.'

The babies that are strong are cared for, and lucky. They don't have mothers whose wrists shake, whose feet stamp on their syringes.

'You're frightening Mia, Cath. You're frightening her.'
The babies that live.

'If you don't snap out of it I'm calling your mum.'
The babies that live a little longer.

'Cath, for God's sake, what are you looking at? Where have you gone? Look at me. Look at me, now.'

The babies that don't live, they run to God, leaving their mothers to howl their names into all the empty years that lie waiting for them.

Chapter 5

Of all the things you could have smashed up, why her medicines?

That's what Dave said in the kitchen when I finally met his gaze. His eyes brimmed with black disappointment, as if it was Mia I had broken.

And I had wanted to say, *Taste the salt on my lips, taste the evidence of how much I kiss her. How much I love her. I would do anything to take her place.*

But I didn't say any of that because the anger in his face was like steel. His baby was crying and compromised, his wife's wounds self-inflicted and his house needlessly broken by her.

Bad, bad, bad wife.

I had tried to explain but he had heard all those things before, about my mother and father, about our child. He was tired of hearing about these things that never changed but got talked about, round and round, without resolution.

And it occurred to me: a symptom doesn't have to be a change. A symptom can be no change at all.

* * *

So I left to get help.

As soon as I was in the car, breathing the smell of its upholstery still warm from the day's heat, I was calmer. I dialled the registrar and explained that I had dropped Mia's antibiotic in the sink by mistake and needed a replacement. *Yes, of course*, she said, as if it happened all the time. *That will be fine.* Calmer still. *We'll leave replacement antibiotics at the hospital pharmacy but you'll need to hurry because they will close soon.*

I would return with a blue-and-white paper bag and Dave would see that I was not a bad mother and wife, after all.

I could emerge from these shadows.

By *atoning*, as Mum would say.

I turned the keys in the ignition. Underfoot a crisp packet crackled and slid. I moved it aside and felt biscuit crumbs and a balled tissue at my fingertips. A bottle that had been there too long, abandoned and half-drunk, the water unable to evaporate into thin air because the lid was closed; bacteria multiplying, toxicity intensifying until soon it would be too dangerous to water plants. I needed to throw it away, as soon as possible, before it leaked and caused damage.

As I drove, I thought of how Dave had looked at my bleeding wrist. He had been concerned but also suspicious, I think, as if it were not the glass from shattered bottles that had caused a slow trickle of blood. As if I was now capable of anything. A new problem in his life, something to monitor and perhaps to contain. Another item on his long exhausting list.

And in that moment I had imagined Richard. The thought had come unbidden. Would he have picked me out of the glass? Had his wife ever fallen apart, and had he held her then, instead of clearing up around her with a face full of cold contempt?

I drove through the neighbouring streets with their red-brick houses and plane trees, past playing fields and a football pitch where boys stood in a huddled mass, like petals on a stem. We'd chosen the area for the schools and the borough football club. We had come for the village feel. We had come for the small shops and the busy swings. We had come for the many speed bumps designed to keep children safe, which I now sped over.

I arrived at the local hospital. The last time I had been there my womb had been contracting and Dave had held me up as my legs gave way, my arms stretched wide against him – an eagle, grounded. Only an hour before we'd been sitting on the living room carpet watching *Friends* re-runs with him feeding me bits of bagel, and Fanta from a straw. Occasionally I'd gasp and he'd say: *contraction or carbonation?* And I'd laughed every time.

It was this hospital that had delivered all we'd ever wished for. Us. A family.

I walked through a crowd of Accident and Emergency patients – antiseptic and alcohol in the air, a child cradling

an arm, a waxen wheezing man – until I reached the
pharmacy.

A queue moved in fits and starts until finally it was
my turn.

'It's Cath, Cath Freeland.' My voice quivered at its
edges. 'Here to collect Augmentin for Mia Freeland. Dr
Korres will have rung it through.'

The woman, whose hair swept across an acne-pocked
forehead, lowered her gaze to a screen. She tapped and
stopped. Tapped and stopped. 'The pharmacist has gone
home for the evening so can you come back tomorrow
morning?'

'No, I'm sorry but I need it now. They said it would
be waiting here.'

'Your request has come from the children's hospital.
That needs a pharmacist. We're only open for non-
prescription items now.'

'Please,' I said. 'This is urgent. My daughter needs
antibiotics. She has cystic—'

'If it's urgent you can bring your daughter to A & E
and they might prescribe? Depending on the circumstances?'

'She needs her dose. I give it to her every eight hours.
I dropped the bottle. It smashed. I didn't mean to drop
it. It's Augmentin. 125 milligrams.'

'As I said, if it's urgent—'

'But she's got cystic fibrosis!' I could feel my voice
getting shriller, more panicked. 'I can't bring her to A & E.

There's a guy back there coughing up his lungs. I can't put her near that.'

'I'm sorry. All I can suggest is that you come back in the morning.'

'Wasn't it rung through?'

'I can see it on the system, but it needs a pharmacist to handle it as it's a prescription drug. If you'd been here an hour ago . . .'

'This is ridiculous.'

'It would be illegal for me to give it to you, OK? I can't do any antibiotics because I'm not licensed, all right? All I can do for you is whatever's not on prescription. For anything else you have to get a doctor.'

I turned away and leaned against the wall, the metal roll and close of the shutter unpeeling my nerves all over again.

I couldn't go home, not until I had atoned.

I walked out on to the street and looked toward the entrance of the birthing centre. I looked up and counted quickly – one, two, three floors up to the ward where Mia had been born in a room bordered with mauve butterfly stickers.

Mauve: to calm the mother through her birthing ordeal.

Butterfly: average lifespan, one month.

I wanted to go back to the birthing centre reception. I wanted to sit on the single orange plastic chair that I had sat on eight weeks prior when it had been me, Dave and Mia for the first time. A family. I wanted to sit on that same chair. A chair that a thousand new mums before me had sat on, waiting for their partners to collect them and bring them home – sore with their ordeal, new life in a car seat at their feet.

I wanted to sit there until a security guard became so discomforted by me not having a baby at my feet nor any sign of someone coming for me that eventually he would ask: *Can I help you with anything?*

And I would say:

Yes, I am looking for something.

I didn't know my newborn baby was the messenger for a new life.

And I need to find my old life because I didn't have the chance to say goodbye.

I want it back, I need it, I miss it. Can you help me find it?

But the security guard would say: *I'm sorry, I can't help you and would you move along, please?*

And the hospital would not come to my rescue if I sat motionless in an orange plastic chair, as it had not come to Mia's rescue by prescribing her replacement antibiotics.

My life would continue as it was and Mia would continue to hold a death sentence in her cells.

Then I felt the essence in me that kept me upright and moving, drip lower and lower into my feet – filling them, pinning them to the lowest ground. A seabed, somewhere.

I tasted salt – my salt – on my top lip and thought of how much warmer it would feel on the surface of the sea.

And I thought of Richard and how he had offered help. Help is what you call out when you're drowning.

Back in the car I retrieved the piece of paper from my wallet, with Richard's mobile number and email address written in looping blue ink.

I dialled his number and left a message explaining that I needed replacement medicine. Augmentin. Because I'd made a mistake. I explained that I needed it as soon as possible and perhaps he, being parent to a kid who'd need antibiotics on a regular basis, might have a spare bottle in the back of a cupboard.

Then I drove towards Hampstead.

I got his text message. Beep, beep, at a set of traffic lights, red. I checked it. It was his full address followed by a cross: a kiss, a hug perhaps?

Green, go, and up, up into leafy Hampstead where strong sun had followed the day's earlier rain and people had probably bunked off, escaping the dry air of the office onto the heath because *how amazing did this day turn out to be?* Wandering around, sweating through a film of sun cream, holding hands or playing football. Resting against grassy banks or standing outside pubs, dewy pints in hand. Nuts in glasses, chips in bowls. Nothing else to do for the evening but talk and laugh.

The last time I'd been in this neck of the woods was visiting my almost-friend Julia, who lived nearby in

Gospel Oak. We'd met while we were both pregnant. Her baby was born a day after mine, we had the same make of buggy and a shared taste for romantic comedies. It should have been the start of something beautiful.

The last time I'd seen her, we'd met on the heath with our babies, and, for about fifteen minutes, it was all I had hoped for; all smiles and sunglasses and normal talk about breastfeeding and TV binges and bad sleep and I thought well this is going to be fine, I don't need to tell her about Mia. Mia had been diagnosed a week earlier.

But then she said her baby had a cold and that the doctor had prescribed saline drops to put in his nose and wasn't that wrong because you weren't supposed to give a baby salt *like, ever?*

When I swallowed it was like there was a big round pebble stuck in my gullet. Looking back, I should have turned the pram around and gone home but I kept walking with Julia at my side, clinging to the day.

Soon enough Mia needed feeding and I had to stop the pram and get her medicine. Julia saw me prepare it all and although she didn't comment, because we didn't know each other well enough for that, I did think: perhaps I should tell her about Mia's CF anyway? Maybe if I share it all with her she'll reciprocate by telling me she's in an abusive relationship, or that she's dying: something terrible like that. We might have a motherhood of shared loves, shared heartaches, that kind of thing.

But when I told her all she said was: *Gosh, I'm sorry* and: *Is there a cure?*

And I said: *No. There is no cure.*

Then she fell silent and she had to look down at her shoes trimmed with scarlet, which only made me feel bad for her so I said something like, It's not as bad as it sounds because medical science is very hopeful in the current climate. Which seemed to make her feel better.

We pushed our prams around the lake and I wondered about the fountains spraying bacteria into the air. What does a single bacterium weigh anyway? Do they float like pollen or sink like fish eggs?

Julia confided that her best friend's middle child had recently been diagnosed with asthma.

Did that count?

No, Julia, it did not.

On the far side of the heath the roads were broad with gaps between each sprawling, wide-fronted residence: some gated, others hedged. I found his road easily. No house numbers, just names. His was The Cedars.

I parked on the road, wound down the window, breathed an early evening air that was still thick with summer warmth.

The driveway to his black-and-white house was big enough to have a garden with a shed in the front. The shed was painted pale grey and guarded a side path that, I imagined, led to something landscaped and lush – space enough for a dozen picnic blankets in the sun. A place for watering cans and wine bottles, teapots and teepees. I pictured a woman lying there, her face towards that sun, hair fanned like a halo. His hand stroking her forehead, or maybe holding her there.

Even as I stood at his doorstep, even as I rang the bell that trilled like an electric bird caught in a brass cage, I didn't know what I would say. Richard had a wife, and a daughter I couldn't be near; whose air I didn't want to breathe. I tried to remember the rules for cross infection. Was it twelve feet between patients? And no shaking hands. A distance to leave between us.

What if she answered the door? What if she spoke and the air carrying her words wafted an infection that stuck to my clothes, perched in the strands of my hair? What if I carried it home to Mia's skin as I bowed my head to feed her, to kiss her?

I stepped back abruptly and turned to walk away when I heard, 'Cath.'

It wasn't a question and there was no surprise in his voice. It was a statement, said like I'd been standing in front of him, all day.

When I turned around I saw that there was no surprise in his eyes, in the creases around them or the circles under them. His mouth was a gentle smile which suggested I was not a hindrance, not a hindrance at all in fact.

'I'm so sorry to interrupt you,' I said. 'I left Mia's

medicines out in the heat. I forgot to put them back in the fridge and they won't work for her now . . .'

'I know, I listened to your message. I can help. It's nice to see you.' He smiled. 'You look . . .' I didn't know how I looked. I hadn't checked for a long time, not since before I'd got ready to go to the supermarket with Mum that afternoon. Suddenly I was conscious of what I might look like; the tangled hair, the mascara that had probably run, the eyes all puffed and glazed with tears.

But he smiled like he didn't mind any of it. 'You look like you've just woken up.'

For a moment we stood there – him inside his house, me on the doorstep – listening to the sounds of fun in the background. A music track with a sing-song voice, bass and drums, a party popper, laughter, the high pitch of a woman's voice. And then he was stepping over the threshold, quickly, to me, and pulling the front door to, slowly and silently – as if he were trying not to wake a sleeping baby.

'Dinner. I'd ask you in, but . . .'

'No, God, no, thank you—'

'Believe it or not it's only the three of us in there. We try and make sure we eat together once a week, on a Sunday usually, because things get so busy. There's school, treatments, work and the charity. Rachel, that's my daughter' – he said it like I'd forgotten, but I'd remembered – 'she likes to get out the party poppers and streamers. And she loves her music. Sometimes we save time and she uses party blowers as part of her physio. Like now, can you hear? You have to blow through them really hard to get your lungs moving.'

'Sounds like a lot of fun,' I said, imagining the scarlet and emerald shine of coned party hats, a pot roast, wine, talk and laughter. And the muted and colourless dinners I'd had with Dave since we tried to make a family.

'It is fun,' he smiled. 'But it's also loud. I could do with a break. Come with me.'

'Are you sure? I don't want to take you away from your family. I need, I only need . . .'

But he took me by the arm and led me towards the entrance of the grey shed. I hesitated at the threshold, looked up at the trees – all willowed and gentle, their leaves like black paper cut-outs against the darkening blue of the sky – and felt him stand behind me, for a moment, as if he too felt the shape of another person between us.

'Cath?' He said my name again, this time like he'd read it from the engraving on a precious antique. Curious about its provenance. Amazed that its shape had survived time.

I stepped out of the twilight and into the darkness of the shed where I breathed damp wood and engine oil. He grabbed me abruptly, painfully, by the elbow before I even knew I was falling, over a coiled snake of hose on the floor.

'I'm sorry, I . . . There was . . .' My hand went to my hair.

He let go.

A standard lamp with a pale silken shade sprang to glowing life as he hit a switch behind me. 'Sit down,' he said, as if my clumsiness had never happened. He pushed a wooden tea box towards me, borders thick with rusted metal, brushed it down and motioned for me to sit. There was a rich Persian rung laid across the concrete floor, and candles that had guttered leaving stunted stalagmites of wax. Underneath the shelves of engine oil, spanners and metal tins of this and that, stood a wooden trestle table with TV, a closed laptop and at least two cups of greying tea.

'Who lives here?' I said.

'No one! This is my shed and my island. It's where I come to get some peace and quiet when Rachel has her friends round. Another rule for dealing with cystic fibrosis and children: always have somewhere you can escape to for a moment. You are that rarest of things: a guest here.'

His eyes were shy but his smile sparked – so bright and wide and inviting, it drew my gaze to his lips. I looked into his eyes then and away again, towards the glow of the lamp. Confused and delighted by how he made me feel as if he were reading something in me that I didn't know how to.

'The pharmacies are all closed,' I said, too abruptly, wanting to move on from that moment with him and yet wanting to stay. 'The hospital pharmacy is closed. I didn't know where else to go. I need to give her antibiotics before tomorrow morning. She shouldn't miss a dose. She's got a cold, she'll have got it from Dave or me. It's not a cough, yet, but—'

'It's OK. Really it is. I'm always talking to the pharmacy for Rachel's meds and I've built a stockpile big enough to get us through the most violent of atomic wars.' He smiled and I smiled. 'Seriously,' he said. 'I can give you anything you want. How much do you need?' His voice was gentle and his gaze steady and I didn't look away.

'One bottle. I, you see . . .'

He was the one to look away then, leaving without further remark and returning only a few minutes later with a blue plastic bag.

I took it tentatively, hooking it with one finger. His brow rumpled in confusion at my hesitation.

'Sorry,' I said. 'It's only that I've read so much about cross infection, perhaps too much, but anyway, you know, like the woman at the parents' meeting said. I don't want our children to pass anything between them.' I looked at the silver-grey concrete beneath me – striated with veins of deep purple, like a steak on the turn – and the dark vermillion, Persian rug with its soft, deep pile. I should go, I thought. 'We wouldn't want to be *unknowing vehicles*. Isn't that what she said?'

'That's unlikely. It's not like we're touching each other right now.'

I looked down before I said, 'No.'

'You're safe,' he said. 'These antibiotics come from my

store cupboard and Rachel is far more interested in boys than her medication stores. These will be a different concentration to the one you're using for Mia. Do you know how to check dosage equivalents?'

'I think so.'

'Good. This stuff's still in date. Small miracle really. Almost everything else she takes is a tablet now.'

'Thank you, I do appreciate your help.' There was a beat. 'And how is Rachel at the moment?'

'She's great!' His smile was so wide and his eyes shone. There was so much . . . I couldn't put my finger on it . . . *life* in him. 'Great, actually. We're in a calm waters phase. She's got the usual, but—'

'What's the usual?' I said. 'I'm sorry to ask, and I'm just checking, is all, because I've read that some bugs are more persistent on surfaces than others.' I felt for the packet of antiseptic wipes in my jeans pocket because despite what he said I would use them to clean the boxes when I was back in the car. 'I'm sorry, I hope what I'm saying isn't offending you. It's the bugs, not the people I worry about.'

'I understand.' His words were slow, like he was thinking too much between them. I hadn't offended him but I'd done something else, I wasn't sure what. 'You'll be all right, Cath. I promise it will get easier. At the start it's impossible to see the wood for the trees. Everything is a threat to your child's life. Every wood, every tree, as it were.'

'Yes,' I smiled.

'Anyway, that lot should see Mia through,' he said. 'And this is for you.'

He put a foil-wrapped chocolate star in my palm, and smiled.

I laid the bag of medicines on the floor, where I could not see it and it could not see me. 'Thank you,' I said, unwrapping the chocolate and putting it in my mouth.

'What happened to your hand?' he said, and I held it up so we could both examine the trail of dry blood that disappeared under my sleeve. I looked on the floor, expecting to see the kitchen towel Dave had given me to soak up the blood where broken glass had cut the skin. But it was gone – discarded somewhere between here and home.

Richard didn't wait for a reply and took my hand in his, holding tight where there were other cuts I hadn't yet noticed. I flinched, because it stung and because . . .

It had been so easy to hold hands when Dave and I only had each other. We held hands all the time when we'd first met because we wanted to touch each other all the time, intoxicated by the newness of it all. Then, when the miscarriages happened and the IVF started and the miscarriages continued, we held hands all the time because we'd been scared we might lose each other if we ever let go. But I couldn't remember a time, not since diagnosis, when we'd really wanted to hold each other's hands again. Perhaps because we'd had to let go when our burden got harder and heavier, our grips taken up with what we held on our shoulders – wrist tendons stretching with its awkward shape, back aching with its terrific weight.

Perhaps it hadn't been practical to hold hands as we once did.

Richard let go and leaned against the wall, like he was resting.

'Sorry, I'm keeping you from your family dinner,' I said. 'You should get back.'

'Please, it's fine. Honestly? Rachel's in a bit of a sulk. I'd booked tickets for us to see *Tiger Love* at the O2. Most teenagers wouldn't be seen dead with their dads at a rock concert . . .'

He looked out into the distance somewhere far beyond my eyeline, like what he'd said had triggered a vision or a memory in him.

'Then what happened?' I said, bringing him back into the room.

He smiled brightly. 'I was asked to drinks with some MPs and it's a rare opportunity to collar them on the subject of those new medications I was telling you about. The Americans have found ways of fixing CF at the source instead of treating symptoms but the catch is that the treatments cost hundreds of thousands of dollars per patient, per year. This drinks is about communicating the human story to MPs so when it comes to lobbying our government they really understand the difference these drugs could make to people's lives. If Rachel gets this new medication it will change her life . . . But try telling that to a teenager whose greatest love is rock music. You know?'

I nodded. 'It sounds like you do so much to help. Rachel must be very proud.'

He smiled. 'She's proud most of the time. Between the moods and the worrying about boys and parties.' He adjusted the carpet at the door with his foot. 'I know her. I know why she's upset. It's for the same reason I'm upset. Those concerts are when we get to spend our best time together. To gossip without her mum being there. She had a crap winter and the spring was, well . . . Fun times together are important.'

'Hard for everyone, trying to meet all those needs.'

'It's OK, her band will be back in town soon. Meantime I'll try and get her excited about learning to ski with me this winter.'

'Sounds fun.' I brushed hair away from my eyes. 'I thought the newborn years were hard.'

'They are. It's all hard! You must be having a tough time: all that sleep deprivation alongside dealing with CF.'

We smiled at each other as if we had silently agreed on something. A language, perhaps.

'All that hard work and anxiety are what make vices all the more important.' He stood up and slid a cigarette box out from behind a well-thumbed book on the shelf. 'Smoking. My one and only vice and, therefore, extremely important to me. No one knows. Or at least, if they do, they're kind enough not to say anything.'

He held out the packet.

I hadn't smoked for over ten years. Dave and I used to smoke incessantly, with coffee and pints and wine, in parks and pubs and restaurants. It seemed to go hand in hand with talking about films and our friends and our weekend plans.

And now, with Mia's lungs so compromised, the idea of destroying my own repulsed me. 'No. Thanks. That's fine. I'm fine.'

'Suit yourself.'

Then there was nothing but the spark of a lighter, a party popper in the background and his deep inhalation. I felt far from the sound of plastic cracking under my heels and from Dave's blaming, appalled cries. Far from the floorboards and the noise of traffic and the pressure in my head.

'I didn't leave Mia's medicines out in the sun,' I said. 'I poured them down the sink.'

He looked up, and moved his cigarette to the side like it had been blocking his view.

'I'd seen my mum,' I said. 'And I missed my dad. And so I don't know why, I broke the syringes and I threw the medicines down the sink. I didn't want CF in my house any more.'

Richard nodded slowly, looking at me with lidded eyes, squinting against the smoke and my confession.

'After Rachel was diagnosed,' he said, 'a whole seven

years and twelve lung infections later, I didn't break medicine bottles but I did do some damage to the lives of people I'd just met. I made huge redundancies in the name of re-shaping my company and increasing profit. My career and business took off but I could only do what I did because the thought of losing Rachel early knocked me sideways. That pain, that imagining, it blunted my feelings towards everything but my family. But we got through it and here we are now,' he smiled. 'Having weekly parties. We manage it. We get by. We more than get by.'

His fingers tremored where they bent round the cigarette. He made me want to join him.

I reached out my hand instinctively towards his words. 'I should go,' I said suddenly, letting it fall by my side.

'How are you getting on with that speech?' he said brightly, stubbing out the cigarette and cradling his hand, twisting the ring on his finger, round and round.

I looked away quickly. 'I'm not. It's not my thing,' I said to the door.

'I think you should do it. And going to the conference might dilute some of the despair. There's no greater high than hearing a medical professional announce he's months away from a cure.' I smiled. 'And it's all quite fun, despite the subject matter.'

I motioned to the cigarette packet. 'Can I? I won't smoke it. I just want to be close to the smell.'

He opened the packet. 'Here, take two. Then they

won't be lonely.' He caught my eye and I caught my breath.

I smiled. 'Thank you. For everything. For your help.'

'Any time.'

When I got back in the car, I wound down the window and used the car's lighter to singe the edge of one of the cigarettes he had given me. The smell of it was everything I knew it would be and yet not enough, so I put the cigarette to my lips and inhaled deeply. Smoke hit the back of my throat, making me cough and splutter. It was all I needed, to be reminded of how nauseating the rush was after such a long time, how it was never as good as I imagined. I threw the cigarette out on to the road. It rolled into the gutter and my face flushed red at the thought of him seeing this. As if I might be someone who was surprising to him. A woman who lay on his lawn and looked up to the sun – burning her face today for a tan tomorrow.

I stowed the remaining cigarette in an empty crisp packet, pushed it to the back of the glove compartment and drove home.

Chapter 6

Saturday afternoon on Camden High Street and a sea of shoppers crossed, idly, in front of the car. There was power in their purpose and in their numbers because they kept on walking – line after linked-line of shopper – all assuming that I wouldn't drive on. But what if I put my foot on the accelerator – defied expectations, overturned their assumptions, drove over their skinny jeans and satchel bags?

'Bloody, touristy bloody Camden,' grumbled Dave.

I waited for a break in the flow then accelerated sharply, gripping the top of the steering wheel like a naval captain steadying the boat in a storm. The heat of the day made the skin beneath my nylon dress itch with salted sweat. I hated the heat as much as I hated the bitter chill of winter. I craved average – a temperature without remark, a family without remark.

A woman ran in front of us, arms flapping in the sleeves of a scarlet kaftan. She cleared us, easily, but Dave pushed back into his seat as if the brake pedal was beneath his foot. 'Should have got the tube.'

Words of blame and disappointment, his first of the day. *Reckless* was the last thing he'd said to me the moment I stepped back into the house from Richard's. I hadn't even taken off my shoes before he handed over Mia, as if she had only been on loan to him for the few hours I was gone.

He'd given me the silent treatment all through breakfast even when I'd made him coffee and suggested a trip to the zoo that morning. *A family trip. I even invited Caroline and the boys. You've been wanting me to see my sister for ages. Come on, let's go. Why not? It's on one of your lists. Our List, actually.* He washed up his cup and silently helped me pack Mia's nappy bag.

'Our List' wasn't the same as a shopping list or a DIY tasks list or even the inventory list Dave had pinned inside the linen cupboard to keep track of the sheets (cot, single, double, dust). Those lists were instigated and executed by one person, usually the one who thought them most necessary. Usually Dave. It's not that I didn't shop or clean or tidy – I did all those things – but I didn't have the same need to document them in linear order.

Until the day I'd had an extra scan at six months pregnant.

Only then did the need to document overwhelm me. Like a tide I'd been holding back.

After the scan – *Looking great*, the radiologist had said, *absolutely viable now, even if she makes an early appearance!* – we went to a nautical-themed café with painted ash floors and a table by the window where we could watch the snow fall and blunt the corners on everything.

We smiled at each other, a lot, over hot chocolate and a plate of scones to celebrate. But that sense of things *looking great* hadn't lasted long as one set of anxieties was replaced by another, as I said something like:

'Now the life inside me is looking like it might well, live, shouldn't we make a list?' The café felt too hot, the chatter around us too sharp and loud but the way his eyes lit up like he'd won the lottery – lovely, really – I thought, Maybe this will be all right? 'We should list the places we could go together as a family, like the Natural History Museum?'

He laughed, loudly, as if I'd told a joke. 'But she won't be old enough to understand what a T-rex is!'

'It's not about the details – the dinosaurs, whatever – it's about listing ways of spending time together. As a *family.*'

He looked confused – either because it was a completely obvious thing to say or not obvious at all – and I realized I didn't know which it was, because we'd never spoken about what our family would actually *be* like. We'd become too scared that what we hoped for might never happen.

So I took a deep breath and tried not to cry because I worried, then, about all the things we'd never said and never had consensus on. 'I thought we should agree on some fundamentals, like spending time together. And *re-assurance*. Even when she's a tantrumming toddler, it's our job to listen to her, and always be there for her. More than anything, it should be our job to reassure her.'

'That's not a list. That's a conversation.'

Perhaps he caught something in my expression, because he tipped his head to the side, smiled, and said, 'We can visit anywhere you want – the museum, the zoo, wherever makes you happy – but I don't think we can plan for the kind of parents we'll be. We won't know until we're in it.'

'We can plan to be *good* parents. And what I'm saying is that I think we need to write some of these things down in case there are times, difficult times, that make it hard to remember what a good parent is.'

Then he looked confused again because I'm not sure he could imagine what such a time would look like.

But I could.

The traffic concertinaed in and out and I said, 'I was thinking that if you enjoy the zoo today then maybe we could adopt you a penguin for your birthday?' I put my hand on his knee to try and seal something there – a memory, whatever.

But he turned away from me to look out of the window, hair licking over his collar, his eye caught by something – a girl, a tramp, a shop selling ankle boots, neon fabric, sandals in white legs, a face with almond eyes, spike heels. One of those things, maybe all of those things.

'I'm sure that's something Mia would like, when she's old enough,' he said, his tone sarcastic as a glowering teen. I took my hand away. 'I don't understand why we're going to the zoo. She's not old enough to appreciate a zebra.'

'Caroline and the boys will be there to enjoy the picnic benches and the gorillas and the ice cream. The point is that we spend time together. Remember?'

He craned his neck further away, toward something that had caught his eye.

'OK,' I tried, squeezing the sigh out of my tone and glancing in the rear-view mirror at Mia, as if she might back me up. 'Maybe we should think of other nice things to add to our family list? Like the countryside, or a little turquoise beach hut on the Norfolk coast? On your actual birthday, why don't we get out of the city to a place like that, where we can all just . . . breathe?'

'Birthday isn't for weeks,' he said, sucking through his teeth as a motorcyclist weaved a few sharp angles to avoid hitting the car in front.

I needed to be calm; it was the only way I would transition from retribution to reparation. It would be a gradual process. We'd been there before when the doctors told us how unlikely it was we'd ever conceive a child naturally. Failure had felt branded to every cell and organ in me and I had exploded with the pain of being unable to escape my own broken body. I'd thrown an empty laundry basket and the willows in its weave had cracked and splintered down one side. Dave had been shocked by my behaviour but there'd been tears in his eyes, too, and I think it was because we were sharing that pain.

But the destruction of Mia's medicines was different. He'd worn the same confused expression as the day I broke the ribs of the washing basket.

But there had been something new.

I put my foot on the accelerator.

Disgust.

Dave turned to face the dashboard. 'The traffic light. Stop, you won't make it over the yellow box.'

'Your birthday,' I said breathlessly, my palms sweating, slipping against the plastic grain of the steering wheel. I cleared the yellow box with several feet to spare and joined another queue of traffic. 'We need to do something nice. Please let me do something nice.' I turned to him and gripped his shoulder, like that would bring him back to me.

'I think you've got enough on your plate.'

'But that's OK, your birthday is important,' I said, returning my hand to the wheel to steer us through the traffic. 'Maybe we could get Seb, Andy and Darren round? With their wives and girlfriends. Like we used to. Let's get some of your favourite people and I'll make food. It'll be something to look forward to. I could make a big lasagne?' As I edged the car forward I could feel Dave looking at me, seeing how obvious my attempts at reparation were. I rarely made lasagnes and pies, the kind of efficient thing people did when they wanted to spend more time with the people they love. 'Or not, whatever. I'll never forget the surprise lunch you threw me at that Argentinian place. God that was nice. I don't know how long it took you to organize it. Getting all those people in one place at the same time. And Charlie over from Canada. Do you remember those trousers Dan had with zips up the side that he took off on the dancefloor? It was my best birthday ever.' The memory of it made me smile sincerely. I took my eyes off the traffic to face Dave, but I was seconds too late and he'd looked away again.

'Have you called Caroline to tell her we're going to be late?' His tone was brusque. I would have to try harder still.

'When would I have done that? I'm driving.' Exasperated, exhausted suddenly.

He craned round to look at Mia slumbering in the back. 'That seat belt is threaded through the wrong bit on her car seat.'

'I asked you to check.' I wiped a palm impatiently on my dress so I could grip the steering wheel tighter.

'I don't think you did ask me to check. It's not safe. You'll have to stop.' He fiddled with his seat-belt clasp.

'Don't do that now. We'll be there in a minute.' Annoyed, I glanced in the rear-view mirror and was unsurprised to see that the seat belt was doing a good enough job. What surprised me more was my own reflection: the clench of my jaw, the shallow trenches of my brow, the

do that . . .' He paused, looked out of the window again. 'We need to think about getting you another kind of help.'

It was a relief in a way, to hear him talk about the past. 'I don't need that again. It's not the same situation as before. It's not like someone died.' He was worried about me. I felt my breathing slow and I put my hand on his leg because I wanted him to know that I was grateful for his concern, that I understood it. 'Yesterday . . . the medicines. Can't you forgive me one outburst? Please?'

'You walked out and left us!' He shouted it. A bookend to his slammed door.

I felt shame at having read him wrong and took my hand away.

'I went to get medicine,' I said. 'I went to try and make it up to her.'

'Yes, but I didn't know that at the time.'

'Because you didn't ask.'

Because you never ask.

'And anyway, what about the rest of her medicine that you . . . that needs replacing?'

'I can call the children's hospital on Monday and sort all that out. I just thought about the antibiotic, the urgent stuff.'

'Where did you even get that from?'

I tore a piece of skin off the side of a fingernail with my teeth. It stung. I knew it would bleed. 'I don't know, does it matter?'

'Where did you get it?'

'I called the out-of-hours registrar, explained what happened and he rang a prescription through to Boots in Piccadilly. They're twenty-four hour. One of the only places.'

I read something, once, that said it's the people who claim they can't lie that make the best liars.

'I didn't know that.'

I stopped the car at a red traffic light and we looked at each other. I thought I saw a change, a tenderness in his eyes, but blasting car horns broke the thread between us.

'I'm sorry,' I said. 'I was sad and overwhelmed and I didn't know what to do with any of it . . . I can have times like that, surely? I'd actually been feeling better. Going to that charity thing a few weeks ago helped. The people I met there. Talking about it.'

'Well, that's great.' He looked so relieved, like he'd found a missing key. 'I thought you'd written it off because you hadn't said anything about it.'

Because you never ask.

I kept my eyes on the road but I felt him turn to me, his voice soften, his eyes probably too. 'I didn't want to push you because I know you wanted it to work out. I didn't want to upset you by asking you. I wish you'd told me. Wanted to give you a bit of space, you know?'

I knew.

He touched my knee. A brief, warm, press before he took his hand away.

And then it was as if we had run out of things to say.

'Do you want me to come to the next parents' meeting thing?' he said eventually.

'No, no, you were right,' I said quickly, brightly. 'It's not your kind of thing. It only needs one of us to be there. I can always feed back anything useful.'

I sucked at the blood on my fingernail and it tasted of iron and salt.

'And the main point,' I continued, 'is that I can see the light at the end of the tunnel. I know about the drugs pipeline. People have told me that Mia will be fine. She'll be one of the lucky ones because she was diagnosed early and if we can keep her healthy—'

'Slow down, we're in a residential area now.' He was sounding short, aggravated again.

'Things are looking better now than they have ever done.' I spoke quicker so I could get it all out, make him hear and understand, before he interrupted me again. 'There are medicines in development that Mia could have access to as early as six years old that will slow down, maybe even reverse the illness. There's one treatment being developed in Britain . . .' I remembered how Richard's eyes had sparked as he'd explained it to the group. 'It's called gene therapy and it's quite far down the line. Mia would inhale something that corrects the underlying cause of CF so it'll be as if she never had it at all.'

'Cath.' Dave leaned his head against the window like it was a pillow. 'All that stuff is light years away. Even I know that the success rate for clinical trials is barely more than ten per cent or whatever. You can't live your life in a fictional future. And you're still going too fast for a residential area.'

I put my foot on the accelerator and turned on to the main road, driving at speed past the entrance to the zoo. My palms were slick with sweat again. The sun above me, the upholstery under me, Dave next to me felt too close and thick, like I had no choice but to breathe in their heat and fibres and words.

'Stop. We're here,' he said.

I put my foot on the brake and turned the wheel too abruptly, Dave swearing as the car wheels scraped and mounted the kerb.

I brought the car to a stop and turned to him, voice torched and flaring. 'Me, living life in a fictional future? And you're doing a great job of the here and now, are you? At least I'm trying. I'm reading and researching and engaging with this. And what are you doing? Playing football and going out with the boys – I don't call that engaging. I don't call that *trying*. What do you actually feel about all this? I don't think I really know.'

'I'm getting on with it.' He was calm. Disappointed in us. Disappointed in me.

'Just say it.' I unclicked my seat belt so I could face him.

'OK, I will.' He unclicked his seat belt and twisted to face me. Now I was close enough to smell the mints on his breath, see the scatter of widened pores across his nose, the bristles, the flakes, the place where his eyelashes faded to nothing. 'I can't let it go,' he said, his spittle hitting my face. 'I can't just write it off as a *nothing*. Your behaviour was dangerous.'

'I would never have done anything to hurt her.'

Did he think that little of me?

'You complain about people not helping you, but you don't take their help when they offer it. Your mum says you don't even return her calls. You need to accept help, if not for you then at least for Mia. She deserves a mum who's not mental.' He sat back and gripped the headrest with both hands, like he was reclining on a lounger, only full of tension in every sinew.

'Are you saying that I'm not doing my job as a mother? Perhaps you should adopt me a penguin so I can practise.' I'd aimed for the joke to show him he hadn't hurt me, but my voice wobbled. I hated the betrayal.

A black-and-yellow-clad warden approached us, pad and camera in hand. I reignited the engine, put my foot on the accelerator and the car's wheels bumped heavily off the kerb.

A screech on tarmac . . . I was a mother, I was a teen-ager taking the moped out for a spin.

'That's not what I'm saying. I'm not saying you're a bad mother. Of course not.' He buckled his seat belt again and his tone was conciliatory and tense – like someone trying to calm a hostage situation. 'Let's step back for a second. The point here is you need to look after yourself.

Maybe that charity meeting wasn't as helpful as you thought. If they're feeding you false hope, you know? Maybe it's as bad hearing that stuff as all the websites and the forums and the googling? Honestly, Cath?' He lowered his tone, as if what he was about to say was confidential. 'A bunch of strangers won't give you what you need. Try talking to family and friends. For a bit, at least. See if it helps?' He reached over and brushed my cheek. The gesture was everything we had once been, back when nothing had smudged our horizons.

We drove round the block for a bit in silence. And then we had to decide if we were going home, which meant calling Caroline to explain, or not. And in the end it seemed simpler to go to the zoo despite it all, so I slowed the car and looked for a place to turn. As I stopped at the next junction I caught Dave's eye. 'OK, I'll try it. Why don't you go in and meet Caroline while I park? I'll see you by the gorillas.'

Caroline and her two boys were standing with Dave outside the zoo gates when I arrived, Mia still in her car seat at Dave's feet. Close by, one man basted peanuts in caramel in a metal drum and another sold helium balloons in bunches – Mickey, Minnie, Mickey, Minnie.

'Hello, Catty,' said Caroline. She was wearing her customary skirt and tucked-in T-shirt and had done something to her hair, pinned it up, perhaps added a new colour to the mix. She looked flushed, juggling a juice cup and split bag of popcorn haemorrhaging kernels.

I kissed her on both cheeks, smelt washing powder. 'Hey.'

'You look gorgeous, Sis. As ever. I wish I could wear dresses above the knee like you.' She looked wistful. 'My kneecaps are so much bigger than my calves.' *Upside down chicken legs* is what she used to call her calves.

Dave crossed his arms and pretended to be interested in the conversation although he had about as much interest in Caroline's body neuroses as I did.

I bent down to meet Mia lying drowsy in her car seat on the pavement. 'We're going to have a great day,' I whispered, and leaned in to kiss her. 'We're going to see the elephants,' and her eyelids fluttered with the struggle to stay open.

I stood up. 'Sorry, it took me ages to find a parking space. Dave, we should get Mia away from these car fumes and into the zoo. Why didn't you go in without me?'

'The tickets are on your card. But I was thinking, I've got a lot of work to do, maybe I'll leave you two to it.' He looked at me knowingly: *Remember what we said?*

'Stay,' I said, gripping his arm.

'Oh yes, do stay,' said Caroline in unison with me, making me wonder whether she didn't want to be alone with me any more than I didn't want to be alone with her. I was surprised when she said, 'Why don't I come and get the tickets with you? Boys, come away from the side of the road. Annoy your Uncle Dave until I get back.'

I knew Caroline, I knew how she worked and I knew what she'd say. *There you go, all you two need is a bit of organizing and everything will be all right.* She had no idea of the mountain we had to climb. Rearranging the trees was pointless. The summit was still out of sight.

We left Dave moving Mia's seat from the kerb and the kids running round him in circles. He looked miserable.

When I'd handed my credit card in to the kiosk, Caroline said, 'I'm worried about Dave.'

'You're worried about Dave? Why are you worried about *Dave?*'

Her eyebrows arched in mock sadness. 'We all are. Mum included. He's very unresponsive on email and text. We don't like to bother you direct because you've got so much on with the baby, and so we write to him, to ask how you are.'

'You can ask me direct. I wouldn't mind.'

'You don't reply to messages. I get it,' she said quickly. 'I do. I know how it is with a baby, always feeding or crying or whatever. They are so exhausting and you've got so much on, I don't want to overload you. It's OK, I don't take it personally. Besides, when I do hear from him, Dave says you're all getting by.'

'Right, sorry, hold on.' I dipped my head into the kiosk and retrieved my card and tickets.

'Map over there,' said the kiosk man. 'Have a lovely day.'

I turned around and Caroline was standing closer than I'd been expecting. 'He completely fancied you.' So close I could smell popcorn on her breath. She pulled an invisible hair from her tongue. 'Did you see the way he looked at you? You didn't, I know you didn't. You're getting, what, half the sleep you used to and everyone still fancies you.' She nudged me and smiled. 'It makes my day if a few people like my new profile picture on Facebook – don't ask me how many shots I take to get one that doesn't make me look like a camel – but you get "Likes" in real time. So jealous.'

I smiled because, despite my age, Caroline continued to try to cheer me up as if I was still the younger sister whose black mood could be temporarily lifted by knowing a boy fancied her.

'You were saying about Dave?'

'Nothing much, really. Apart from wondering how you guys were supporting each other, wondering whether he could do with a bit more support. That kind of thing?'

'What makes you say that?'

'Just something he said to me the other day at Mum's. That you're a bit in your own world, I suppose. Not very present, as the Buddha would say. It's understandable. Don't get me wrong. I wondered if—'

'What else did he say?' I resisted the urge to defend myself because that would have caused a row and then I'd never know the extent of my husband's betrayal. If I criticized her, she'd shut up like a clam.

'Only that he misses you, I guess. I don't want to stir, I just want to pass on morsels, you know, anything I can do to help, which isn't much at the best of times.' She propped sunglasses on her head. 'Listen, I wouldn't usually "go there" but it's so important to keep marital relations going through this period. Even if you don't feel like it – and God, why would you feel like it after everything that went on down there? But you know, sex saved our marriage in the sleep-deprived newborn years. Rory said that without it—'

'Did Dave say we weren't having sex?'

We weren't. The birth had left me in pain but even when that abated my head was full of Mia, attached to Mia, belonging to Mia. Then after diagnosis I wanted sex even less because my head was crowded with the opposite of everything that sex had once meant to me. From creation to destruction, my libido in ruins.

Each time I'd say: *No, I can't, not now*, and each time it took longer and longer for his smile to return. At first he apologized for seeming churlish, then later he stopped apologizing but took pains to reassure me, and now he said nothing, simply turned away.

'Aren't you having sex? God, no, what I mean is, well, that's not what he said. He was only letting off steam. He just said he wished it was the way it used to be.'

'Which was how? How, exactly, did it *used to be*? I mean, look, yes, of course we had sex the whole time at the beginning, but what else was there to do? We had nothing to worry about then.'

'Don't be so hard on him. He was good when Dad died. He understands that you kind of, you know, mentally disappeared for a bit then. I think he might have been saying that he was frightened, for both of you, I mean . . . at least, that's the way he talks about it to me.'

'He talks to you? And, what, I *frightened* him?'

'Only in the way he can't seem to reach you . . . is all . . .'

Fuck Dave for hefting our private life over the walls of our house like a thief in the night. What gave him the right to cough up our problems, my problems, making me look bad and flawed and like I wasn't coping while he sat on the sidelines and criticized and failed to forgive my mistakes?

Me and you? You and me? Written in blood-red ink on the back of our wedding programme. What bullshit.

Caroline rearranged the strap of her handbag and looked down at her feet. 'You're taking this the wrong way. All I'm saying is, I'm sure he understands that people deal with things differently and the way you deal with things is . . . probably one of the many reasons he's married to you and not to me, for example. Right?'

We arrived back at the entrance to collect Dave and Mia. Caroline corralled her boys, breaking up an argument over a tractor in patient tones while she handed out grapes from plastic Tupperware. She was everything the ideal, supportive, talkative, balanced mother and sex-giving wife should be.

'Everything all right?' said Dave.

'Fine,' I said through pursed lips, unstrapping a now wide-awake Mia from her car seat then slotting her warm limbs into a sling on my front.

We walked down a wide stone path towards the gorillas, in silence.

'Let's go and see the giraffes,' called out one of the boys.

'I can't take Mia in there,' I said. Dave's eyes were blank. 'Wet straw is marinated in the aspergillus fungus?' Dave looked sad, as if he were being reminded of the facts all over again.

'Fine. Let's go to the aquarium,' said Caroline.

'I'll have to wait outside with Mia.' Caroline and Dave both looked at me then as if I'd told them I was taking off for Hong Kong. 'Fish tanks. Aerosolized pseudomonas bacteria. I'm not trying to be difficult.'

'Why are we even . . . ?' Blame sweated out of Dave's pores.

'Time,' I snapped. 'Family time. I knew you didn't get it when we first talked about it, I knew you didn't . . .'

Dave and Caroline looked at me. Speechless.

'Let's just go and get ice cream,' I said.

The boys ran ahead and we three walked in silence.

We arrived at an ice cream vendor and queued, all looking anywhere else but at each other.

Eventually Caroline said, 'Have you thought about telling work when you're going back? Will you take the full year?' I looked up in time to see her cast a knowing glance in Dave's direction.

Dave took a step back and reached into his pocket for his phone to read something that would remove him from the conversation.

'I haven't decided when I'm going back to work. Perhaps you and Dave could discuss it and reach some decisions on my behalf?'

'Can we go and see the penguins?' said one of the boys in time to deflect any response.

'No,' said Caroline sharply. 'We can't. The splashes of dirty water are bad for Mia. Right, Cath?'

My heart slowed and softened. There were times I really loved my sister. For rising above herself. And me. 'Yes,' I said to the boys. 'That's right. But you're OK. As long as you don't get your hands wet with dirty water.'

'Are you sure?' Caroline said.

'Yes,' I smiled weakly. 'They should go and have fun. We're all supposed to be having fun.'

She smiled. A thaw.

'Besides,' I said. 'When Mia is the same age the boys are now, hopefully she'll be able to splash about with penguins as much as she likes. The new medicines sound that good.'

Caroline's smile was big and relieved. 'That's great.'

'That's what one of the charities says, at any rate. I'm thinking about volunteering to make a speech on newborn diagnosis at their annual conference this year.'

Dave looked up from his phone. 'Really?' He leaned into the freezer chest and chose five of the same gold-wrapped ice creams. 'I thought you were going to keep a bit of distance from that kind of thing?'

I looked at him firmly. 'The subject would be newborn diagnosis. I feel like I could say a few things that might make other parents feel . . . less lonely.'

'Right,' said Caroline.

'What do you mean by that?' I said to her.

'By what?' She looked surprised.

'By saying *Right*, like that, like I've told you I'm campaigning to be the next prime minister, or something.'

'Don't be so touchy.' She tore the foil from her ice cream. 'I didn't think you liked talking in public, is all. You get so nervous.' She was right, I hated standing up in front of people. 'Remember that time at school when you had to do that *Phantom* duet and you completely froze up? I'm definitely not saying I'm any better, but I guess I get a lot of practice with my job. Marketing is all about PowerPoint presentations.'

'Thanks. If it weren't for you I'd lose track of my own character flaws.'

'Don't be like that. I was only saying, thinking, maybe I could help out, if that's what you want to do.'

'Cath's keeping a bit of distance from the charity. Aren't you?' Dave said – quicker and louder than the last time.

'I thought Caroline might know that already,' I said. 'Given she seems to know everything else.'

'What's wrong with you?' he said. 'What are you talking about?'

'The tent show is about to start and we've come to the zoo. We're not leaving until we've all had some fun.'

Inside the covered auditorium I took a seat at one end of the front row and curled my arms around Mia. The place was full of trumpeting and drumming, of children's screams and their parents' high-pitched cajoling, a restless jumble of seat-moving and bags pushed under chairs. I closed my eyes, longing to escape to a place where I could imagine him fully – the way I thought he'd looked at me that time and how it would feel on my skin and in my heart for a man like that to take my hand again and draw me closer.

'Do you want me to take Mia?' said Dave, edging around me in the space between seats, knocking against my kneecaps so he could pass.

'No, thank you.'

'Go on, go and sit with Caroline. Talk to her.'

I glanced at Caroline a few seats over from the boys, pretending to look fascinated by the cloth-covered dragon on stage and the plastic monkey puppets waiting to be pulled into life.

'I don't need to talk to Caroline. I've already talked to Caroline.'

'What's wrong with you?' he hissed.

'I've changed my mind.' I stood up then, the fire building

in me. 'Take Mia.' I unravelled and unclipped the sling, gathering Mia's warm limbs into my arms. Dave's hands were at his forehead – exasperated, resigned.

When she was safely in the sling and attached to her father, I took her hand. 'I'm sorry for smashing your medicine,' I said, feeling an angry ache in my jaw and tears in my eyes. 'I never meant to do it. I never meant you any harm. I love you. Do you believe me?'

I was speaking to her but I was still looking at Dave.

The lights went down then and a white spotlight swung quick, quicker and quicker, drunkenly quicker around the auditorium. And that's when I saw it, flashes at a time, as the lights caught his eyes like the beams of a lighthouse picking out a shipwreck. That something in me frightened him.

Chapter 7

A seagull – grown plump on discarded chips – shat between the letters R and G on the platform sign for Margate, and took flight, heavily, into the clouds. I filled my lungs with air that tasted sweet and salt, and savoured how easily it moved in and out of me; so unlike the smog of the city that felt like it left plaque in me.

I'd arrived in Margate clutching my speech for the conference. If things had been different, normal, I might have called Dave. Once our calls had punctuated our journey on any days away from each other; they were how we stayed together even when we were apart. Lunch breaks too, sometimes more than one call – a status update on the day's soup, a headache brewing, what we should eat for dinner, office politics. If we had nothing to say we might simply text Hello, Hi or I Love You. A small way of saying: You are missed.

From Margate's railway platform I might have left a voicemail that said, *I'm here. The journey was fine but the air con was broken. How are you? I miss you both. Just checking in. It's nice to be beside the sea. I think I needed a break. To be out of the house. How was she after I left? Tell her I love her. I'll call again when I'm getting back on the train.*

But since our trip to the zoo earlier in the summer so many of the words we spoke or sent to each other had been stiff with practicality, the cold civility of making necessary arrangements. It felt like we were safe so long as we kept to the subject of tasks: size two nappies and carrots on the shopping list, a note to get new syringes from the hospital, the bathroom needing a clean. Any diversion from those tasks – the things he did, the things I wanted to do, what he wasn't doing, what I was already doing – often led to fraught misunderstandings, raised voices and then my tears behind closed doors. So often, it was as if we were talking at each other from opposite sides of a busy road, the sound of traffic drowning out anything more nuanced than simple gestures and one-word shouts.

I set off down the hill towards the seafront. There was some afternoon sun, not enough to burn through thick cloud but enough to shine a half-light, a discomforting post-nuclear kind of light. As the camber of the hill increased, my strides quickened.

That morning I had dressed in front of the mirror; stockings with lace at their tops and a green silk dress that fitted me again after weeks of wearing nothing but leggings and maternity shirts. I tried on all my shoes and chose a high-heeled pair whose straps twisted round my ankles like thorns.

Mother

Dave had come to me as I dropped silk over my shoulders. He was wearing his dressing gown like a pregnant woman, belt lashed comically high above the waist.

'I remember those stockings,' he said, before putting his hand on my thigh. It was the first time in weeks he'd touched me like that.

But before I'd had a chance to think about it, to really think about the meaning of his touch, I recoiled. Our eyes met in the mirror, both of us surprised.

'Sorry, I'm late for my train.' My words were quicker than I intended, quicker than was needed.

He was hurt. 'I still don't understand why you're doing this.'

'Please don't let's start this again.'

'What exactly are you hoping to get out of it?' he said, as if I'd said nothing. But I didn't reply because I wasn't going to be dragged under again. And besides, the real truth would have hurt him. Which was that I needed to hear different things. Things he couldn't tell me. Things he didn't know how to tell me.

My silence seemed to rile him further.

'Can you buy bread and milk and a lemon on the way home because there's nothing in the house.'

That was an untruth. There were things in the house. They just weren't the things he wanted.

'Can't you buy them when you're out with Mia today? I might be back late.'

'I've got to try and work while I look after Mia. It's a working day.'

'Thank you. Thank you for taking her. Is that what you want me to say for the hundredth time?' He'd done it, he'd won, he'd drawn me back in. 'Thank you for looking after our daughter while I do something *I* need to do. Thank you. Thank you. Now will you please stop punishing me for all this? I'm doing it for her. It's not like I'm off playing football.'

I was going out to fight for my cub. Wasn't that how Richard had described it? It was a good way of describing it. I could possess all the power and purpose and passion of a lion in the jungle.

'I think it's a distraction. Like all those pages open on your tablet.' He said that last bit like he'd found evidence of me having an affair. He raised his eyebrows at me. 'What?'

'Why were you looking at my iPad?'

'I needed to order something on Amazon and it was the closest thing to hand. The point is, it's weird, Cath, the number of pages you've got open on CF. You're tracking stock market shares in pharmaceutical companies. I had to update your software to keep the whole thing from crashing. It's obsessive and it doesn't change anything.'

'But it helps *me*.'

'It's not good for you.'

I wondered what he'd have said if I told him that I

had dressed that morning imagining another man's eyes on me and that what it made me feel was more helpful than any shrink or antidepressant could ever be.

'Will you let me do this?' I asked.

'Will you get in touch with a counsellor?'

'I'm not making deals with you. Please just try and have a nice day with Mia.'

'It's a working day for me. I've told you that.'

'I heard you.'

And on we went.

At the bottom of the hill stood a tower block of flats built in the 'brutalist' style. *Out of concrete, with no concern for comfort or ease* – a line from the books I used to read about painting and architecture, the ones that had always inspired images in my head, that made me feel like someday I might make something myself. But I hadn't created – I hadn't drawn since Dad had gone. I'd become numb and stayed numb for months and years, the impasse happily broken with a decision, *the* decision, to get married, buy a house and have a family.

The numbness replaced by feeling: even if the feeling was the fear of never having a baby.

I'd take feeling bad over anaesthesia any time.

I wondered, did the architects of those buildings live long enough to see them demolished? To see society turning against their ideas, pulling them down, erasing them? Did it hurt or were their buildings only ever meant to last a lifetime or less? Even on the day the first foundations were

111

poured, did they know it would end in demolition, dust and a new blueprint for the space? Was it enough to have had something, once?

In front of a wall covered in spray-paint bubble letters was a police car, parked up on the pavement. No sign of a crime or accident. Perhaps the crime had already happened or was about to happen. A split bag of chips lay open, its contents crushed into the pitted tarmac; the fallout of a crime. Or perhaps dinner slipped from the hand; perhaps just bad luck.

Down on the seafront, I strolled along a promenade dotted with the families and workers cashing in on a few extra hours at the beach before sunset or a late afternoon's drinking. Tacking on a few holiday days to the upcoming August bank holiday. Last chance for a break before the long and dismal haul to Christmas.

I took my time, past the billboard promise of the Dreamland theme park. Dreamland: if it all got too over-whelming and I couldn't face delivering my speech, I could escape on a candy-coloured rollercoaster or feel my brain knock repeatedly against my skull riding a flame-painted dodgem. To my left lay the beach, deserted but for a merry-go-round faded to pink and white in the sun, bolts bleeding rust down its sides. On the other side, over the road, an arcade; shut down and boarded up.

Once, this seaside town had been full of families on their summer holidays. Then everyone had left, as suddenly as Cinderella on the stroke of midnight; rides unridden, drinks half empty, one-armed bandits mid-spin. After years of bleaching and greying, a scattering of new structures had risen up. A gallery. Old buildings repainted – yellow, pink and green.

I took a narrow side street lined with shops selling sweets and vintage signs, and arrived at the hotel. *Better for the staff to get out of London*, the charity had said, *better for them to get out of their environment and think of new ways.*

Yes to the new ways!

I took the steps like a hiker tackles the start of a hill. In my handbag a lipstick and a pen and a shawl and a breast pump but no nappies or wipes or bulky cooler bags of medication. This was a chance to feel lighter again.

The interior of the hotel was all grey, white and maroon, like a thousand others. A fan of brochures on a low table. Black leather sofas that weren't made of leather at all but were easy to wipe down. Black-and-white photos on the wall, one of water tipping over rocks. A sunset, or sunrise – I could never tell them apart.

I saw him, then, in reception – the man whose gaze I had imagined when I dressed that morning. He stood straight, his back turned to me, a phone clamped to his ear. The height of him. The breadth of his shoulders. The way he stood there, like that, so invested in whoever he was speaking to. He rested his hand on a sign – one used for a thousand other conferences that pointed delegates like me in the direction of the Nelson Ballroom.

I smoothed down hair that had been bullied by the onshore breeze, and took long, purposeful strides – the heels of my shoes clicking noisily on the marble. I turned my head as I passed him, not enough to make eye contact, but enough. He saw me.

I felt bad, for a moment – for having thought of him as I pulled up my stockings that morning. For having adjusted my hair as I passed him. But then I thought about what I'd said to Caroline as she'd sat in my kitchen only last week, mascara running down her cheeks, a second bottle of wine drained. Grown tired of waiting to be asked round, she had knocked on the door one night holding a bottle of Rioja and apologizing for making it sound like she had been talking with Dave behind my back. That it was a difficult situation for everyone. I had been exhausted, in no mood to talk about my own feelings, and so she'd talked about her own – once she felt assured that I wasn't angry with her. She'd cried about the diagnosis. *Sorry*, she'd said. *I have no right to hate the world, but I do.*

You can hate the world, I'd said, *just don't buy a revolver when you feel that way.* Because my daughter was her niece and of course the diagnosis was difficult for the other people in Mia's life.

Just don't buy a revolver. Just don't hurt anyone.

I wasn't hurting anyone by looking at him like that. As if he were special.

At the end of a beige corridor there was a volunteer

dressed in verdant green, bent over a table of name badges. She told me that the most important directions I would need all afternoon were for the coffee urn, and then she laughed. She took my surname – Dave's surname – and selected my badge. Explained that the green dot on my badge stood for the afternoon's workshop group I had been assigned to. I tried a smile as she handed me an agenda of talks to sit through.

As I fixed the name badge to my T-shirt I looked for his name.

Richard Brightman, orange group. An orange dot, like the stickers they put next to a painting that has already been sold.

The Nelson Ballroom was cold with air conditioning and bright with too many overhead lights. I sat through the opening address – pen in hand, goosebumped arms – but I didn't listen to a single word. Away from the clear sea air, my head felt thick with fog again; crowded with Dave's words, with the knowledge of Richard's presence somewhere and the prospect of stepping into the audience's gaze. I messed with my hair, pulled it back into a ponytail, felt a charge of something through me when the address came to an end and my name was read out: *Cath Freeland, here to talk about the experience of newborn diagnosis*. I felt slippery silk beneath my fingertips and the tug of shame in me. There I was, all bogged down in the arguments, the lipstick and the imaginings of a man I didn't know – and for a moment I had forgotten why I was really there.

To talk about the day I was told my daughter would live a half-life.

Ah, yes. That.

My baby girl back at home, so dear and sweet and unknowing about the mess unfurling around her. So much feeling and love invested in the smile of a barely there child.

I stepped up to the podium and confronted the sea of faces as they fixed their sights on me for the next item on the agenda. My limbs felt skittish and my stomach roiled as I laid my palm on the lectern and a single piece of white paper.

I breathed deeply and looked out into the audience again – one seat in the front row, empty.

Dad. I never got a chance to introduce you to your granddaughter.

Or to tell you our news.

All the speeches I would never make.

Put them aside now. Focus.

Speak.

'When my baby daughter was diagnosed with cystic fibrosis, everything I had hoped and expected of being a mother for the first time was destroyed.' I spoke to an empty seat. 'What had begun with the glory and privilege of witnessing "firsts" – the first time she opened her eyes to the world, the first time she opened her lungs to scream, her first bath and feed – became the terror and pain of witnessing "lasts". If someone had told me, before I became pregnant, what pain and fear I would experience on becoming a mother . . .'

My words shook but I managed to continue talking – about the seismic grief, about the medication. And soon a roomful of strangers came to know more about what I felt than my own husband did.

He hadn't even asked to read my speech.

I spoke about meeting the charity and about meeting people going through the same thing.

Dad, are you there? Tell me, what do you think about all this?

I can't even remember how your voice sounded.

'Strangers change lives forever when they break this news over the phone and in hospital rooms. And it will be strangers again – clinicians, philanthropists and scientists like you – who will change them once more, this time for the better, by helping us find a cure.'

I was finished. Crying now, but with the last words safely out.

Richard was the first person I saw when I looked up again and my face burned from the heat of a gaze that was as proud as a father and curious as a new lover.

I retook my seat and bowed my head as the next guest speaker was introduced, tried to calm my breathing and warm my freezing skin as a research scientist was welcomed from America. Strangers in the seats around whispered kind congratulations. I felt a weight subside.

Then, as the next few hours passed and my words were

replaced with the scientist's theories on macrophages and other things I did not understand and that did not especially sound like hope to me, I began to understand that nobody was going to promise us a cure this year. I tried to focus on the talks and their stats and graphs but my mind kept wandering, wavering and unanchored, looking for what to say, do and think next. The idea of returning home to nothing, nothing changed, nothing planned. A black sea with no horizon.

Soon enough there were questions from the auditorium about how infection was controlled amongst CF patients in America and then I was listening.

'Glove and gown,' the scientist said. 'That is the only way of being sure and even then . . . There is so much that is still unknown about bacterial transmission.'

Glove and Gown. I wished that was the name of a pub I went to and not a policy that was relevant to the life expectancy of my child.

Next somebody gave us instructions to gather in the same place as the coffee urn – *More like coffee altar*, someone heckled – so that the workshops could commence. My breasts were aching now, full of the milk I should have been feeding Mia. I told myself I should go and call Dave, that my silence had been punishment enough. But as everyone stood to leave, I turned around and Richard was there, a few rows back, looking at me. Like he'd been looking at me for some time.

He mouthed: *Hello.*

I smiled, held up a hand, then looked away so that he could not read what was in me.

Back in the room with the coffee urn, I retreated to a corner. Fished my phone out of my handbag and checked its screen. Nothing from Dave. No photographs of her feeding or sleeping. I felt like I had snapped myself from her and needed to get back to mend the break: to kiss her and tell her that I loved her.

I scrolled through my phone, found Dave's number and was about to call when I heard Richard's voice.

'I hadn't expected to see you here.' I felt the silk of my dress gather in my fist because I knew he'd seen me in reception. 'Well done on your speech. That took guts. Bet you're pleased.'

'Thanks for encouraging me.' I dropped my phone back into my handbag. 'And for the medicines, that time . . .' I tried to sound calm, bored even, as if I hadn't thought of him. But the truth was that I'd thought of him every day in the month since we'd last seen each other.

'I'm glad I could help. I've come to join your workshop group. I was put in the nutrition group but there's nothing I don't know about the healing properties of coconut oil, garlic and dark green vegetables. I'm evangelical about that stuff. I bore myself on the subject. Transplants I'm interested to hear more about.'

'Because of how your daughter is?'

He looked surprised, shocked even. 'No, not at all. No, God no, she's nowhere near that. Not even close. I never want things to get that bad. She'll be fine.' I nodded, sorry to have brought up the subject. 'I'm interested because of some more policy work I'm doing for one of the other charities. Our organ-donor system is flawed for so many reasons. Imagine giving people the option of donating their organs at the exact same time they sign their first driving licence? It makes you think about having a car accident straight away. People are superstitious. It's like tempting fate.'

'I suppose so.'

A young woman in overly patterned leggings and charity greens cajoled us to form a circle. 'We need to look at how we increase the number of lung transplants,' she said, too loud. 'How do we encourage more people to sign away their organs? Once we've cracked that, we can hit the bar for a stiff pre-dinner drink or seven.'

The group gathered around an A3 pad and shouted out words that the patterned woman transcribed into red capital letters, as if they were breaking news:

LIFE EXPECTANCY.
BODY OWNERSHIP.
GENEROSITY.
SUPERSTITION.

'Did you know?' said a man, standing up, belly pouring over jeans. 'That someone I spoke to on the transplant list was given an NHS mobile phone so he could be contacted when the organs come in? No one has the number apart from the transplant people and, of course, those bastards that sell life insurance. I mean, listen, Cath, you talked about your daughter up there – can you imagine your little girl is waiting for the call to save her life and some git . . .'

Save her life? She wasn't struggling for breath, she was playing with her dad, she would be missing me and I needed to feed her and be with her to check that she was safe. She would never struggle. That's why I was here.

The skin round my breasts was so taut it itched. I grabbed my bag, murmured an apology and ran to the toilet.

Inside the cubicle was warm and beige and clean. I sat on the toilet seat and pumped milk. Bzzm. Bzzm. I realized I'd have to do this as often as Mia fed, which was a lot.

When I was finished, I poured the expressed milk into the toilet.

'Cath,' said Richard, as I strode out of the bathrooms. 'Is everything all right?'

'Yes. Why?' The simplicity of what he said had shocked me. It was too personal, too intimate for two people who had only met a few times. It was inappropriate. And yet, what he was asking was so simple. There wasn't time to think so I said, 'Yes, no, I mean yes, I am fine. I think.'

'It's only that . . .' He looked at me intensely, stood so close I could smell something on him – cigarette smoke, something else . . . 'You looked pale in the middle of that transplant brainstorm. I know some of that can be hard to hear. Rod has never understood how blunt he can sound.'

'It's OK,' I said, touched by his thoughtfulness. 'I'm breastfeeding, is all. I needed to . . .' I patted my handbag, embarrassed. I didn't want him to think of me as an animal being milked by a machine. 'I should get home.'

'You're not coming to the bar for a drink?' He didn't wait for a reply. 'I wouldn't blame you. After a few hours of cocktails and tequila shots, it's like a school disco.'

'Yes, look, I should go. I need to get home to my baby.'

'I'll walk with you. I could do with a bit of air. And I've got this.' He held up a bottle of something. Tequila. 'Bought it from the bar. I was going to have a quiet little toast to the end of summer as the sun goes down. In case you change your mind.'

'Classy,' I said, amused at how teenage it all felt. 'It wouldn't be the same if it was an upmarket gin, now would it?' I smiled.

Of all the gin joints, in all the towns . . .

'That would be too much like I was trying to impress you.' He stepped forward, opening the door widely for me, catching my eye so briefly I could have imagined it. 'Besides,' he said, when we were out in the street, 'spirits are only good for one thing.' He held the bottle up to the darkening sky: 'Oblivion.' The lines around his eyes crinkled as he smiled. His skin shone, clear and tanned. He offered me the bottle.

I laughed. 'I can't do that. I've got to breastfeed my baby in a few hours. I can't mainline her tequila.'

He shrugged and took his first swig from the bottle. 'Lucky baby, to have such a thoughtful mum.'

Dave used to laugh when I came home drunk but after the birth he'd drawn a line. A few days before diagnosis, I'd returned from a mother-and-baby lunch after too much white wine and his silence was like being shouted at.

Richard and I kept going towards the sea.

I should have gone then. I should have walked away.

'Do you ever find talks about life expectancy difficult?'

'Nope.' He drank more tequila. 'I don't think about transplants. I think of cures. I think about how the cavalry is nearly with us.'

I nodded, disappointed – wishing for solidarity, an allowance that death was a part of why we were both here. Perhaps I was wrong, though. He knew more than me.

For a while we walked in silence along the seafront and I watched the silver disappear from the underside of fine clouds as the sun sank finally into the sea.

'I am afraid sometimes,' he said, as if he had been considering it while we walked. 'Sometimes I feel very afraid,' he added, quietly. And I was glad of it. 'But Rachel's determination keeps me going through the tough-times. Her strength inspires me. It makes me want to be strong. For her.'

'The day before they confirmed the diagnosis,' I said,

'I had a moment when I thought – no, I knew – that they were going to tell us it was all a mistake. That they had mixed up the papers. Got the wrong baby. I imagined that moment so deeply, so absolutely, that I knew in my bones what it was like not to have to worry any longer. Having that burden go away, having that possibility that your child may face an early death, go away? That felt like the giddiest kind of happiness. I realized I hadn't felt anything like it before. I realized it was the first time I'd felt truly happy. And it was all in my head. None of it real. Isn't that rubbish? The happiest moment of your life and it's nothing but a fantasy.'

I had never told Dave that, but then I suppose our conversations had become crowded with other things. And when they weren't crowded, they needed other things, other distractions.

Dave might have said, *You weren't truly happy the day we got married?*

Not happy like that, no.

'I'm not explaining it right,' I said. 'It's like someone is dying in the desert and they finally see water and they can almost taste it and then—'

'It's a mirage.'

'Yes. It's just more sand. And then you die.' I laughed, but there wasn't any joy behind it.

Richard stopped, then, at the top of uneven, sand-covered steps that led down to the beach. He looked up the hill to the station and turned to me. 'You'll be happy again,' he said, with such assurance that I believed him absolutely. 'It gets easier.' And he turned his back and walked down the steps to the sand.

I followed him, taking care not to slip on the steps. 'And until then,' I said, 'there has to be some fun. Give me that.' I took the bottle of tequila from his hand and drank; one gulp, then several more. The liquid stung my throat, like antibacterial gel stings cuts on your hands you didn't know were there.

The tide was coming in on a black and blue-lit beach, long-billed birds skewering the mudflats for what wriggles and tunnels beneath. A mile away, fairground lights at the end of the pier flared red, green and gold across dark water.

My breasts ached and burned. My fingers felt them instinctively before I noticed he was looking.

'My boobs hurt,' I said. Then I laughed because it was the kind of thing I'd say to my sister or a girlfriend, not him.

'Not sure I can help you there,' he said – amused, surprised, something I was pleased to have made him feel.

'Anything you could do would be inappropriate for a public beach.' I thought too late about what I'd said, the implied image of him milking my breasts on a beach. I would have been mortified if I'd been sober. But I wasn't – so when he laughed, I laughed too. My sober self, my old self, had no place here.

He swerved abruptly, in the opposite direction to me.

'What are you doing?' I said.

'Tidal mud,' he said. 'I . . . we've spent ten years of family beach holidays avoiding it. Nothing like three months of inhaled antibiotics and nail-biting waits for test results to make you regret taking your child to the wrong bit of the beach on an otherwise idyllic family holiday.'

'Pseudomonas aeruginosa,' I said.

He looked up. 'You're learning quickly.'

'Sandpits, lakes and rivers,' I said. 'Proximity to these joyful places will put your child in mortal danger.' I was afraid, then, for who I was becoming; such a fine line between sarcasm and bitterness. 'We have so much to look forward to.'

I sat down on dry sand, suddenly, as if the weight of it all was too much. He turned around and took a step towards me, sitting beside me, and for a while we drank – long enough for my skin to chill, long enough for the silence to feel normal. Side by side, elbows resting on bent knees like teenagers at a beach party. Looking out at the horizon. Saying nothing. Asking nothing as the tequila melted the edges of my thoughts.

I checked my phone. A blank screen. Not even a charge.

By the time I got home they would be asleep – our daughter curled into Dave's chest.

I took the tequila bottle from Richard's hand for the last time, drained it and threw it at the sandbank. I unfastened the straps of my shoes and stood. Waded into the tidal mud so that my legs were covered in it. For a moment I was disgusted but fell to my knees anyway. Then I lay back in that mud, feeling the damp clag in my hair, the tickle of wetness around my head and ears.

It felt cold and dirty, how a pig must feel.

'Why are you doing that?' he said.

'Because I can.'

His laugh was warm and chaotic.

I eased myself out of the mud and ran towards him growling, holding my hands up like a zombie. 'I'm coming to get you.' I growled and laughed, laughed more, growled louder.

He ran into the water and I went in after him, mud slapping on wet sand beneath. Soon I couldn't keep up and the tequila and weight of water against my calves confused me, held me back until I tripped and fell, collapsing into the sea, waves breaking around me, laughing till I couldn't breathe. The water was achingly cold and my breath came in short bursts, reminding me of something – giving birth, having sex.

There were only a few feet of sea between us then. I leaned back so that the water rose to my neck, covered my chest and soothed the breasts that needed a mouth; numbed them so I could no longer feel the stretch and pull of skin. He lay next to me, his face towards the sky. It was like we were both trying to catch the last rays of a sun that wasn't there and all I could think was, *Two people shouldn't be this close.*

'You're funny,' he said.

The tequila was travelling through my blood like a log flume, faster than my thoughts. I wanted to go where it took me and so I did, I went, I said, 'Is there . . . ?'

But then I caught myself – if I said any more there would be no going back, but I was having more fun than I'd had in a long time.

'What?' he said. 'What are you saying?' He smiled because he knew exactly what I was saying. His smile was imperfect and inviting and it made me want to go faster.

'Is there . . . I don't know?'

We both looked away from the sky and sat up to face each other.

His hand reached out of the water and he wiped something from my face with his thumb, so firmly it hurt. 'Mud,' he said. 'There's still mud all over you.' His hand remained on my face.

I held up my hand – like *hello*, like *please stop*. 'Here, have some.' I smeared the mud across his cheek. 'Now it's on you too.'

All at once, the pain in my breasts was too much, too searing even for the anaesthetic cold of the water.

I needed to get home to Mia. To feed and reassure her. To be her mother.

I looked at him again – the last time, I told myself – and waded heavily back to the beach. Back on the sand I ran as fast as I could.

Chapter 8

Scads of wet sand and mud smeared the floor of the railway station's disabled toilet cubicle and the ammonia stench of stale urine stuck thickly to the membranes of my nose and mouth. A mirror pane hung high on the wall – haughty, cloudy with grease – reflecting tribal smudges of mud slashed across my face and bottle green silk clinging across my shoulders in dark, sodden wrinkles.

I scrubbed at my face with an antibacterial wipe and dropped it into the empty tray of a sanitary bin. I used the rest of the wipes on any visible area of me, and thanked God for the coruscating, antibacterial properties of salt in seawater. It would have washed away the worst of the infectious mud from my skin. It would have cast risk and evidence far out to sea.

Still my breasts throbbed with pain and my skin itched with salt. I thought of Richard on that beach – of where he'd gone when I left, and where else he might have gone if I'd stayed. There was a pressure in my chest and a flush of heat through me despite my skin puckering with cold. I unfurled a shawl out of my handbag, strands of its fine mauve wool catching on the zip in my haste to cover myself, and perched cautiously on the closed toilet seat. Tried to forget the mess I was as the breast pump started to pull milk from me.

I took panicked sips of air, not wanting to inhale any more of that environment than I needed. I didn't want spores from the tap's black mould getting into my lungs, nor the gritty flakes from a U-bend's lime green and white cast sticking to my skin. I was sitting too close to a stranger's balled-up and soiled piece of badly aimed toilet paper.

I couldn't stay there any longer. Imagining pseudomonas, E. coli, C. difficile and countless other species of bacteria multiplying in the space around me. Picturing their armies, linked and furred, crawling and clawed, first finding and then touching and finally breaking the skin with poison-tipped talons.

I shut off the pump, the job only half-done, and ripped out its tubes, tipped Mia's milk into the sink. A sleeve-covered hand to turn a tap, an elbow in place of a palm to bear down on the door handle.

On the short walk up the platform I rolled up my sleeves, trying not to touch the areas that may have made contact with the door handle. I would not touch the furniture or carpets when I arrived home later. I would tip my clothes into a bin bag and then I would tip that bag into the washing machine and set it to boil.

Dave had been right; I shouldn't have come to this

seaside town with all those unrealistic expectations of how it might change things for us. I shouldn't have been on that beach in near darkness when everyone else had packed themselves up into hotels and bars and restaurants for the night. I shouldn't have been in that town, on that beach with a man who wasn't my husband.

If Dave was still awake when I returned . . . If he was awake and he asked me why my clothes were wet, I would say there had been rain. The kind that falls like a bathroom shower – but that my talk had been good, thank you, and the journey back uneventful.

I was alone on the platform. The charge of tequila and adrenalin in my blood retreating with the tide, leaving me drained of their sparkling and capricious energy. I pulled the shawl closer to keep myself warm. Only then did I allow myself to think of how Richard had left a joyful imprint on my skin where he'd touched my cheek.

I had felt bound to Dave a hundred times over with that feeling when we first met. It was life giving and mood altering and I had missed it. It was not designed to sustain a relationship throughout its life. I understood that. I understood that it needed to give way to something more nurturing, more suitable for raising a family.

There were no people and no CCTV cameras on the platform and if I were abducted – lifted from the platform with a strong embrace, thrown over a shoulder, silenced with a snowball of fabric in my mouth – no one would see. Even if the track of my damp footprints remained on the platform, no one would think how odd it was that the track suddenly ended, because the track of everyone's footprints comes to an end on a platform like this. It's where trains are boarded. Where journeys are begun and others ended.

Words crackled through a speaker. The train to London, delayed.

Eleven minutes to wait.

On the edge of the platform, I dared myself to stand in front of the yellow line, dared anyone watching to tell me: *Stand back, please, madam*. But they didn't.

A seagull's call. A shout. A catcall, from a human or an animal. But no one with words for me.

Unsure, unsteady – I felt bound to something and yet cast adrift, and I listed the substances that were causing it:

Tequila, adrenalin, cortisol, oxytocin, the possible beginnings of a chemical reaction in me as bacteria from mud or mould twisted its way into my immune system.

And something else.

Once I boarded the train safely I would find a seat and the carriage would be empty because it was late at night. I would be alone. The upholstery would be cold, laid over hard plastic, and the windows left open from the daytime. A shawl would not be nearly enough to warm me. I would sit alone with my memories of the day and the evening and I would begin to doubt whether it had all happened in the way it did, whether it had only been me that felt something deep and changing.

Perhaps doubt would be for the best.

I would think about him all the way down the tracks in thoughts that were neat and disbelieving, parcelled out one at a time like the rationing of a packet of sweets. And as the lights of the city emerged I would break those thoughts up into guilty chunks as images of Dave and Mia intruded between them. Before getting home I knew I would have returned to my memory of him twenty times, a hundred times. A lapsed addict not quite believing her luck that she'd found something new to make her feel so good again.

Richard had altered my physiology, lit up my neurons in a new path.

Seven minutes.

Back at home, I would turn the key in the lock. See the pram in the hall. Think of him, and think of her. Tiptoe to sleep alone in the spare room where the mattress was hard and the duvet scratchy with a nylon mix. In the next-door room Dave and Mia would be asleep, side by side, unaware of my return. But six a.m. would come around and then Dave would drop Mia into my aching, guilty arms, his eyes half closed with the need to sleep again. He would shuffle back to the door without a word and I would turn to her, kiss her and feed her, my heart filling with the joy and relief of seeing her again despite my body craving the oblivion of sleep.

Five minutes.

I had a piece of time that I could do anything with.

Take some time for yourself! everyone seemed to say when I was pregnant. *Because it will be in short supply when the baby arrives!*

So I'd gone to swimming pools and cinemas and cafés on my own like I was living out my last dying moments. Pressured. Overrated.

Three minutes.

If I was at home, the time would come for Dave to leave for work and he would do so without a word. He would close the front door and there would be no conversation or contact until he returned that evening. A day would stretch ahead with no plans because I hadn't made any. I would lie on the rug and look at the ceiling while Mia slept. I would sterilize syringes, pour medicines and thump Mia's chest, imagining mucus and infection dropping off her lung walls with every beat.

Two minutes.

And that night he would say it again and we would go round in circles. *See someone, see someone. See a shrink because I can't seem to say the right thing.*

And I would hear, in the gaps between those words: *See that shrink because I can't do it, I give up. I am not qualified to be your husband.*

I walked up the platform, to see if the train was coming.

But it wasn't. And there was no one.

And there would be no one tomorrow.

Apart from Mia, and my memories.

Memories of Dad, memories of a marriage.

One day I would be left alone with memories of my daughter.

The train rounded the bend, shining its lights in my eyes. It came to a standstill at the platform and I stood in front of its open doors. But I did not board. No one urged me or encouraged or chivvied me – *Come on love, make up your bloody mind* – and after the requisite fifty seconds the doors shut and the train pulled out of the station.

I turned and re-traced the now invisible track of my damp footprints. Slowly at first. Then at the end of the platform I broke into a run, past the toxic toilet cubicle and through the closed ticket hall.

In the night air I picked up pace and ran as fast as my spiked heels and the cutting straps at my ankles would allow. Grateful for the discomfort of leather seams rubbing and cold silk sticking to my skin, displacing other thoughts – better thoughts, committed thoughts, honourable thoughts. Impractical outfit and impractical footwear for the wrong place and the wrong time and the wrong person . . .

And I ran faster, despite the pain.

I had a piece of time that I could do anything with.

Uncounted, it belonged only to me and now I would belong to it.

My throat crackled with breath that was fast and alive. My chest walls strained and I felt the damp sting of raw flesh at my ankles where the straps cut. I was running so fast down the hill and back to the seafront that I nearly hit the wall where earlier the police car had been parked.

I ran back along the seafront.

I looked forward. At the street I had been on earlier.

I arrived back at the hotel and came to a stop in the peaceful lobby – breath hot and impatient in a chest that didn't have space for it. The place was empty, not even a receptionist, and through my caught breaths and coughs I felt the weight of disappointment, seeing then that I had been expecting him to be there. Standing. Waiting for me.

Of all the gin joints, in all the towns . . .

His head full of the same conflicted and wanting thoughts as mine.

In that emptiness my resolve to find him felt shameful and pointless: a drama manufactured in my head, its context and meaning now ripped away.

But as I turned to leave I heard music playing and a cheer raised from the recesses of the lobby. I followed the sounds to the hotel bar where the space reeled with movement; lurching disco lights, staggering charity employees grasping at drinks and each other. Absorbed. Locked into smiles and touches. Dancing. Huddles, riven with secret thoughts and rivalries, loves and crushes. Plans to leave. Plans to stay.

I sat at the bar and ordered a drink – gin, to replace the buzz of the tequila – and for a short time I felt comfortable. But as the music got louder, chants and conversation more in tune with each other than before,

I felt different to them. And alone. It made sense; the charity employees in that bar had begun the evening at the same time, like they'd all caught the same train together.

But theirs wasn't a journey I was on, so I drained my glass and left.

Back in the lobby, the beginnings of rain outside stopped me. It fell lightly at first until, within seconds, it was driving itself with such force into the pavements that it danced back up towards the sky in sharpened swords. It was sad, to watch the rain launch a pointless and pitiful battle to return to the clouds, to see how far it would have to go and how it would never succeed because the essential nature of rain was to fall.

'It's not like you can get any wetter. Going out in that.'

Him. Like a thunderclap. Sending a thousand charges through my blood.

I turned to find Richard standing by the lift door, wearing a sweatshirt that was navy and dry; the opposite of the sodden white T-shirt I had last seen him in.

He walked towards me and held my arm by the wrist. 'You're cold,' he said.

I became aware of more than the itch of salt on my skin. Of how my skin attached to the flesh, and how the flesh attached to the bones that protected my organs. He was holding the skin that held together everything that was me and he was holding it like it was precious.

He took off his sweatshirt and draped it round my

shoulders, then took my hand, walking me towards the lift. His hands were big and rough and mine felt small and smooth and protected inside them. If anyone we knew from the charity had seen us like that and raised an eyebrow, I wouldn't have cared. Our indiscretion would have been worth it for this, the first time, my hand in his.

The lift doors slid open, just as the train doors had on Margate's platform. But this time I didn't hesitate before I stepped inside.

There were no words as we ascended. Only breath. Only us, side by side, hands held, fingers intertwined, as we rose higher and higher and higher. And outside the lift he turned to face me, closer that time, and looked at me as if to say: *You can turn back. I would understand.*

But I held his hand tighter than before.

His hotel room was beige and brown, striped and draped, and I stood at its threshold. A black leather wash bag lay open on a glass side table. A can of shaving foam; a well-known brand, a missing lid. A tube of toothpaste and a toothbrush; still wet and pooling dilute paste. A bottle of contact lens solution. His wet, white T-shirt lying lifeless at the bathroom door. The room smelt of soap and him and he ushered me in with a hand at my back.

Then it was just us, hermetically sealed from the rest of the world by double glazing and door locks. Us, our breaths and the low hum of an air-conditioning unit.

I would be asleep, otherwise. At home, in the spare

room. But here I was awake, standing at the centre of this new piece of time I had given myself.

'You can go,' he said. 'Whenever you want.'

He lifted his palm to my cheek, as he had done on the beach, and I tilted my face to fit it. For a moment we stayed like that and I was happy not to be held because I needed holding together.

I took his other hand in mine and we linked fingers, the action of it bringing us closer still so that I could feel the heat of his breath on my face. I leaned forward and kissed him once. He closed his eyes tight like he was experiencing a slow and agonizing pain, a needle finding its way into a vein.

His hand traced a path down my neck and my breath quickened; his fingertips rough against the thin skin along my collarbone, drawing a fine line along the top of my breasts where there was still pain as new milk continued to rush in. I looked into his eyes, gripped by self-consciousness and the thought of him seeing the blue blood striations caused by multiple breastfeeds. I grasped his wrist tight and stopped him, held his palm to the flattest plane between my breasts, as if it were neutral ground. But his gaze was full of such longing that it drowned any anxiety and the moment passed quickly. I released my grip and allowed him to slip the sleeves of my dress off my shoulders, to pull down the straps of my bra and reveal the map of blue veins. He stroked away the throb and the pain across the flesh and I closed my eyes as he unhooked my bra and kissed areas so tender I flinched. I closed my eyes and kissed him again. We kissed each other – and for a time I was something other than fundamental to another's survival.

I grasped his hair, soft and rough under my fingertips, ran my hands under his T-shirt and down the curve of his spine. I undid his belt, felt where the band of his boxer shorts met skin and banished thoughts of how different his skin felt to Dave's, of how I wanted to touch this man's skin like the coat of a soft and dangerous animal. I kissed him more, everywhere, the smell of him familiar and yet new. Then it wasn't enough only to be touching each other. I needed to be part of him and I needed him to be part of me, for us to map ourselves to each other. Empty of resolve, no part of me wanting to turn back, defeated by a need stronger than any I had felt for anyone before. Feeling, in that moment, that the meeting of that excruciating, extraordinary desire was fundamental to my survival.

As his hand moved over the loose and soft flesh of my belly, I thought of how unacquainted with this body Dave was. Dave had made love to a long and taut body before pregnancy – passionate and quick and often in the early days. And then later to a body that had swelled with hormones during IVF – clumsy and functional, needing and wanting. And sometimes, not often, to the body stretched and filling with a child – cautious, afraid of causing pain or damage. But he had not touched the new body, the one that had been excavated, left limp and soft.

He had not touched the body that had become food for a child. He had not touched the new body because I had pushed him away, afraid he would find it as alien as I did. Afraid that in comparing me to the past, he would not like the woman that I had become. The woman that life had forged in front of him.

I held Richard's arm tight, bit my lip and held back tears as his palm pressed between the elastic of my knickers and belly. I bit my lip so hard it bled. I tried not to cry at the thought of a person and a past I was unravelling, at a loyalty I was burning, as he held my gaze and kissed me. As his hand moved between my legs, to the very place even I had been anxious about touching or seeing for fear of discovering the truth: that I had been sewn up in a grotesque manner. That I had not been mended properly.

Richard seemed to sense my anxiety and whispered, 'It will be OK. I won't hurt you.' But I didn't know what kind of hurt he was talking about – there were, after all, a hundred kinds of pain. It wasn't the pull and catch on skin as his fingers went deep into me because I knew how much I wanted him and that was the opposite of pain. 'I won't hurt you,' he said again as he laid me down on the bed and kissed my breasts and belly and I kissed him back because I believed that he spoke the truth. He entered me and then it hurt. But even then, the pain was the most delightful I had felt; it came as quickly as it went leaving something lasting and warm in its wake.

There was no past, no future and no consequence.
There was just us. Us and our breaths.

He had not hurt me.

He had healed me.

Chapter 9

When I woke I was tragically grateful for rest without the snapped and shredded images of dreams because for months, years even, sleep had dismayed me with quests that were bruised, bloodied and always without resolution.

I opened my eyes to the darkness and the shapes it made had a clarity and calm. Thin slices of midnight blue framed the blind. On one patch of quilt, moonlight shone through in matchsticks. On the carpet, a pool of golden light emerged from a slash of space beneath the closed bathroom door.

It was the sound of things moved and used behind the bathroom door – the complaint of a tap being shut off, a glass knocking against metal – that disturbed and reminded me that I was somewhere I shouldn't be. I pulled the sheet around my torso, and sat up, searching desperately for my clothes and shoes. My dress lay flat on the floor, damp and abandoned, its arms outstretched and skirts full as if it had been sucked dry of the woman that belonged in it.

But before I had a chance to find anything else the door opened and there he stood, a towel wrapped tightly around his waist. I felt the heat in me as I remembered how my arms had reached, how my fingertips had touched where his shoulders widened and swelled. And how those shoulders I had held on to did not belong to my husband. Did not belong to me.

But Richard looked happy. Childishly so – as if I were new to him and endlessly delightful. I found it hard to look away, as there was childishness in me too and then he said, 'Please, don't go,' as he sat down next to me and held my hand in his.

I looked at the sheets bunched around me and how they pooled and scalloped like the skirts of a gown I would never wear outside that room. I knew I had to leave and that one look, if held too long, would draw me in and make me bury the truth of it; which was that I was not someone who could float in gowns and lose her slippers at midnight. Not when I had made promises to honour and commit to another human being, several times over: I had made them the day I first kissed Dave, the day I moved in with him, the day I married him, the day I fell pregnant, the day I gave birth and a new role was conferred upon me to maintain the new, precious and precarious life we had both made.

My life, a legion of promises, mangled and mutated in a single night.

Richard pulled at the sheets that bunched between us

and I resisted him at first, until he drew me closer so that I could smell his skin again.

One moment more. But only one. So safe and warm and out of sight in that sealed hotel room. Then I would go.

I felt his warmth on me, his arms cast around me and his breath, deep and slow, against me. He tucked hair behind my ears and kissed my neck slowly as if it were made of fragile material.

How quickly this had happened. How quickly I would need to forget it.

I closed my eyes and released myself from him. Reached down and gathered up the green silk dress in my fist, cold and stiff with salt, and stood up.

He held on to my hand, even though I had moved away from him.

'I haven't stopped thinking about you since the day we met,' he said.

I looked into his eyes, the light from the bathroom casting a triangle of gold and shadow over his face.

He didn't ask me whether I had thought the same, and I was glad of it because the moment I had given myself was this. Nothing before and nothing after. This time with him would be the isolated mutation of my life that I would throw away and forget.

Not the rest, not the other promises and people.

'This can't happen again,' I said, pulling the dress over my head, the material catching and failing to unfurl as easily and smoothly as silk should.

'No,' he said. But his eyes said the opposite.

'Never.' But I couldn't take my hand away from his. I picked up his other hand and held it in mine, feeling the warm metal of his wedding ring between my fingers, then returned his hand gently to his lap.

He laughed softly, sensing my hesitation. 'Are you going to ask me?' he said.

'No.' But my eyes were dipped again, afraid they would betray what I wanted to know.

'If you did ask me, I'd tell you that she and I are all but over. We only stay together for Rachel's sake.'

He pulled me down on to the bed next to him and kissed me. I kissed him back and it was as if the bookend of sleep had never happened and what we had done together was remembering itself and starting again. For a moment, a few at most, I allowed myself to drink in the memory of that, as if I was fuelling up for a long journey.

He broke away first. 'And if I asked you about him?'

'Let's not . . .'

'OK,' he said quietly. 'But I want to know more about you. How to get more information out of you, though?' he said thoughtfully, his smile then so childish and mischievous that I laughed. 'What about a game? Snap? No, not that: we've both got kids with CF, both in unhappy relationships . . . That would be a short game.'

'I'm not in an unhappy relationship . . .'

'Happy Families then! No, not for me. Twister? Boggle? I've got it: word association. Would word association make you feel less like you're going to say something that will ruin your life?'

'Probably.'

'I'll start then.' He returned my hand to his. 'Light.'

'Fairy,' I said, smiling.

'Wings.' He stroked my shoulder blades and ran a line where wings might have grown in another life.

'Bird . . . stork.'

'Aeroplane.'

'Cracker.'

'Cracker doesn't have anything to do with aeroplanes.' He kissed me quickly, repeatedly; the kind of kiss you gave someone that was newly yours. Dave and I had kissed each other like that once. I still kissed Mia like that.

I should have turned away and picked up my stockings and handbag, to go to her, but instead I said, 'Crackers are everything to do with aeroplanes. I love them. They're the only plane food I eat.' I brushed away the hair from my eyes. 'I ate them the first time I flew. They remind me of how exciting it is to be in the air.'

'We should fly together sometime. Let's fly, to New York, so I can see the look on your face when they put the tray down in front of you.'

I laughed and stopped, as joy was suffocated by a membrane of sadness. There would never be a time we shared a flight together, and he knew it.

There would never be a time when we met again.

There should never be a time.

147

There was no future for us, either as lovers or a family.

Our children couldn't even breathe the same air. They could never go to each other's birthday parties or share a room on holiday in a place with sun and sea. They could never sit at Sunday lunch together or kiss each other good night or read together or watch television on a sofa next to each other. They could never become sisters.

If they did any of those things together, their germs – strong after years of growing and changing – would infect each other's already weak lungs.

And bit by bit our children would fade faster before us.

They couldn't be with each other any more than Richard and I.

'I have to go,' I said, glancing around the room for my handbag.

His face softened and he held me there. 'Tell me one more thing. Please, tell me what you wish for most. I want to know.'

I sat up, lifting the bed's blanket around me because the cold damp of the dress and the air conditioning was making me shiver.

I took a deep breath and looked into his eyes, hesitating for a moment because I worried that what I most wanted to say would make him see a woman that was weak and unformed. But the way he looked at me? There was only warmth and desire, as if nothing I could say would change that.

'I wish I was a different person. No, a better person. I wish I was a better person in so many ways. A better mother, wife, friend, sister, daughter. Mostly I wish that I was the kind of person who could cope.'

'You can but you don't know it. It's early days.'

I smiled, pleased at his faith in me. 'I don't know, I've been doing some strange things.'

'Long may that last.' He pulled me back down on to the mattress and swung one leg across me. He brought my face to his. 'Every time I look at you . . .' His hand tracked up my thigh, running circles at my waist, along the top of my leg, between my legs. 'Every time I look in your eyes I just want to hold you, hug you, kiss you, fuck you until you know there's something else you can feel.'

I felt him against me, next to me, with me – so close in mind, so entirely without the impediments of character or history. It felt so pure, so strong, so impossible to imagine that anything could ever come between us. 'You tell me now. What do you most wish for?'

'Other than wanting you to stay all night and all day tomorrow and the next day?' He lay back and I rested my head on his chest, his arm drawing me close. I laid my palm against the soft fur of his chest. 'I wish that Rachel had been born fifteen years later. Things would be easier.'

'But she's doing so well. You said.' I shifted a bit, my legs stiff and uncomfortable.

'Yes.' But there was something, a minor inflection in

his voice that forced my thoughts into order. His daughter was in her late teens and it would be unusual, nearly a miracle, for her not to be culturing something in her lungs. I'd asked him, I know I'd asked him. Hadn't I asked him?

'What does she have? What is she being treated for?'

'Oh, God, not much. The usual.'

'What's *the usual*?'

His throat rippled as he swallowed. 'Oh, I don't know. Pseudomonas aeruginosa.'

My palm sprang away from his chest as if it had set light. There was the tingle of something on my fingertips as I felt myself at the end of a chain:

Rachel kissed Richard. Richard kissed me. K.I.S.S.I.N.G.

I sat up to look at him, picturing infectious bacteria moving from Richard's chest into the recesses of my mouth, my pubic hair, my eyebrows, burrowing down and hiding where no soap or chemical could find them.

He sat up too. 'What's wrong?'

'Nothing,' I said breathlessly. 'I mean, everything. I thought you said she, I thought you said Rachel was doing OK? Didn't you say she was healthy?' My eyes darted to the sheets, now rumpled and pulled from a mattress that was brown and water-marked.

'I don't know what I said. She is, mostly, healthy. She was very—'

'But we were talking about pseudomonas on the beach and all those family holidays when you tried to avoid it. Why didn't you say anything then? I don't understand why you didn't say anything?' I felt displaced, like a warm-blooded reptile tipped on to raining city streets.

He pushed himself up against a bank of pillows. 'Because it didn't seem relevant.'

'How wasn't it relevant? We were naming bacteria.'

Word association: tidal mud, family, bacteria, pseudomonas, Rachel, Richard, Cath, Mia . . .

'Because, well . . .' He turned around and patted a pillow flat against the headboard. 'I suppose because Rachel's pseudomonas isn't the kind you get in mud. Or anywhere else in the environment, so it didn't . . .' He paused. 'It's the other kind.'

'The clinical kind?'

I was cold then but not the kind of cold caused by the outside – by wind and rain and snow or air conditioning and damp clothes. I was primal cold, cold caused from the inside – by the blood rushing away from the extremities towards the major organs, to keep you alive in the face of threat and danger.

'You *have* been doing your reading. Yes, it's hospital-acquired. The worse kind, the harder to treat kind. But what you have to understand . . .'

I glanced around me; at the wash bag and the sweat-shirt all creased and cast aside on the smartly upholstered armchair – all of it came from his house, their house, his daughter's house, a house that was colonized with bacteria that would make my daughter ill, that could reduce her capacity to breathe in days.

'I have to go. Where is my handbag? Why didn't you tell me before we did this?' I motioned around the room, at the mess, and at him, at the thought of everything we'd done and everything that could mean. I grabbed my shoes, a tangle of straps between my fingers, fitted and coiled them around the sores on my ankles, feeling the sting of it all, the terrible chest cracking guilt of it all.

'You were rolling around in the mud, which kind of implied you didn't feel that strongly about bacteria . . .'

'What?' I saw the strap of my handbag looped under the bed and pulled it out like a hiding child, a tumbleweed of grey dust following in its wake.

I bashed the side of my handbag to rid it of dirt. 'I can wash the mud off. Antibiotic-resistant strains are different. I don't . . .' I felt the tears coming. 'I can't wash you off, and that bacteria, I don't know how . . .'

He got out of bed and walked to me, holding out his arms. 'Please, come here. You're so upset. It's OK. I really don't think those bacteria are as virulent as you think.'

I stepped away and held my arms out so he wouldn't come closer. 'You don't *think*? You don't know! No one knows, and I'd rather not take the risk. You heard them this afternoon at the glove and gown talk. No one knows the true extent of bacterial infection and virulence, but they seem to know enough . . .' I pressed my palm against my forehead. 'They seem to be afraid enough in America to take real precautions. You heard them, Richard. In America the consultants have a shower, they change their clothes and wear new gloves and gowns every single time they see a different cystic fibrosis patient. That's six showers and six changes of clothes if they are seeing six patients in a single afternoon. They are that worried about becoming the vehicle for infection.'

And yet I continued to stand in that room, with that man, wearing a skin that was toxic with infection, crowded with bacteria waiting for its moment to jump on Mia and crawl into her lungs where it would bed down and erode and infect and kill.

'You look so afraid,' he said. And for a moment he looked so sad, and I was so confused I stepped back. But he grabbed me, like he was trying to stop me from falling.

'Why didn't you say anything?' I tried to let go of him, I did, my hands clutching and unclutching his sleeves, fingers unwilling to let go and afraid to cling on.

'It's OK. You don't need to be afraid. Everyone with CF cultures pseudomonas at some point. It happens. And this, Rachel's kind, it's not as bad as you think.' His smile was so warm and intense and heartfelt that I smiled back, like a baby mirroring the smile of her mum. 'She's cultured and then eradicated so many bugs in her life . . . It's always a worry that something will stick and never leave, but it usually works out. We get through it. It's not so bad.'

I looked up at him. Waiting for what he was about to say.

'The strain Rachel has . . .' he said. 'We were lucky. It's not as nasty as some of the ones out there.'

'I understand, I do . . . But I have a new baby.' I felt the tears behind my eyes as I said it, at the realization that as I had turned my back for a moment . . . 'It's my job to look after her and I can't do that without the right information.'

Maintain your promise. Maintain life.

I pulled away again, turned to the door but he held me tighter and pulled me to him.

'I'm sorry,' he said. 'I guess I'm used to these things. But you don't need to worry on this one, Cath.' He smiled and looked up at the ceiling like he was thanking a benign deity. 'I was so relieved when they told me that it was sensitive to one antibiotic. One! Can you believe it? Thank God! All we needed was one.'

He reached out to stroke my hair. 'How can it be that bad if tomorrow I'm meeting Rachel at the airport? I'm taking her to Rome to see *Tiger Love*.' He glanced over at the tan leather suitcase lodged in the corner of the room. 'Rachel may be fighting something but she's still having fun. Life with CF – a normal life – can be done. Remember?'

I leaned back and saw his eyes blaze with the need for me to understand. I smiled partly because he asked it of me and partly because I was happy to hear what he'd said. So happy to hear that life carried on and in a way that was joyful. And yet . . . 'I still have to go. I can't take these risks, not with my daughter's health.'

'It's not even light,' he insisted. 'The first train doesn't start running for an hour. Please, stay.'

I was crying again, but perhaps I had never stopped. 'I don't know what we did. I don't know what we're doing. I don't know how we can have a conversation about our lives without discussing our marriages. This whole thing is, is . . . dangerous.' My breath was short, unable to find its boundaries in the lungs.

I picked up my shawl and stepped towards the door, holding my breath as if that would reduce the amount of bacteria entering my system.

'Stay, please,' he said. I felt his hurt gaze on me as I slung my handbag over my shoulder and twisted the lock in the door. 'I'm sorry I didn't tell you,' he said quickly, as I pressed down on the door handle and stepped back into the dim light of the hallway. 'I didn't tell you because . . . the tequila, the beach . . . and you. For a moment you made me forget it all.'

I looked back at him before I closed the door.

I knew. I had felt the same.

And it could cost me everything.

Chapter 10

I fell asleep at some point along the ninety-mile stretch of motorway and woke only as the taxi drew into a parking space outside my front door. I saw Dave's bike chained to the railings, the bins wheeled out for collection and the greying orange light of dawn.

I closed the front door softly behind me. Stripped off my clothes still standing on the doormat. Slipped on other shoes, taking care that my bare and contaminated feet didn't touch the floor. Crammed my damp and filthy clothes into one of the bin bags I had left by the door to ring-fence and capture the toxic grimy drops of other people's umbrellas.

I couldn't guarantee that the most scalding wash would do the eradication job I needed, so I said goodbye to that bag of clothes – both sad and relieved to see the last of that green dress. I tied off the top of the bag with a yank and hurled it on to the pavement with the rest of the rubbish.

Finally, I put my handbag and heels in another bin bag by the door to remind me to disinfect it all – with bleach, the strongest substance I could think of – and covered my hands in antibacterial gel to eradicate the whorl of Richard's prints on me.

Tiptoeing to the landing, I snapped on the bathroom light and twisted the dial on the shower to its most urgent temperature. I stood in front of the bathroom mirror and watched my reflection escape behind a cloud of steam.

'Sleep well?' Dave said, somewhere on the landing outside, and my breath faltered.

'Yes, not bad, yes, fine, thank you . . .'

He appeared at the doorway, bleary-eyed and yawning, holding a bundle of wriggling Mia in his arms. 'How was it?'

'Fine,' I said to the steam cloud in front of me.

'Good news,' he said, as I turned to him. 'This one slept through from ten last night. Didn't need a bottle or even a cuddle. How great is that?' He looked thrilled. It was a 'first': hers and also a joint family achievement. I should have been delighted at the hopeful beginning of us all sleeping through the night again. And yet it felt like a loss, a hollowing at the pit of my stomach that ached for not having been there to witness it; the first time she didn't need me.

'It's great, wonderful.'

Mia began to cry, escalating to fire-alarm sobs as I held back my own.

'That means she hasn't eaten since six last night because she hated her bottle at dinner. Hated that it wasn't your boobs. Give her a quick feed before you get under the water?' Mia's screams intensified.

'I'll have a quick shower first.'

'Can't you do that after you've fed her?'

'No, look, I don't know. I should shower. I was on a train last night. The seats were dirty, I've been around people with colds and so many of those people at the conference have kids with CF . . . what if I've carried something back with me?'

'Wash your face and antibac your hands? Have a shower later?' He held her towards me like he was offering up a gift. I wanted to take her in my arms and cuddle and kiss her but my skin fizzed with what lived there. 'God, Cath, come on. Please feed her.'

I stepped back because an awful thought occurred. The steam would be picking up the bacteria on my skin and aerosolizing it into the air towards Mia's airways. I reached forwards and slammed the door with the force of my body.

'Bloody hell, what are you doing? Are you OK? Are you drunk?'

'I told you, I don't want to feed her until I've had a shower,' I called over the sound of running water, through the thick glass of the door. 'There was a street cleaner outside. I didn't mean to stand so close and it sprayed up some dirt in my direction. I don't know what kind of grub has stuck to my clothes. Or my skin. I'll be quick, I promise I'll be quick.'

'Cath, you're being neurotic.'

I ignored his call and grasped a spray bottle of toilet cleaner from the floor, spritzing my arms and legs, belly and hair – everywhere but my face.

I stepped into the shower and sucked air through my teeth as scalding water burnt my skin pink. I stood under that water in fits and starts, for as long as I could bear, but it wasn't enough – not really, not unless my skin boiled to a hundred degrees. I poured a mound of shower gel on to a flannel and scoured the surface of every limb, between my legs, down my neck, through my hair – everywhere he had been. I scrubbed until the water swirled pink then red down the plughole from a place on me that had started to bleed.

I cried in pain as another patch of skin on my inner thigh thinned and split and bled. But my cries were silent and the tears were without shape – washed away with the water as soon as they fell. Yet my chest heaved in time with Mia's loud and desperate sobs outside the door.

Mia cried because she needed feeding, and to be loved.

I cried because I couldn't see him again.

I cried because I was supposed to be a mother and I had acted like the child.

I cried because I needed feeding, and to be loved.

When I couldn't take the water any more, I wrapped a clean and dry towel around me like a short and cheap sundress. Only then did I open the bathroom door, halting Dave's impatient pacing and gathering up my daughter into arms that stung so much they were scarcely able to hold her.

Dave followed me to our bedroom and watched me struggle as I tried to hold Mia in my arms and the bath towel around my body. I should have let the towel drop – the curtains were closed and I was in my own bedroom – but my husband was looking at me like he could see through the towel to the scrapes and trails of blood underneath, and it was a short hop from there to a place where I would have to lie to him.

So I lay Mia down on the bed and refolded the towel around myself. Then Dave lay down in the still-warm crumple of bed sheets and closed his eyes to it all – expelling a final, sorrowful sigh. As if he'd witnessed a death.

Nothing more could be done.

I lay down on the bed next to him and held Mia to my heart. Her legs frog-kicked joyfully at the prospect of food, a smile rooted in her cheeks as she locked eyes with me and latched on. In that moment her joy – despite it all – spoke of *This*.

This moment is wonderful.

But that moment – for me – was fleeting, its strings snarled in branches and tugged back from the clouds.

How irreversible the processes of birth and growth, decomposition and death.

And Mia fed, as Dave and I slept.

I woke as Dave moved – a subtle shift, a righting of his limbs – releasing an odour of sleep and washing powder from the duvet. An escaping beam of sunlight traced the body that was turned from me – the line of his head, down his neck and over the curve of his shoulder. A bodily halo for a good man: the kind that would buy pale pink roses for me every Sunday the first few years we were going out. The kind of man that bought a new pair of pyjamas for me every time I came back from a hospital stay, when the pain of having lost life again had made me want to burn alongside all the other clinical waste.

Dust motes danced like fairies above him; I closed my hand around some and released them with the stretch of a magician's palm. I did not deserve their magic.

'I should get up,' said Dave, his voice clear and untainted with the gravel of sleep. It was hard to tell how long he had been lying awake, or what thoughts he had been thinking on the other side of the wall that lay between us, its foundations reaching deeper and deeper into the earth's core.

He rolled out of bed, back still turned to me. He walked toward the door and busied himself at the drawers, pulling out T-shirt and shorts – his shoulders hunched and his arms drawn close to his heart as if he were trying to stop the overflow of something. He turned to me, a tangled expression on his face: not knowing where to begin and so beginning nowhere.

As he left the room I saw his bones, the architecture of him, poking through at the shoulders, and I thought of Richard – of the curve and surety of his arms and how their arrangement of fibre and tissue made it look as if he were armoured. I thought of how those arms had circled me and how I had felt the heat of his breath on me again and again as he asked: *Are you all right?* I covered my face with the duvet, like I needed hiding, because I worried: I worried that although Richard's cells and scent were washed from me, he was still daubed on my skin in thick and luminous brush-strokes and Dave could see it, like the shine of still wet paint.

I drew Mia closer because as long as I was holding her I couldn't do any damage – not to her, not to Dave.

And a few moments later he shouted, 'Tea?' Disinterested, from the floor below.

'Yes,' I said. 'Please.'

Bin men on the street outside shouted jokes, jibes and asides at each other. A gutsy laugh and an angry shout as the heavy plastic flump of something hit the pavement.

It would be too easy to call him. Even easier to text. Any words in any order would be enough to start it all again:

A *Hi.*

Or: *Hello.*

And weeks or even months later: *It's been a while but I wanted to say Happy Christmas / Sunday / any day of the week . . .*

Thunderous footsteps and a slammed front door.

Mia's eyelids tremoring as she fell into sleep.

The pained steel crunch of the rubbish truck's claws sounding for another round; tearing easily into the plastic, digesting the contents messily and carelessly because what did it matter? It was all rubbish.

The pained steel crunch inside my mind as I realized what had happened.

I lay my sleeping baby down on the duvet. Even as I ran to the top of the stairs and opened my mouth to begin a shout down the hallway, I ached with the pain of it . . .

Yet felt relieved at its simplicity.

'Dave, the bag that was inside the front door. What have you done with it?'

'The bin bag? I gave it to the bin men.'

No more digesting sounds outside, the truck long gone. A crushed phone. A splintered SIM card. Not even the page with the looping inked scrawl of his name and telephone number, now shredded between the family photos and debit cards and flaking leather of my wallet. Even the keys to my home would be disfigured.

No more contact with Richard. It was for the best.

A loss. The aching hollow pit at the bottom of my stomach.

'Are you all right?' said Dave, coming up the steps to meet me. 'What was in it?'

'Nothing. I mean, my handbag.'

'Your what?'

'It was only that cheap green one.' I plucked at words,

the simplest I could find from the mulch I was sinking into.

'What was in it?'

'My phone and wallet.'

I could remember where he lived. If I tried I could get there again. But I wouldn't. That meeting in the hotel room had simply been a piece of time with a beginning, a middle and a rightful end.

It was for the best.

Nothing more could be done.

Pulled down and down, toe by toe, into the gloom of the underworld.

Dave's eyes filled with alarm. 'The wallet I gave you on your thirtieth birthday?'

'Yes.' I blinked back tears, as I realized at the same time. 'I'm sorry. I'm so sorry.' He had saved up for that wallet a decade ago, on a wage that had barely covered the rent, and I'd used it every day since. It was packed with pictures – stupid, drunken passport photos – of us in our twenties. But the seams were un-picked and clagged with dirt. The zip, unusable. That kind of decay was inevitable, after ten years of daily use. 'No. Oh no. I'm so, so sorry.'

I sat down heavily on the doorstep and held my head in my hands. 'I put my bag by the door to remind me to clean it with bleach after I got sprayed by that street cleaner last night. I'm sorry, I'm so sorry about it all. I'm so sorry.'

My body heaved with sadness and I couldn't find the breath. It was how I imagined the beginning of drowning to feel as three hundred million air sacs inside the lungs clogged with mucus so there was no space to expand or to live, any more.

Dave gently shoved me over and laid his arms around my neck. 'Come on, breathe. It's OK. We'll get you a new phone. It's not like someone died. Please, look at me.'

I looked up, longing for the face I knew, but his eyes were questioning and his concern tentative.

'Is this it?' he said. 'Is this what's going on? All this obsessive cleaning for Mia – I understand it, I do – but it's interfering with our . . . with your life. Cath, look . . .' He took a breath, a hesitation. 'Your history, your . . . anxiety. All this cleaning, it's a . . . it could be, I'm not saying it is, but it could be the way your anxiety is expressing itself. A kind of Obsessive Compulsive Disorder.' His eyes brightened as he grasped desperately for something he could at last see the shape of. 'And if that's it, if that's what you've got, then we can get you medication for that. Just to give it a name or label, even it's only for a bit, while we sort you out . . .' He smiled gently. 'That could be a real relief for you.'

I looked up at him with his labels and lists, his clean, neat boundaries and his good, good intentions and part of me wanted to rally against it but then I thought perhaps I could do this. For Dave, for us, for Mia, maybe even for me. If I healed, if I tried to be better, then maybe we would start to feel like a whole family – one made of stronger fabric, with seams that would never come apart.

A new start.

'Perhaps you're right. I'll stop. I can stop. I'll be better. I'll try not to be so obsessed with it all. Get earlier nights, eat better, that kind of thing. Talk to Caroline. See more people. Think about a psychologist. I'm sorry for being . . .'

He held me tighter, in a gesture that was supposed to comfort and reward because I'd said what he wanted to hear, but his grip pulled at me and hurt my neck and then I panicked because I couldn't find his smell beneath the washing powder on his clothes.

I drew away and he looked disappointed again.

'You don't have to do this alone,' he said, because that's what you were supposed to say in a situation like that. Those words were a place-holder: only we never seemed to work out what to replace them with.

But maybe it didn't matter because things were going to change.

I would be the one to break the cycle. I would be better.

Marriage was hard work. Everybody said it.

You had to *work at it*. Keep on going until things changed.

My bag going, my phone crunched into a steel maw – it was all a sign. A sign I had to work harder with what I had.

I would be content with the memories of Richard. They

would sustain me until eventually they faded through overuse, and then I would be left with what mattered.

'It's OK,' I said, resting a palm on his cool cheek. 'I'm fine, honestly I am. The conference was a bit overwhelming and I wasn't expecting it to be. Too much CF, perhaps.'

'Definitely too much CF. Shall we just get rid of it?'

'I'm over it.'

'Me too. Did they say anything about progress?' He looked hopeful.

'Not really. I think it's still a way off.'

'So we're stuck with CF.'

'I think so.'

'Well, she's worth it, isn't she?'

'I'm tired. And I'll have a think about seeing someone. You go back to bed. I need to cancel all my cards. Then I'll make the tea.'

'She's worth it though, isn't she?'

'Of course she is.'

Chapter 11

The days grew shorter and darker – an unremarkable autumn – and we became the not-the-most-recent trauma in our circle of friends and family. A distant cousin had been in a car accident on her way to pick up the chops for Saturday lunch and an entire A-road had been blocked off for three hours while they cut her free. An old school friend suffered a third miscarriage and was having tests after a shadow was discovered on her ovary during a routine scan. Our situation – our *diagnosis*, our new way of life, whatever – was still in the deck of people's concerns, but it was no longer the card at the top.

One day I got a text from a number I didn't recognize saying, *It's Richard.*

Please don't contact me. The simplest response, though I'd drafted others.

And meanwhile I watched and waited for Dave in an uneasy present: hoping for a glimpse of the past (unasked for tea, porridge in bed, an unexpected kiss), watching for signs of change (say something different, see that I was trying, speak, ask . . .). Hoping for a different future.

I watched him as we ate the healthy food I cooked and waited for him in the moments before I turned out the light at nine p.m. to pointedly get enough rest. Watched and waited as I made a show of seeing Caroline once a week. As I closed down the pharmaceutical stocks and shares pages on my iPad and opened up new ones on wellbeing and mindfulness to show him how useful the breathing exercises were, how interesting the visual-izations.

I watched a slow and contented change in him as the raw conflict between us diminished, as the words I spoke held fewer problems, meant less stress for him.

I suppose sometimes I hoped he'd say something like: *Isn't this still as terrible as the day we were first told? I feel angry, the way you felt at the beginning. Do you remember? I understand why now, I do. I feel sad. I feel resentful. How did we get here? Do you ever think that? Do you ever feel trapped by it all?*

I kept hoping because I knew he was capable of more. There'd been a time, during IVF, when, for a moment, he had allowed himself to face the possibility that what we were going through was his fault. He'd cried like a baby as I held him in my arms and we glued together again. At the time it felt like a breakthrough so I didn't give much thought to the fact that we never mentioned the episode again. For a while it made me forget how lonely and messy of mind I'd felt at all other times.

But as the autumn became colder and darker my watching became less intense and less efficient. So unfocused, in fact, that Dave started to blur before me.

And when I didn't think my arms could take another session of Mia's physiotherapy – it was Richard I thought of.

In the early hours when Mia woke to feed and I couldn't sleep again for the thoughts crowding my head – him.

Through the anxiety of the month-long cough Mia developed – him.

With every test that came back showing she hadn't, despite that hacking cough, in fact cultured anything deadly in her lungs, no pseudomonas – thank God no pseudomonas – I thought of him. Each negative test was proof that my contact with Richard had not hurt my daughter. Each test was proof that my concerns about cross infection had been unnecessary, a symptom of anxiety, hysteria even. And as the evidence mounted that I wouldn't be made to atone for my sin, the truth is that I felt less and less guilty. And I allowed myself more than memories.

So the internet searches began.

The website for Richard's company. A business photograph of his head and nicely suited shoulders. Head and shoulders above the rest. His hair brushed to the side, a dashing airline captain from a bygone era.

And then a hundred photos reeling on someone's social

media page of Richard at another man's stag do, a mid-life party heralding a second marriage. Boy-men on a beach in summer with a campfire burning. Trousers hung on hips, beer bottles swaying off hooked fingers. A cigarette burning in his hand, a half-smile on his face. The way he held himself, so sure of himself: a thousand others would have thought, yes, him. His wife had. I had.

In the same collection of photographs there was one taken of a smaller group, sitting on the same beach at dark, elbows resting on knees, heads bent forward in conversation and thrown back in laughter, their faces half lit by the fire. Eyes smudged with tiredness and heads full of conversations that would never make it back home. This is one I looked at often. And another one, near dawn. Perhaps a conversation had after too many beers about feelings held for someone else. Despite the marriages and the promises and the children, what greater commitment, despite the ferrying to and from piano lessons and rugby practice and the ideas for birthday presents and things that always needed to be done back home: *Yes, her.* How many in that group of bleary-eyed men had fucked a woman that wasn't his wife? Was it a habit in the wider world, or was my sin an outlier, the ugly choice of a failing woman?

But looking at those pictures and imagining, just imagining, was like fuel.

Calmer, is how Mum had described me to Caroline. *Is she taking medication?*

Well, are you? said Caroline.

Not that kind of medication.

Less distracted, is what Caroline had said to Mum. Well.

I can't believe she makes vegetarian lasagne now, Dave told his parents.

And as each of Mia's cough swab tests came back negative – six, seven times over – the pictures stopped being enough and I gave myself more.

On a day when there was nothing planned I drove back to the tree-lined streets of Hampstead. To be close to him, to increase the chances of seeing him. Mia slept in the car seat. I wore a new red lipstick (matt, *fever blush* etched into its round base) and a skirt that rode at least a foot above the knee when sitting down. I'd made up a reason for being there in case I bumped into him – I was in the area visiting a friend, going to the ponds, for a walk. Just to get some space, you know.

I never went to his actual house. I would never have done that.

And if I'd seen him on the street, from the car window? Perhaps that would have given me enough fuel to keep going. But the not-seeing? It made me want to light a match and burn what fuel I did have so that he would see the blaze.

A few days later I tried to nail a whiteboard to the kitchen wall. I regretted how I'd dithered on wall colour, allowing

Dave to choose a yellow that looked pallid and sickly rather than the healthy glow we'd hoped for. I swung the hammer hard at the nail, confident of my aim.

'Ow. Bloody . . . Ow!' I sucked air through the gaps in my teeth.

'You all right?' said Dave, glancing behind him, then flicking on the kettle. 'No point in hammering there. It's brick. You need a drill.' He opened a kitchen cupboard and tried to fit boxes of dry-powdered antibiotic into an already over-packed space.

It was the cupboard I had emptied of tea and jam and then assigned to the special storage of Mia's medication. I had painstakingly filled it, building stocks of antibiotic and pills as if the doctors were going to suddenly stop writing prescriptions. If I ever dropped or spilt or broke anything, I could replace it. Immediately. There was absolutely no danger of doing more wrong on that front.

'It's fine,' I said. 'The whiteboard can stay propped against the window. I was only trying to find a place for it so it's not covering the window. We could do with more light in here. It might make the walls a bit less sallow.'

Dave shrugged his shoulders, unconcerned with the level of detail. 'Are you off somewhere?' he said, glancing at me again.

'No, why?' An A4 sheet with the children's hospital masthead flapped to escape its magnetic fastening as I walked past the whiteboard.

'You're wearing lipstick.'

'So I am.' I felt my brow wrinkle in expectation.

'It's very . . . red.'

When it became apparent that he couldn't find the words to express what he actually felt about the fact of my lipstick, I spoke, 'Seeing as it's Sunday, shall we go to the seaside or something? You know, cross something nice off Our List. Whitstable?'

'It's a long way.'

'It's not that far, and I need some sea air in my lungs. Wouldn't that be nice?'

'It's been a long week. I'd rather hang out here.'

'I spend my days hanging out here. We could get your mum to look after Mia and go watch the announcement of the gene therapy results at the university, if you don't feel like the coast?'

Dave laughed as he poured boiling water from the kettle into a pan crusted with dry porridge. His laugh had always been high-pitched. This time it was more mocking than amused. 'Pointless pinning your hopes on that.' He turned from the pan to look at me, and the amusement fell from his face. 'God, you are, aren't you? Pinning your hopes?'

'What, on the very real possibility of an inhaled gene to correct the defect caused by CF? Of course I'm pinning my hopes on a positive result. It could change everything for Mia.'

'Be realistic. New drugs go through lots of different trials and most fail. It can take years for things to get to the patients. Never mind the process that these things need to go through to get approved by the NHS. And even then, there's no money. There's no money to fight cancer, let alone our niche little illness.'

'Niche little illness? You sound so defeatist. If you're interested in NHS funding for expensive new drugs, I can give you a paper to read on the most recent parliamentary debate—'

'No, that's the point. I'm not that interested. I don't need to know what they're doing, I only need to know when they've done it. Meantime, I refuse to spend my Sunday listening to . . . I don't know . . . stuff that may never come to pass.'

'Caroline's going.'

'Why is *she* wasting her time?'

'I guess she wants to be supportive.' I crossed my arms. 'By showing some interest in what the future could look like. And I guess this is a weekend event so she doesn't have to miss any work.'

He shrugged his shoulders. 'I'd rather spend time in the here and now with my baby bean.' Dave scooped up Mia and admired her against the hot bright glow of the ceiling lamps, jiggling her up and down like a captain brandishing a trophy above his head.

She smiled at him in appreciation, then gurgled with joy as the bouncing continued. Then he admired her again and she gurgled and the circuit of delight continued.

It occurred to me that if I stepped back two quiet paces in socked feet, if I left the kitchen, the conversation between Dave and I would be over but the circuit between him and Mia would continue to flow unbroken.

I felt a sting of pain, outrage even, that they weren't bringing me into their circuit. Every strong family was an unbroken circuit. The light bulbs wouldn't go on otherwise.

I thought of my own family then. Mum and Caroline. Dad and I. A family never separated by geography, but by other things: personality, interests, understanding, empathy.

Mum and Caroline. Dad and I: two distinct circuits that never joined as one.

My fault then, perhaps, now, for feeling on the outside: I was so used to being one of two. Maybe I'd never known how to be more.

'Personally, I'd like to know what the future looks like, so if we're not going to the seaside as a family, can you mind Mia while I watch the results online in the living room?'

Dave lay Mia down on her playmat then began slotting plates into the lower rung of the dishwasher. 'I suppose so.'

'Great, thank you. And maybe when I've done that we could go for pizza or something? To that new place?'

'That's a nice idea.' His eyes brightened. 'But hold on. We should finish that casserole in the fridge. Loads of it still left.'

'But that's leftovers.' I felt the words snap off my tongue. 'I've eaten them three times this week. They're dull. There's a new noodle place, or we could get takeaway Vietnamese? Chow mein?' I smiled, I tried. 'Please, anything but that casserole. I stay at home all day, every day doing the same things, eating the same things. You get to leave this house each day and see the world in all its variations.'

I remembered a higgledy pile of dirty plates smeared and scattered with food on the floor of Richard's hotel room that night, and how he'd told me that he'd ordered one of every type of sandwich on the menu because he wanted to taste it all. See it all. Try it all. *You never know what you might like until you try it*, he'd said, kissing me, again and again.

Dave didn't say anything in response and watched me bow my head to the floor tiles. Then he leaned down and tickled Mia under the chin. He pushed a syringe of medicine into her mouth and, grasping her round the trunk, lifted her to standing. He held her there, as if to see what she might look like when she was older, more mobile and able to communicate with him as part of that ever-strengthening circuit. 'Look at those fat juicy legs in woollen tights. You're a gorgeous little winter sausage, aren't you?' He planted a big kiss on her cheek and she smiled at him again, something huge and heart-warming.

And then she coughed and we were both silent and still – as if any movement would send an undercurrent through the thick worry that lay between us.

'Her last cough swab test was negative, right?' Dave's voice was quiet now.

'Yes, of course it was. I would have told you otherwise. There's nothing to worry about, but I don't know why—'

'That's fine then. You know what,' Dave said brightly, as if the cough had never happened, 'I know what we can do today. If you want to get out of the house let's go to the Great Big Warehouse off the Westway and buy Mia her first trampoline!'

'That wasn't quite what I had in mind, Dave. And the crowds there, they'll be way worse than the seaside.'

'This is important though. We need to get her on that trampoline. Get her jumping, get the mucus moving in her lungs. Better out than in!' He grinned at Mia.

'Dave.' My face flushed with frustration. 'She can't walk, let alone jump. Let's wait a few months and get one that's the right size. Otherwise we'll only end up chucking it when she grows out of it after a few weeks.'

Mia squeaked out in happy agreement.

'We don't have to chuck anything. We'll use it for the next baby.' He looked at me searchingly. 'Don't you think?' His question seemed pointed, loaded, and I felt compelled to answer so I said:

'I can't think about another baby right now. I'm exhausted.'

Then I looked up at him and his eyes were pale and glassy and clouded with frustration and I felt like a fool because he hadn't asked me that question, not directly anyway. But before I had a chance to say anything else he said:

'Everything I suggest, you just . . . I can't win, I—'

'I didn't know you were trying to win and besides,

you're doing the same to me, stepping on everything . . . I . . .'

Silence fell between us.

'Why don't I take her to buy a trampoline and you can spend the time watching the gene thing?' He sounded kind, then, either because he regretted his tone or because he wanted to put space between the two of us as soon as possible. 'Then we can all eat together? I'll do something fun with the leftovers. Put chilli in there or something.'

We exchanged insincere and formal smiles and in that moment I decided to give myself more. Decided to take myself to a place I knew He would be.

'Fine,' I said. 'If that's what you want. Maybe I won't watch the gene results, I'll actually go to the announcement at the university. Let's call it my equivalent of you buying a trampoline. I need to know what's being done to help her. Then I can help in other awareness-raising kinds of ways.'

'Fine. If that's what you want. Will you be back for chilli leftovers?'

'No.' I was on a roll now. 'I might go to the drinks thing after. Maybe I'll meet some of those scientists. Maybe I'll have an idea or something, to help more.'

'Meet whoever you need. Mia and I will be here.'

Yes, of course they would. Strengthening that circuit, mapping the course for the electricity, lighting their bulbs so they glowed together.

Chapter 12

Caroline and I took our front-row seats in the university lecture theatre. Directly opposite us, a small group of men and women dressed in suits perched on the edge of a table consulting notes, exchanging encouragement and finally calling for hush as the lights snapped out.

A dark room, a bar of midnight blue light through the window.

As a bright rectangle of light beamed from projector to wall it occurred to me that this was the kind of hope people had felt in wartime when communities came together in cinemas to watch propaganda films: to feel reassured that there was a vast net surrounding them doing the most that could be done to save lives. And that there were others feeling the same kind of anxiety and desperation. That, above all, they were not alone.

He must be here. Had to be here.

The more I thought about it, the more amazed, appalled even, I felt at Dave's insistence that these things weren't relevant to him. There was no way most people would have brushed off today's announcement – the culmination of years of scientists working together to achieve great things – with the same lack of curiosity. These scientists were not buttoned-up freaks to us, like they were to Dave. They were gods who had the answers to life.

Was he looking at the collar of my coat, the curve of my neck? How impossible not to turn my head and find him. My transfusion: a charge of warmth and life in my veins again.

I listened to those gods paint hope in broad strokes across bar graphs to show that an inhaled gene to correct the defect caused by cystic fibrosis was a real possibility. More tests and doses and trials were needed but yes, there was definite hope. By definite they meant cautious. They were very clear when they said there was some way to go but things were as good as could be expected at that stage.

Cautious, tentative, definite, rabid, whatever you choose to call it. It's all still hope. Isn't it?

He'd know.

They had a vision for what could be. But a vision is worthless unless you do something about it. Unless you make something happen.

How and when would I see him next if he wasn't here?

They had a vision for a cure but what exactly were they going to do next? What, when and how will this end?

How will this all begin again?

The talk ended and Caroline squeezed my arm but we didn't look at each other. We sat for a while as the lecture theatre mumbled into life. We waited as if the scientists were going to say: *Sorry, one more thing! We forgot! From this day onwards, your daughter will never suffer again because she will be cured.*

Silence.

I looked around for him then, watching each doorway as it opened, scanning the sea of anonymous carers carrying their blunted hopes toward the exit.

In the concourse, Caroline swung her handbag over her shoulder. 'Coffee, I need coffee. Are you OK? Is that what you were expecting? That science was way over my head. Not exactly what we were hoping for, but sort of positive, yes?' Her eyebrows arched in anticipation.

'Yes, I think so. Maybe.'

'Do you want one? I'm totally desperate for one.'

'What?'

'Coffee!'

'Yes, please.'

Caroline set out purposefully for the concession stand and, in the shadow of a brick arch, I combed the parents and carers and scientists again.

But I was gripped with anxiety at a new thought: that his wife had attended instead of him. And that my gaze might have passed over her a hundred times without knowing.

She was the tall woman with the glossy black hair and grass green espadrilles. She was the mid-height lady with indigo jeans and a red and orange handbag. She was the woman with the huge eyes and the woman who was shorter than I but far better looking, and the woman with the hay-coloured corkscrew curls and a smile that told you she was a kind and generous person.

I knew nothing about her. I didn't know whether she was tall, short, thin or fat. I didn't know whether she ate chocolate and broccoli or had allergies to alcohol, nuts and bath oil. I didn't know whether she ran marathons or liked crocuses, whether clowns scared her or if Italy was the country she dreamed of living in.

I knew nothing about her other than the experiences we had in common. The ones I counted were pregnancy and childbirth. I counted having a sleepless newborn and a cystic fibrosis diagnosis.

I counted marriage.

I counted sex.

My face flushed and I wanted to wipe away the powder and the blusher, the mascara and eyeliner. I wanted to scrub at my face so it blotched black and red and pink. I put my hand over my face so that I couldn't see the woman I had stolen from. And I walked, almost ran, toward the double doors.

'Cath! Wait!'

I turned to address Caroline urgently, to tell her that we had to leave as soon as possible but she grabbed at my sleeve, the cardboard tray of coffees shuddering in her other hand.

'Bloody hell,' she said, standing so close I could smell the previous night's garlic on her breath. 'Are you OK?'

She held up two white paper cups garlanded with coffee drips. 'Where were you off to?'

And behind her, Richard walked towards us – at first dawdling, hands in his pockets, unaware of us, and then approaching quickly.

'What are you looking at?' Caroline looked behind her, trying to find the thing that had caused my face to change and my pupils to widen. She looked back at me, unsure of what to make of it, and of me, because she was my sister and she more than anyone knew how my face morphed with fear or longing or pain or expectation.

'I thought you might be here,' he said, arriving at my side. The breath clogged at the back of my throat and I couldn't say anything.

Caroline moved an inch closer to me, like she used to when we were little and sensed I needed back-up in a conversation I was stuck on, with a person that made me clam up. I hadn't felt protected by her like that for a long time. The days when she needed to talk on my behalf were long gone. And yet, I leaned in towards her.

'Caroline.' She thrust her hand forward. 'Cath's sister. Older, in case you were in any doubt.' She laughed.

I laughed.

We all laughed.

'Richard,' he said. 'Friend of Cath's.'

I looked away towards the doors as she handed me a paper cup, licking a trail of coffee from the back of her hand.

'Very good,' said Caroline, although her words were filler and we all knew it. 'Well, yes. Lovely.'

'Richard and I met at a CF parents' meeting at one of the charities,' I said.

'Oh, yes, I remember,' said Caroline, relieved. 'That's good. You've always said that was a turning point for you.'

'Yes,' I said, willing my shaking voice not to betray me. 'Richard was encouraging. You know, hopeful about the future.' I felt my face redden with heat and lowered my head to my chest.

'Amazing developments in CF at the moment,' he said. 'Mia has been born at the right time. Great news today, I thought.'

'Really?' I said, hope igniting in me. 'It sounded to me like they had quite a way to go.'

'It'll be fine. Scientists are always cautious and conservative. Don't want to be caught out saying the wrong thing. But I just chatted to one of them and they're further along than you think. It'll be in clinic pretty soon.'

I smiled. 'That's good to know. Great to know.'

'Yes, great to know,' echoed Caroline.

'How's Rachel getting on with her treatment?' I said.

He glanced across the concourse, distracted by something. Raised his hand in a wave.

'Yes, sorry,' he said. 'Colleague over there, from . . . So gene therapy, yes, I'd say it'll be available to patients within two years. All quite positive.'

'Great,' I said.

'Yes, great.' Caroline turned to me. 'And who's Rachel?'

'She's my teenage daughter,' Richard answered swiftly. 'She's been on a lot of medication recently. It's tiring for her.' He had heard my question. 'And how's little Mia getting on?' He scratched at his hairline.

'OK,' I said. 'She's got the usual viruses; a persistent cough, that kind of thing, but nothing the consultants are worried about. The cough swabs are all negative.'

'Oh good,' Richard said. He sounded amused – vindicated, perhaps – that my panic that night had been unfounded.

'How old is your daughter?' Caroline asked him.

'Seventeen.'

'And how does she manage her CF with school and everything? If you don't mind me asking. I'd like to know, so when the day comes—'

'We should get going.' I gently nudged my sister, trying to steer her away from the subject.

'Rachel does great, she has a great attitude. And you know, she is so much better than the last time we spoke, Cath. It's a slow path but we're getting there. We're on four nebulizers a day at the moment but we still managed to pack a few suitcases – an entire one for her medication! – and take her to Spain for a week's holiday. That was fantastic. The weather was perfect. And we've almost finished re-reading the *Harry Potter* series: I read them to her as she does her nebulizers. She loved them when she was little so we thought we'd do it all again.'

'What a super dad you are.' Caroline beamed.

'Four nebulizers?' I said. 'That must be taking a lot of time out of your day. You can't be getting much sleep,' I said.

His eyes held mine a beat too long. 'It's one of the reasons.'

'So she – your daughter, Rachel was it? – Rachel could really benefit from this gene therapy business?' said Caroline.

'One day,' said Richard, hugging his arms tight to his chest, tapping out a soft rhythm with his foot. 'But there's so much being developed that it'll probably get beaten to the finish line by other things, other drugs. There is an excellent—'

'But what about the price of these things?' said Caroline, excavating further.

'What about it?' said Richard, his head tipping to one side, checking his phone and slipping it into his back pocket.

'It's one thing these drugs coming through, but how is this country going to pay for them? I read about it in the press. Doctors and nurses are being asked to work for less and less money. Then these big new medicines come through, priced in the hundreds of thousands of pounds. I can't see how they'll afford it. Frankly, it's heart-breaking to think . . .'

'The government will find the money.' Richard cut her off abruptly. 'Not a problem at all. There's always a way. It's all politics and grandstanding.'

'But how are they going to conjure that money out of thin air?' said Caroline, clutching her coffee cup to her chin in thought. 'I worry about it.'

'I'm actually involved in one of the committees that lobbies parliament on these issues. We had a meeting about it quite recently. These things take time. Bureaucracy, that's the problem.' Richard's eyes darkened and he looked over his shoulder, distracted or agitated perhaps. And something in the finality of his statement made Caroline turn away from him and look around as if for the exit.

'Look at the time,' I said. 'Caroline, aren't you on a meter?'

She looked at her watch face and swung round. 'Absolutely right. Listen to me. I could talk for hours. We should head off.'

I realized that I was holding my handbag very close to my chest, which was silly because it wasn't a baby that needed looking after.

'I was thinking,' I said. 'Dave is expecting me to be out for most the day, and I left a few bottles of milk for Mia. I thought we could go to one of the museums, take advantage of the opportunity. You know . . .'

Caroline rolled her eyes to the ceiling. 'I'm sorry. I'd love to come with you. That would have been so great, but I've got to get back. Jules is struggling with maths at the moment. We need a good long division session this afternoon to crack it.'

'God, no. You get on. You go.'

She gave me a warm hug. 'So pleased for you that the findings were good. Up to this stage, you know. Cautiously optimistic. Things can only get better, and all.' She turned to Richard. 'Pleased to meet you.' Then she stepped backwards, slowly at first, as if she should be taking me with her. The designated driver. The responsible older sister.

'Bye,' I said, holding up a palm.

'Bye, then,' she said, before turning and walking out of the revolving doors, phone in hand.

'So which gallery are we going to then?' said Richard, when she was out of sight.

I smiled, nervous and terrified and excited. 'Presumptuous of you. What if this is the only time I've had to myself since . . .'

'Since the walk to my hotel room?'

'Yes,' I said cautiously. 'What if that was the last time I . . .'

'Then I know how that kind of walk ends.'

I looked away. Heard more smiles in his words. Should have gone, should have run but instead I said, 'Shouldn't you be getting home? I thought Sundays were when you and the family ate together?'

'Oh come on,' he said, smiling and taking me by the hand. 'Dinosaurs or Science?' And then I looked up, smiling a smile I couldn't have stopped even if the whole room had been watching me.

Chapter 13

The Science Museum was crammed with crying, shouting, musing people who moved too slowly. Despite the cold outside I sweated in the dry and artificial heat of the concourse. An advertisement for a new exhibition, *Our Planet*, a giant sphere – half recognizable as earth, half the flooded and scorched remains of global warming – swung violently from the concourse ceiling, sending out semaphores of green light across all our faces.

'I used to love this place as a child,' I said.

'Me too,' he said. 'But then I also used to love chocolate milk. How quickly childhood pleasures get eclipsed by good food and great whisky and sex.' He put his hand on my lower back and I fought the urge to look at him. 'How's your marriage then?'

I stepped away. 'What? No, look, you know I don't want to . . .'

He looked at me with raised eyebrows as if he wasn't going to accept that answer, as if he'd prefer to wait until I gave the right one.

'We're good,' I said. 'Much better recently. Thank you. Things are really good.'

'I don't believe you.'

'Don't then,' I said, as we walked down an aisle lined with cases of rock – moon rock, land rock, I couldn't see for the bank of children – a foot apart, as if we weren't actually there together. For a minute or so I wondered what we were doing. There. Anywhere. But then he said,

'Do you want to know why I don't believe you?'

'No,' I said. But I did.

He cut across me and between the gang of children, leaning into a model volcano, peering into its crater, stabbing at a button to make its inside glow with the embers of an impending eruption. He leaned towards me and spoke into my neck. 'I don't believe you because you just looked at me like you want to fuck me.'

I pushed him away; annoyed, embarrassed, and yes, wanting to. Trying to imagine Dave ever saying that to me or me saying that to him, counting how many years it had been since we'd felt like that about each other – if we ever did. Seeing the want in Richard's eyes. Ceasing the count.

I set off towards the interior of a 1950s living room; beams split and tipping, bookshelves at mismatched angles, furniture broken and smouldering, the TV spilling stage smoke. Examples of destruction caused by earthquake.

He stood close behind me. 'Were you disappointed in the gene therapy results?' he said.

I turned to face him. 'Do you think there'll be something real in time for your daughter?'

His brow crumpled in annoyance. 'Of course. Besides, I can always take her to the States to get medication there. I'll get it all on health insurance if I need to.' He was gripping his own hand so tightly I saw the blood drain white from his knuckles.

'How would you get insurance if you don't have a green card? Can you go and work out there, just like that? And I thought you said other therapies were on their way to the UK—'

'What does it matter?' he snapped. 'There are options. Things are being developed. It's good. It's fine. We're all going to be fine.'

I stepped back. 'Good. I'm glad for you all.'

His brow softened. 'I mean . . . it's complicated. Medically is one thing. But our family isn't . . . things aren't going to be fine with Nancy.'

Her name was like a firebrand on my skin. I turned away and began walking.

'Where are you going?'

'I didn't want to know her name.'

'Look,' he said, 'I know you care about me.' He caught my arm and turned me to look at him. I couldn't look away because it was the truth. 'Can I at least talk to you about something as a friend? As someone who understands the pressures of living with this fucking illness in their life, day after day after day? I have to talk about this.'

'Yes,' I said. 'Of course. I'm sorry.'

'I'm trying so hard to make it all work. Doing the parent support stuff with that charity. Working with a separate committee on drug funding and organ transplant policy. Working on my relationship with Rachel and at her treatments. Not to mention working on my business. Working, working, all the time working.'

His eyes narrowed and his skin seemed to grey before me. He suddenly looked so very tired.

I reached out to hold his hand. He squeezed it.

'I booked that holiday – in Spain, by a beach with dry sand, no river tributaries, no tidal mud, not a single threat there, God, the research it took! – thinking it would be good for us all to get away and have a break. But my wife and I argued the whole time. She was annoyed with me before we even got there. I happened to book it in a week that coincided with some kind of *Tiger Love* secret gig and she usually takes Rachel to those things because that's what they've always done together. I think she thought I'd done it on purpose, like I was competing or something. Never mind that I'd booked something for us all to do together. Toxic . . . she's—'

'I thought *Tiger Love* concerts were your "thing" with Rachel? You were going to one in Rome the day after we were together at the conference? That suitcase—'

'No, no,' he said shortly. 'I would have been going to Rome on a business trip.'

'Oh. I must have misunderstood . . .'

'Anyway, my wife didn't want me there, in Spain, is the point. All that stuff about me booking the holiday for when she takes Rachel to a gig, it's insecurity. I think she's quite envious of my relationship with our daughter.'

'I'm sorry things are so bad.'

He took my other hand so we were facing, like we were the ones at the end of a church aisle making final promises to each other.

'I missed you so much,' he said, his face flashing red and white with the on, off of a neon sign that read: *This Way to the Moon*, in bulbed full-stops. 'I'm so tired of it all. But you and Rachel? You're the best things in my life.'

'You barely know me.'

'I don't think that's true. I don't think you feel that way about me either.'

'Come on,' I said, leading him through a corridor, under speakers playing Bowie – the one about sitting in a tin can, about being far above the world, about there being nothing I can do. 'The moon is this way,' I said.

We walked down a flight of steps, through another corridor and outside into the paved concourse with queues tailing and sirens wailing in the distance.

I led him to the entrance of a red tarpaulin circus tent and spoke to the lady at the kiosk. 'Just the two of us, please,' I said to her, though I was looking at him. 'Two pairs of roller-boots. Size six for me and . . .'

'Eleven for me,' said Richard, glancing around and

taking my hand. 'What are we doing? I haven't done this since Rachel was ten.'

We stepped inside – into the lights, flashing red and white – and watched dodgem teenagers ricocheting off each other on the roller-rink, like we had something to learn from them. Watched them taking tumbles and righting themselves as quickly as they fell: wondering if they knew what an advantage it was to be that young when it came to making a quick recovery from life's bumps. How rapidly their cells regenerated, how their bones were less brittle and less likely to snap. How much easier those things made it to recover and move on to the next thing.

We sat side by side on a low wooden bench, and he moved close, nudged me, smiled, as if to say: *It's good to be here. With you.*

And I thought, *There is nowhere I'd rather be.*

Threading laces and tightening the corsets of our boots.

'Come on, let's go to the moon,' I said against the music, standing uneasily, a newborn foal taking its first steps.

And then the memory of how to skate came dripping back – push and flow, push and flow and trip, push and flow until finally . . . balance. Push, flow and balance; they all had to happen at once in order to stay standing, to keep moving.

Then speed took over and the pushes became secondary, the balance innate. I felt like a bird taking flight, riding slipstreams in the air. I was swimming and flying at once, as if I was on my own and far from the crowds of the museum, away from shops that sell trampolines, floating high above the city's parking spaces and traffic jams, its jostling pedestrians, pushbikes, babies trundled in prams, its dogs held back on short leads.

'You're good at this,' he shouted over the music as I skated past him, holding out my hand to his, expecting him to hold on tight and come with me but his stasis instead whipped me back into his arms. We faced each other, as close as I would a mirror to my own face, to see the bloodshot capillaries of my own eyes. I felt myself reflected in him, felt his amusement at the same joyful hysteria I'd felt as a child when my breath was stolen by high winds on a beach.

I squeezed his hand tight. 'Come with me.'

He followed, in slow and small steps, as together we edged into the fast-moving lanes of roller-booted traffic. I sped up and felt the weight of him behind me until he too found his pace and was travelling next to me.

Us, together. Hand in hand, two teenagers on a first date.

I sped up to pull him faster. Let go of his hand and he glided behind me.

I held out my hand to catch him again and this time he sped ahead, pulling me along, letting me go so that I glided. He waited for me to catch up and we glided together – hands out, fingers touching sometimes, flying separately and together. We rolled round and around that space threading through and across the disco lights, joined by our smiles when not by our hands.

I skated faster and faster, giddy with it all, and he laughed, trying to stop me, bringing me back to him with a touch and a grab. But each time he took my hand I unfurled it, let go and skated again.

The last time, I reached out to grab a hand that wasn't there and felt myself fall, in slow motion, on to a surface that was cool and polished, where my wrist slammed, a pain reaching through me like a knife slicing through skin and flesh.

I wondered why it was that falls always seemed to happen in slow motion. Perhaps it was the job of every synapse, cell and fibre to make you feel pain – slowly and excruciatingly – to remind you fully, remind you entirely, to be careful, much more careful, next time you try and go somewhere you shouldn't.

I held my wrist close to my chest as if my heart had the energy to heal, and shuffled to the side of the rink, out of the traffic.

I squeezed my eyes closed and waited for the pain to subside.

And he was there, by my side, as if we were huddled in an alley together, away from the rain, his arms round me, whispering. 'Breathe deeply. It will stop. The pain will stop.'

I looked up at the shadow cast across his face now we were sheltered from the lights. He held my hand and drew it away from where it was sheltering at my chest. Kissed it. Held my hand in his like it was a broken bird and he knew how to heal it.

'Your eyes shine,' he said, his lips sweeping my cheek. 'It's like you're always on the verge of tears but not because you're sad. You're beautiful.'

I smiled, a tear tracking its way down my cheek. God, it hurt.

'I have tried to remember how your skin tastes,' he said, so close to me I felt his breath cool my tears. 'And my favourite memory is what you did to every cell of my body the first time we kissed. I remember that a dozen times a day.' He kissed my wrist, in the area where the joint was hot with pain. 'Sleep with me again? Even if it's only one more time. I want more memories of you.'

I knew I would, as I kissed him. As we kissed each other, backs to the ice-rink barriers, holding each other like there was no one else. Like there had never been anyone else.

We went to a hotel – a faceless place booked by tourists on last-minute trips to the city, a few minutes' walk from the museum.

I didn't want it to be the last time. I wanted there to be one more time, and one more after that until we knew, perfectly, what each other liked to read and eat and watch and dream.

I wanted it to happen again and again, for us to keep travelling together.

Further and further up towards the moon. To stay there, through the cold of the night. To be heated by the rays of the next rising sun, our bodies melting together, annihilated.

Chapter 14

Dave slung Mia's car seat into the crook of his arm like a trug of vegetables, and stepped over the threshold.

'Stop,' said Mum, raising a policeman's palm and falling to her knees. She adjusted the doormat to sit flush with the doorframe. 'Good God, I can't be responsible for you falling head first with that little princess in your arms. Such a hulk of a chair. Why are they so heavy? Come,' she said, clamping Dave's arm firmly. 'Lay it down there, careful now, no not there – under the stairs, so she can snooze a bit more.'

She turned to me as I followed Dave, 'You look nice, dear. Don't bang the . . .' I pulled the front door closed behind me. 'Door. Oh dear.' Mia's eyes blinked open. 'What a shame my house woke the baby.' Then she added, 'That blusher washes you out a bit, darling.' Because that was how she punished me.

'Perfect time to wake up, Mia. Lunchtime!' I said, hanging my coat on a hook.

Dave wrestled a bottle of red wine out of the nappy bag and handed it to Mum as he curled Mia into the other arm. 'Lovely of you to have us over, Sheila.'

'Ooh, watch that precious cargo in your arms. Careful with Mia too!' She laughed. 'You shouldn't have. We've got acres to drink. Absolutely acres. But if it's a good one, perhaps I'll save it for lunch with the Sullivans next week?'

'You mustn't waste it on us,' said Dave, his eyes twinkling with amusement. He caught my eye and we smiled at each other knowingly – perhaps both realizing how long it had been since we joked about how tight Mum was when it came to buying alcohol. How long it had been since we'd joked about anything.

Mum had little regard for wine: a crushed-grape drink at best, its only saving grace that it symbolized the blood of Christ and therefore how could any pinot, chateau or cabernet in the world be good enough?

'What I'd really like, Sheila . . .' Dave choked a giggle. I knew which story he was remembering, and it made me laugh, seeing the naughty glee in his face. 'What I'd absolutely love is a snifter of that Communion wine you bought back when Gordon Brown was made PM.'

'Oh, you *must*,' said Mum delightedly. 'I've got heaps of the stuff. I can't give it away. You *must* help me drink it.'

'I'll take that bullet, Sheila.' He shrieked in mock horror. 'Cath! Get the ambulance on speed dial!' And both Dave and I collapsed into giggles at the memory of an uninformed individual putting Mum in charge of the Communion wine and her buying something so cheap and awful – *like white spirit*, said parish-member Graham who'd been the first and only one to try it at Communion and spat it out on the priest's robes. The four cases she'd bought were returned to her that same afternoon.

'You are naughty.' Mum hid a smile, catching on. 'I've got treats for you all. Roast chicken with all the bits. And pudding. Trifle, dear.' She turned to me. 'I made a trifle with those toasted nut things you like.'

'Not sure you'll be here for that, will you?' Dave unbuttoned Mia's cardigan and handed it to me, still smiling, and I wanted to take a picture of his face like that. A reminder of something.

'I can't stay long, Mum. I'm doing a radio interview for the charity.' I folded Mia's cardigan and held it to my chest. 'I'll have to head off in an hour or so.'

'Oh yes. Very good,' she said through pursed lips. 'Why on earth are you dressed so nicely if you're going on the radio where no one will see you? A shame to waste that red lipstick on a room and a microphone.'

I managed a smile where sharp-edged words might other-wise have had their say, because the warm memory of Communion wine was still with me, and in a few hours I would see the look in Richard's eyes before he kissed my lipsticked lips. That look was everything to me, the vision I held in mind as I signed up for too many charity events and workshops – talking, participating, fundraising – weaving in ways of spending time with him afterwards.

Virtue followed by sin.

I grasped Dave by the shoulder as Mum disappeared around the corner. 'Did you tell her it was national radio? That I'm going out to fight for her granddaughter on national radio? Couldn't she bring herself to ask me a single question about it? It's not like I'm on the radio every day. If she bothered to even ask me what station it was airing on she'd go crazy with excitement because she could tell all her friends and they could listen while they eat scones and knit scarves or whatever it is they all do on a Wednesday afternoon.'

'Give her a chance,' he said. 'We only just got here.'

The windows in the kitchen were frosted with cooking steam. Caroline and Rory sat at opposite sides of a Formica fold-out table sipping sherry from small glasses painted with European flags. They set down their small drinks and we gave each other our warmest hugs.

The house was situated between two towering plane trees in such a way that it lay in perpetual shadow whatever the weather. The narrow windows and low ceilings and dark carpets didn't help.

'Can we please turn on a light so it doesn't feel like we're sitting in a crypt?' I said. 'It's going to get dark in a few hours anyway. We might as well prepare.'

'I'd rather you didn't turn anything on, dear. My cataracts are playing up.' Mum turned her back and began slowly, deliberately, skimming fat off the gravy with a teaspoon.

Caroline cleared her throat and raised her eyebrows: *Why do you even waste your breath on the subject?*

'Can I pop Mia's medicines somewhere in amidst all this amazing-looking grub, Sheila? Is there space?' Dave surveyed the carefully tessellated Tupperware inside the fridge.

Mum took the medicine pack from him and studied the card on its underside: a timetable of Mia's daily medicines and important phone numbers that I had painstaking written out and laminated against splashes. 'Look at you. So organized. No wonder Mia's doing so well. Such a super dad. There's precious little space in the fridge. You'll have to pop it outside on the windowsill. It's cold enough out there.'

Sheila returned the medicine pack to Dave. He looked up at me as I shook my head. He shrugged his shoulders.

'Takes you ages to get all that medicine stuff sorted and ordered, doesn't it, Sis?' Caroline dried her hands with a tea towel.

I gave her a grateful smile. 'Where are the kids?'

'Athletics camp. Any opportunity for those two to burn off energy. They'll be running laps all day.'

'Sounds intense. I actually tried a bit of yoga this morning for the first time—'

Mum turned to me. 'What? I don't know how you manage anything, let alone yoga, with that wrist of yours. Shouldn't you see the doctor? You've been wearing that grubby support thing for weeks. You can't even carry the child's car seat.'

'I can carry the car seat,' I said. 'But Dave was the one who got her out of the car.'

'Right. Very good.'

The worst of the pain in my wrist was long gone but in the last month I'd found comfort in the bandage, like a scarf to soothe a throat on a day that wasn't even cold. Beneath the warmth of that bandage was an ache that reminded me of Richard. Reminded me of the first time and the second time and the third, fourth and fifth times after that. And the time that would soon come again.

I wore that bandage like some people wore wedding rings.

'Are we ready to go in?' said Caroline, arming herself with vegetables and hooking a finger through the gravy jug. 'Lovely dress, Cath. Gorgeous print. You look amazing.'

'Nice of you to say,' I said.

'Well, it's true.'

I delighted in dressing for Richard. Every frill and flash of colour, every band of lace and trail of necklace, every cuff and stocking and slick of mascara: he named it all, appreciated it all, saw it all.

'What are you smiling at?' Caroline said to me outside the door of the dining room.

'Nothing,' I said. 'Nothing at all.'

Despite the chill of the autumn day, the dining room was stifling. Mum had closed all the curtains and turned on the electric heaters. The room smelt of singed wool and boiled vegetables. She filled her wine glass to the brim and started the rounds with everyone else.

I opened the curtains and she shielded her eyes dramatically with the back of her hand, as if she were a vampire.

'Sorry,' I said. 'Forgot.' Before closing them again.

Dave lay Mia in his arms and began coaxing milk into her from a bottle.

'So Davey, Leighton Orient. That new player has brought us nothing but bad luck,' insisted Rory, rubbing his nose with the back of his hand and unzipping a chunky knit cardigan to reveal his supporters T-shirt.

'Judgement,' said Dave, adopting a deep and considered tone, designed to give the impression he possessed superior knowledge on the subject. 'That's all it is. Starts with management. A few bad choices. It all stacks up, then you turn around one day and you're bottom of the league. You've got nothing.'

'Maybe the manager was having a difficult time the day he made his first bad choice,' I said.

'You shouldn't be a manager if you let your bad day interfere with your judgement,' said Rory.

'But you have no idea what might have happened to that man, he might—'

'Will you look at that gorgeous girl feeding from her daddy?' Mum clamped her hands on her hips and gave a proud smile. 'It's so different to my day. Your father never so much as changed a nappy, Catherine.'

'Dad came into his own later on,' I said.

Mum filled my glass to the halfway mark before getting distracted and putting down the bottle. 'That he did. Help yourself to veg, everyone. Don't stand on ceremony.' Then, despite what she'd said, she piled everyone's plates on top of each other, noisily scraped potatoes out of the roasting tin and slid them across each plate as if there was no time to spare.

'Your father was such an eloquent talker,' she said. 'If you got him on the right subject. Which I rarely did.'

'Loved hearing your dad talk about toys of the late forties. Wind him up and hear him talk about tiddlywinks and model plane kits.' Dave laughed and adjusted Mia on his knee.

'He held such a lot of useless old information in that head of his.' Mum rolled her eyes and smiled; it was rare to see both criticism and fondness reflected in them.

'It wasn't so much the talking, as the fact he listened,' I said.

'To some of us,' said Caroline.

'Oh yes, some of us,' said Mum, shaping green beans and sprouts at the border of each plate.

Dave cooed at Mia and kissed her forehead as she drank.

'Dave'll be a good talker with Mia, you can tell,' said Mum.

'Good talker, good carer, good car seat carrier,' I exclaimed. 'It's almost like he's her father!' I covered the words in layers of smiles and singing tones so no one would see the toxic cracks in me.

'Sarcasm is so unattractive,' said Mum, surveying her plate work.

'I don't need to be attractive now I've bagged myself a husband and can change a nappy. You too, Caroline, wipe off that lipstick, you tart.'

Mum flinched and pretended to pull a hair from her lip. 'Stop that.'

'Who's going to carve?' said Caroline, smiling

I caught Mum's eye then and saw her brittleness fade. Her eyes filled with sadness and she sat down, as if to conserve energy. Her thin-boned wrists pushed against each other in a pyramid. Without an answer, for once. Carving had been Dad's job. It had been one of his specialist subjects.

She dipped her head to her plate and, despite my irritation, I saw something in her that I recognized. I saw for a moment how tired she was of managing the house. How tired she was of having to look strong and stop her environment from overflowing with domestic and administrative rot. How someone else doing the carving, performing an act of kindness, might bring such relief to an overburdened existence. If only she had been the kind of person to let her guard down and tell me how hard she found it all. If she'd been different, perhaps me having a baby would have brought us closer together, not further apart.

'I'll do it, Mum,' I said. 'I'll carve. Dave changing nappies, me carving the roast. We'll be swapping underwear in a minute.'

'I do hope not,' she said. But she smiled, and took a deep breath. 'So lovely to have you all here. So rare for us to spend time like this together as a family.' Which is what Dad used to say when he carved. 'We're all so busy we never get to sit around and catch up, do we? The good Lord ate with his disciples and thus we shall eat together.'

'So which one of us is the Lord?' I said.

'That'll be you,' Caroline said, smiling. 'At least a bloody saint for all that charitable work you're doing.'

'A heap of it,' said Dave. 'A workshop last weekend, something each week, so much going on. And then this afternoon, with the radio show.'

Everyone dipped the crowns of their heads to clatter and scrape at their plates.

'I think it's great, said Rory. 'Plenty in your position wouldn't make it out the house, let alone stand up on a soapbox.'

'So this radio show then,' said Mum. Dave looked up at me as if to say: *I told you she'd ask*. 'What's the subject matter?'

I was pleased she'd asked, too pleased perhaps. I wondered whether she'd finally asked because I'd shown her some compassion. Maybe she'd seen something in me like I'd seen something in her. Seen that I needed to be asked. That to be enquired after, thought about, was nearly as good as being looked after.

'The subject is mothers who care for children with life-limiting illnesses,' I said.

She paused, looking up from piling gravy on to her fork like it was a spoon. 'I see.'

'See what?' I said.

'It sounds interesting, that's all I meant.'

'Good,' I said briskly, keen to take the subject away from me. And we didn't need to wallow in it anyway. I knew why I was doing it. Giving Mia and her condition a voice. It was like Richard said: I was fighting for my cub. Doing what mothers do. 'How's work, Caroline?'

'It's just that . . .' Mum continued. 'Why is it only mothers?'

I put down my cutlery and drank the few sips of wine Mum had poured me. 'Well, I suppose it's the mothers who are on maternity leave when newborn illnesses are diagnosed. It's the mothers, mostly, who give up their jobs to be at the hospital when young and teenage kids get sick. Not all the time, but mostly, it's the mothers.'

'You must be careful with that. Because Dave is doing a lot. Dave does a lot with Mia, don't you?' she nodded towards Dave.

Dave cleared his throat and dipped his head. 'I like spending time with my daughter.'

'Speaking of my work, I've actually got some news,' said Caroline, spooning extra peas on to her plate. 'Been promoted to Deputy Head, Regional. It's a full-time post.'

There was a full-mouthed chorus of relieved congratulation.

'Oh, darling,' said Mum warmly, her head snapping to attention, eyes lighting up like a fairground. 'That's wonderful news.' She lay down her cutlery and went to kiss Caroline on the head.

'Pay rise, tick,' said Caroline, loading her fork. 'One office away from the corner office – watch out Michael Dickson, I'm coming for you. Company car, tick.'

'Bingo!' said Dave. 'Living the dream.' He filled Caroline's glass and toasted it with his before she had a chance to pick it up.

'Well done, Caro,' I said, when the tide of congratulation and relief had retreated.

'Excellent,' said Mum. 'Now we need to get Catty sorted out.' She pyramided the pads of her fingers and chewed thoroughly and efficiently, beginning her next sentence before the job was complete. 'Who thinks it's not right she should be bandaged up like that after all this time?'

'Mum, let it go. It's fine. This kind of thing takes ages to heal. The railing nearly snapped it.' I scratched my forehead. 'What did you mean when you said I needed to be careful with the subject matter of the radio show? Dave does some of the work caring for Mia – maybe a bit more recently. It's not like we have lots of extra hands. His parents still work and you're so busy with the church.' I drained my glass. 'The point is that I still do the child-care, sometimes round the clock. But no one sees me queuing at the GP or pharmacist or hospitals to get the right prescriptions, or getting Mia weighed and inoculated. All you see is Dave at the dining table – effortlessly feeding her the milk I made and pumped in the middle of the night, from the bottle I bought and sterilized and packed in the nappy bag.'

'Come on,' said Dave, not unsympathetically. 'She's not saying you don't work hard. You keep Mia happy and healthy.'

'Are you going to be mentioning Dave at all?' said Mum. 'On the radio show?'

Dave held up a palm. 'Sheila, it's fine. To be honest, I'd rather not be mentioned on national radio. She's doing an awareness thing, that's all. She works hard, so do I. You all pitch in when you can. We all have busy lives. We all do our bit.'

'I suppose I'm saying, if Cath's pursuing her own projects—'

'My own projects?' I said. 'Awareness-raising for our daughter's life-limiting condition is a project for *me*? Fighting for my daughter, our family – is a project for *me*?'

'It is, in part, dear. You've chosen to do it. When you're talking, all I'm saying is be honest about what it takes.' She paused. 'It takes a village. Isn't that what they say? Give your supporters credit. We make sure to acknowledge helpful people in the church newsletter. We name them. It makes a world of difference.'

I swiped at my forehead, now crackling with heat. 'If

211

Dad had been here he wouldn't have made this all so bloody difficult. He'd have been proud. Simple as that. He'd have said: *Would you like me to run through some of the possible questions with you?* Then maybe we could have talked through some of the grey areas. But, Mum, you sound like—'

'We certainly agree your father had his uses,' she said. 'We all miss them. I cleaned and cooked and disciplined, and he was your sounding board. He certainly picked the prime cuts of parenting. But, it made sense for him to be a sounding board because he knew about *things*. And I knew how to run a home.'

I stood up suddenly, my cheeks flushing in that warm and airless room, my heart hammering to transport the fury in my veins. 'He wasn't my sounding board because he knew *things*, he was my sounding board because he asked questions. You could have done that too. You could have asked me questions instead of cleaning the cooker. You chose not to.'

'Sit down, Cath,' said Caroline.

'You never wanted to know anything about how I felt,' I continued.

'I suppose I should have left the cooker filthy?' Mum's eyes filled with outrage. 'Chatting away, leaving the rubbish to overflow? You never complained about being fed, and having your sheets washed, having your dishes washed!'

'I have to go, I have to leave for my interview.'

Caroline laid down her cutlery. 'You don't need to go this minute.'

I looked at her: *I think I probably do.*

Dave downed his glass. 'Can you give me a hand doing Mia's antibiotic before you go?'

I took Mia from him and whispered the things in her ear that would prepare her for medicine. Then I held her up to face Dave, who put the syringe to her lips.

'What's that you're giving her?' said Rory, eyes focused on Dave's action.

'It's OK, it's all over.' I held her to me as her face contorted in disgust and she broke into tears. 'An antibiotic. Co-amoxicillin. For her cough,' I said, wiping traces of the sticky liquid from the corners of her mouth.

Dave looked up in surprise. 'It's not actually. They switched it to a stronger antibiotic yesterday. Because her cough's still intermittent?'

'Why have they done that? And why didn't anyone ask or tell me? Her cough is almost gone. Why are they giving her more medicine?'

Dave looked perplexed. 'They kind of did ask you. We were all on an email loop together. I assumed that your silence meant you were in agreement with the doctor's opinions, and you didn't mention it last night, so I thought . . .'

'Silence doesn't necessarily mean I am fine with something,' I said sharply.

He looked at me, shocked. 'Did you even get the emails?'

I closed my eyes to give myself a moment to think, to step outside the glare of all those people in the room who felt like they were reading everything in me. I'd been in the park the day before, standing under a tree whose peeling bark surface looked like a map of the world, pushing Mia back and forth in the pram so she would sleep. There was no one around, no one to talk to and I saw those emails come in and thought I will read them, of course I will, but at the same time a text arrived from Richard and so I checked it first because I knew it would make my heart lift, not sink. We were making plans for the future. Plans to meet. And then there were more texts from him and I could think about what I would wear and how I would look, rather than: I should wake Mia at three and do we have enough bread or what TV show will Dave and I watch on the sofa tonight before going to bed in our separate rooms?

I would always have checked my emails from the hospital. Always. Eventually. 'I'm sorry, I obviously missed them . . . I thought you might tell me if it was urgent.' And I put my hands to my cheeks because they burnt with shame and my stomach ached with the anxiety of unanswered questions.

If they were still medicating her for a cough then they must be worried about something . . . But her cough was just a virus; *in all likelihood*, is what they'd said. All her tests, all the cough swabs, had been negative for signs of bacterial infection.

But I'd missed something. What?

There was a silence and then words were exchanged between Caroline and Rory about more carrots and more chicken; as if to imply they weren't actually listening to our conversation so that the rest of us didn't need to feel so exposed and awkward.

'I'll get the other peas,' said Rory.

'There aren't any other fucking peas,' I said, and he recoiled an inch as if I'd thrown a sopping flannel at his face.

Mum coughed pointedly and nodded at me. 'Play a straight bat. That's all I'm saying. Be honest in the interview. You'll feel better about yourself in the long run.'

'Better about myself?' I snapped, wanting to stamp my feet like a child. 'I feel fine about myself, thank you. And by the way, I am a good mother. And I manage to keep our cooker clean on top of everything else I have to do.'

'Why don't we all have a nice cup of tea to calm down?' said Caroline. 'I know! What about Christmas? Only a month away. Who wants to come to ours this year?'

'I kiss my child a hundred times a day,' I tried not to cry, not to undermine the point I was making. 'I breastfeed her six, sometimes ten times a day. I change countless nappies and medicate, medicate, medicate. I spend the first two hours of my day medicating and feeding my child before I even think about what I might need. I take a few afternoons, a few days off, I miss a few emails and suddenly we should give Dave a medal because he can actually tip a bottle of milk into her mouth at the right angle?'

'Can you stop going on about me and the bottle?' said Dave.

'Well,' said my mother. 'I suppose we can all agree that none of it's very fair. No one truly sees the person we try to be. When Jesus—'

'I know what it is now, Mum.' I stood taller, my chest puffed out in victory, intoxicated with the need to win. 'You're jealous.'

'Of what?'

'Cath, please, we're trying to have lunch together,' said Caroline.

'No, let her say it,' said Mum.

'Dad and I talked. He never talked like that with you. You're not capable of it.'

'Don't flatter yourself,' she said, her mouth set in a rigid line, her wrists shaking. 'It's not all about you. You try filling in the gaps when someone leaves you for good. You imagine trying to be two parents – which, for the record, is all I am trying to do by giving you good advice. I'm obviously failing. You've got a lot on your plate, more than most, I know that.' Her voice cracked on her last word. 'I don't think you're being honest about who you're trying to be.'

Even if she'd asked me in calmer, more private circumstances, I wouldn't have told her the truth. Which was that I'd lost track of who I was even *supposed* to be.

She put a fist to her mouth to staunch the flow of emotion in her and I closed my eyes because the sight both repulsed and broke me.

The room was silent but for Mia's wriggling and cooing.

'I have to go now,' I said.

Dave shifted. 'Are you back for bedtime?'

'I don't know. I doubt it.'

The dishes were cleared swiftly as Dave and I made arrangements.

I kissed Mia and made to leave.

'Cath,' said Dave quietly. 'I thought you hurt yourself at home?'

'I did.' I concentrated on fixing the buttons on my coat, on closing my handbag.

'Why did you say you hurt your wrist on a railing earlier?'

'What do you mean? I didn't say that.' I collected the napkins from the table and layered them on top of each other, lining up each right-angled corner against the next.

'You did, you said railing.'

'Railing, banister. Same thing.' I flattened down my hair with a palm. 'I'm sorry I didn't read the emails properly. They're obviously worried about her cough if they're changing her medicine. Do they think it's going to get worse? Are they worried it's something else? I thought all the tests were negative. It's just viral, isn't it?' I put down my bag. 'I'll cancel the interview. If they're worried about her, I should stay.'

217

What was I thinking buttoning up my coat like that? If something was wrong with her child, a mother always stayed.

Dave's eyes softened. 'Calm down. It's no big deal. They want that cough gone. They want her to return to her baseline, which is no coughing at all. You don't need to cancel your radio interview. The doctors are only being cautious.' I breathed more easily then. Regained my composure. It was like Richard had said. The research scientists are over-conservative with their reports. Doctors are over-cautious with their patients because no one likes to be caught out having over-promised.

And so, reassured and uneasy, I left.

Chapter 15

I arrived at the hotel room clutching a wine bottle by its neck, an inch still sloshing about at the bottom. Richard squinted when he saw me, as if I was a blinding light.

'Your mascara is very smudged. It's quite sexy,' he said.

'Fuck me then,' I said, stepping forward and tripping over his foot on to the ground, where I stayed, cheek pressed against the soft pile. Dampening the carpet with tears, adding to the mess of wine already spilt and staining. Blotting the clear lines and shapes of that hotel room with my messy pile of limbs and crowded, heavy head.

He lifted me up into his arms and laid me down on the iron-flat, hospital-cornered bed. The room was bright, bleach white, and I smelt clean sheets and the alcohol tang of his aftershave.

I pushed myself up, head tipping with the buzz of alcohol.

'What's wrong?' he said. 'What's going on?'

'It doesn't matter.'

He turned my face to his. 'Of course it matters.' He drew me into his arms and I was soothed by how gently he stroked my hair. Like a child. A few moments passed before he squeezed my hand. 'Tell me, what's wrong? Did the radio interview upset you? What did they ask you?'

'It wasn't that . . .'

'I've got something that will cheer you up.' He brought out a glossy flat black box crossed with wide scarlet ribbon.

I felt my eyes widen with gratitude because he was the gift really; every moment with him clearer and sharper and more charged with life than any other high. I pulled at the ribbon with shaking hands and opened out the tissue paper to reveal a pair of black silk pants lined with white lace.

'I'm going to fuck you while you're still wearing them and then I'll keep them so you'll be with me even when we're apart.' He trailed a hand up my dress.

I laughed. 'So you've got me a present to cheer yourself up?'

'Yes, but we both get the advantage.' He drew me close, pressing his hands further between my legs, making the heat rise in me – burning away the shame and anger of earlier. He kissed me deeply on the mouth as if he were sucking away the pain, and his hands were on me and in me, and his breath warmed my lips as he said, 'Tell me what's wrong. Tell me while I make you come.'

I moved toward him so he was deeper, so he was closer.

'Tell me why you're so sad. I'll always want to know.'

He grasped at the opening of my dress to feel my breasts. 'What did they say?'

'I didn't do it.'

'The interview?'

'Yes. I thought about it and I couldn't do an interview about being a mum. It wouldn't have been fair to suggest . . .'

Richard removed his hands from me, face full of disappointment – I had done something wrong and now I burnt with shame. 'Why didn't you do it?'

'I realized I didn't want to talk about those things.'

'Didn't you *think that through* when you first agreed to do it?'

I rearranged my dress so I was covered again. I edged away from him. 'Maybe I didn't. I agreed to do it because it was an excuse to get out of the house, and a chance to see you afterwards.'

'But . . .' Anger flared bright in his eyes. 'Look, I appreciate that. Of course I do. But opportunities for the charity to have someone on a primetime show like that come up about once every five years. Surely they told you that?'

'No.'

'Well it should have been obvious.'

'It was just one radio interview.'

'No, but this is a crucial time to get a message for cystic fibrosis out there and a good personal story can make all the difference. Changing the law on opt-in transplants will give people . . . Haven't you seen the numbers for people who die waiting?'

'I'm sorry for letting you down. I know your daughter—'

'This has nothing to do with Rachel.' His words travelled through me, shock waves from an explosion. 'Transplants have nothing to do with her. Stop saying that.'

I stood up uneasily and collected my coat from the floor. 'Don't shout at me like that.' I yanked my arms through the sleeves.

'Don't go,' he said suddenly, eyes softening and flooding with regret, reaching out for my hand. 'I'm sorry.' I pulled at my coat buttons, struggling to fasten them. 'Cath, please. I don't sleep, I can't sleep . . .' He bowed his head as if to hide something from me, tears perhaps. 'People are dying in the time it takes for decisions to be made about access to drugs and new organs. I sometimes feel that the lives of these people are in our hands.'

'But it's not all on you. There are all sorts of committees and charities and qualified individuals working to try and change things. You're generous with your experience, but it's up to the people whose actual job it is to campaign and—'

'I know, I know, and I am on at them, day after day, to fucking hurry up.'

'I understand and I'm sorry about the interview. But Mia isn't even six months old and I don't even know if I've learnt how to be her mother yet, let alone . . . Look at me.' I ran my fingers through a tangle of hair. Felt mascara logged tears fall in muddy trickles.

'What was it that changed your mind?'

'I keep leaving my husband and baby to be with another man. I couldn't go on national radio to talk about what a saintly person I am. I'm not. I'd be asking the country for help to fix my family, and the truth is that I betray them every day.'

He turned my face to his and spoke urgently. 'You are the person who cares for Mia, who is making sure that she's delivered into a future where there is new hope for her. You should own that.'

'I'm being unfaithful.' I felt myself pleading to him like he was a priest in the confession box. 'I'm being unfaithful to my child's father.'

'This is about survival. If being unfaithful is what you need to get yourself through these dark fucking woods, then give that to yourself. Stop nailing yourself to the cross. You deserve to be happy. Let me give you good things. Let *me* make you happy. I love you, Cath.'

I didn't know what to say and the words hung there.

Facing each other. I thought I saw every line and tic and contortion in him.

Close your eyes.

He loved me. I think he honestly loved me.

The last time Dave told me he loved me was in the moments after Mia was born. Perhaps he'd told me in the days after that. I couldn't remember.

I kissed Richard because I wanted to kiss him. Because I wanted to suck up those words that still hung in the air.

He searched for something in my eyes. 'Take my love. I won't ask for anything in return. Listen,' he said, pulling me to him, 'I want to take you away. Not for a few hours here and there in a hotel room. A proper trip away. Overnight, so we can drink champagne and make love to each other and actually have breakfast.'

I laughed in disbelief. 'I can't do that. How would I even make that happen?'

'You tell him you're seeing friends. That you need some time to do something that isn't about CF. You tell him it's what you *need*.' His eyes shone with that luminous, fevered intensity I knew well of him now, when it seemed as if he was speaking to someone else entirely.

He kissed me. 'I'll take you winter camping in the moonlight. We'll get a tent with a wood burner—'

'I think it's risky. I think Dave, you know . . . he might be beginning to suspect something.'

He sat back. 'Would it be such a bad thing if he found out? Then life could be like this more of the time. I know what needs to happen.' He looked high on something, engaged and yet entirely removed: his words sparking with energy, but directed into that middle distance again, missing my sight line. 'I'll end it. I'll divorce Nancy.'

'What? No, don't do that.'

'Of course that's what needs to happen. When Rachel

is cured and Mia is cured and the good drugs come through – who knows? Maybe they'll get along and Mia can be the little sister Rachel never had. We can all go to Spain together and stay by the sea. As a family.'

'Richard,' I put a hand on his arm, as though I was calming a bucking horse. 'Whatever drugs come through in the near future – and we still don't know how long that will take – our daughters will both always have cystic fibrosis. It's in their genes and will always be in their genes. They're a danger to each other. We can never be together as a family, not the four of us. You know that. Let's not pretend . . .'

He looked tired for a moment, but his face softened and focused back on me, as if he'd just remembered I was there. 'The problem with you is that you don't think big enough. You don't believe that the impossible can happen.'

'Sometimes it can't. There are some things you can't change.'

He put his finger to my mouth to stop me, and kissed me again, replacing fears with warmth – as he had done, time and again. His best trick, the one I loved most. And yet, in that moment, I knew instinctively that I was not the one who felt afraid. I wondered why the flame that had burnt with such life in him was so rapidly changing into a throbbing, agitated fever.

'Promise me one thing?' he said. 'Tell Dave you're going away for the weekend? Come and make new memories with me?'

I kissed him and agreed and put my arms around him to hold him.

I saw us then, reflected in the bedroom mirror – my head cast over his neck, our bodies close, faces looking at opposite walls.

Chapter 16

I took a taxi back later that night, expecting nothing more than a silent and dark house, perhaps a stick of light under the closed door of the spare bedroom. But even as I stood on the doorstep, I heard Mia's cries from inside and something was wrung out in me, dripping its ice through my veins. I scrambled uneasily through the objects in my handbag – a zip scraping the back of my hand, vain and mocking cylinders of make-up passing through my fingers in the search for house keys.

'How are you, sweetie?'

I glanced round, impatient at the delay, to find our nice neighbour Marian grappling with a sack of rubbish as she checked me over. She had such an attentive look on her lined and furrowed face that I almost stopped and wept. Nearly told that near-stranger everything.

'How is the baby? We don't hear a squeak through the walls. She must be a regular angel.'

'Good, thank you. She's good. Yes.' I turned away, keys found. Tried the door. Once, twice, but in my panicked haste the key slid at the metal surface of the keyhole.

Hands trembling. Heart racing. 'I can actually hear her now.'

Why couldn't Dave stop her tears?

'Having trouble with your door? My Stephen can look at that, if you like. I'm sure doorframes do something in the winter. They expand or lose weight.'

I tried again. Failed again. Rested my forehead against the lacquered wood for a moment.

'Would you like some help?'

'Thank you, no, it's OK, if I can get the key . . .'

She adjusted the sack in her hand. 'I keep meaning to say, if you ever need . . .'

I got the key in the door, barged at the wood with my shoulder. It opened a few inches but stuck obstinately on a thick wrinkle of doormat. I shoved it hard with my shoulder again.

'We'd love to babysit,' she continued. 'We love children. I've had lots of practice with four grandchildren. So if you ever . . .'

'Help, yes, no, thank you. It's OK. Thank you.'

'OK then. But the offer's there if you need it.'

I heard the soft, bottle-clanking collapse of rubbish sack against bin behind me, and heaved the door one more time.

I was in.

The cries grew louder as I climbed the stairs and ran towards the dusky pink light of the nursery. Dave stood – holding her tight, head bowed over her forehead as she cried into his chest.

'She's not well,' he said.

I ran to kiss her, to tell her I was there, that I should never have left her, but no sooner had my lips touched her warm and damp brow, no sooner had Dave's head lifted to watch me and consider me and all that had passed between us at Mum's, than I remembered and stepped back as if our child was molten rock.

I stepped back once more and stood behind the doorframe of her room, wiping at my skin and over my hair until I was damp with antibacterial fluid.

We both knew the drill each time I returned from the charity. Each time I returned from Richard. Scraping away the possibility of infection from under my fingernails, wiping it off my skin, peeling it away as I shed my clothes. Putting on my pyjamas as if the bed I had just jumped out of had been my own.

I returned to the bedroom and fitted my palms under Mia. I wanted to hold her because all children wanted their mothers when they were sick.

But she screamed louder and buried herself further into Dave.

'What's wrong with her?' I said.

'She vomited about half an hour ago and again just now. I think she's got a bug. A few days ago there was a girl at soft play who threw up in the ball pit where Mia was playing. Might be that.'

'What should we do? Should we call the hospital?' I began to cry. 'What if this is to do with her cough? What if these are the signs of a worsening infection? This is awful. I should never have left her.'

I raked at my arms with my fingernails as if I was still scraping and cleaning the skin.

'It'll be a vomiting bug,' he said calmly. 'Let's see how she does overnight.'

She stopped crying, then looked up at us both. In calming me he had calmed Mia.

'Can I?' I held out my arms again, asking to hold her, as if she were someone else's child.

I tried to take her from him a second time but she started to cry again, flinging her head back in desperation and gripping on to Dave as if her life depended on it.

'She'll be fine,' Dave insisted, as my tears worsened.

'But I want to hold her.'

His eyes brimmed with a truth he could have spoken.

But instead he said something about having been with her all day, which was probably why she wanted to stay with him now: *A security thing, you know?*

Despite all the cross words between us in the previous days, he did not allow the truth of it to spill over. No greater pain could have come from his mouth than: *She does not want you any more.*

That night the house would be dark again and the only stick of light would come from under the door of the spare room where I slept.

* * *

230

The next morning I tiptoed downstairs and watched my husband and child at the doorway to the kitchen – expecting the moment when the two of them would see me and turn away. I felt a pain in my chest, something carving its way into what lay there, and I wondered when such a simple love had transmuted itself into a fear of my husband and child's displeasure.

'Why are you standing there? Come in, I've made coffee.' Dave smiled and Mia turned to look at me, holding up her arms in supplication. I went to her, feeling the rim of my eyes sting and my chest rise and fill with gratitude as I lifted her into my arms. As I poured scorn on myself for underestimating how powerful love could be: that Mia had forgiven me and that Dave, having seen my distress, understood how hard I tried to be a good mother.

The mother *he* always hoped I could be.

The mother *I* always hoped I could be.

His faith in me had wiped away regrets and concerns, and, perhaps, for a moment, he had seen me.

I touched Mia's rosy cheeks and held her close to me, like a shield, emboldened by her love. I held my palm to her forehead and it felt cool. 'She seems to be on the mend. Is she on the mend?'

Dave put toast and coffee in front of me and smiled. 'I think so. Look. I'm sorry about yesterday.'

'I'm sorry too,' I said too quickly.

'Your sister tore a strip off your mother and me when you left. Said I had no idea what it's like being alone in the house day after day with a baby and that it was too long ago for your mum to remember. That it was hard work. And it could drive a person mad.'

'She said that?' I held Mia on my hip and kissed her four times. 'You and I are two people under a lot of pressure. It wasn't your fault. I've been spending too much time away. I'm sorry.'

He smiled. 'Hey. You look nice. You have a glow in your cheeks.'

I should have had faith in him and us and our family.

I decided then not to ask him if I could go away for the weekend. He and Mia had forgiven my ills so easily and I needed to repay that faith.

'We need some good quality time together,' he said. 'But not today. Today would be a good time for you to take some time off. Take a swim in Lake Me.' He laughed.

'But it's Sunday,' I said brightly. 'I don't want time alone today. I thought we could go to the local pub for a roast?'

'Mia and I are actually going out to lunch already.' Dave's eyes were bright and his face wide with a smile. And I saw that perhaps his happiness and positive energy weren't simply a forgiveness of me, or a clean sheet for us. Something or someone else, had made him feel generous towards me.

'Oh?' I smiled.

He bent down to button Mia's cardigan. 'Jane's coming

to meet us in the park with her kids and then we're going for lunch. She'll be here in a minute so I should get on with sorting our stuff.'

'That's nice,' I said, my mind projecting a picture before it had a chance to process the facts of her.

Jane with the pretty green eyes.

She was Dave's old friend from college, the one who made him sparkle-eyed with gratitude on the rare occasions she got in touch, the long-time crush he'd spent nights imagining himself with before I came along. It was so obvious in the way he spoke about her. Or rather, the way he didn't speak about her – on the few occasions I'd asked. She'd married a merchant banker called Pete and given up her career in advertising to have two kids that she dressed in tasteful cream and navy.

'If you're going to the park, why don't I come and say hello?' I coughed as I spoke, trying to damp down the niggles in my voice that might betray me.

'You don't need to do that,' he said. And my heart fell further. 'Why don't you have some time to yourself? Plan your next project or something. Maybe something that's nothing to do with CF or Mia or the family. Or read a trashy magazine, catch up on *Housewives of whatever* . . . We won't even be at the park for long. It's nearly lunchtime already.'

I put Mia back down on her play mat, confused at how I had gone from feeling part of the family to cast out in a matter of moments.

I went to leave. Changed my mind.

'How is she then? Jane?'

'I think she's fine,' he said distractedly. 'Doing a lot of childcare on her own. Pete travels a lot for work so they don't get out much together and I think she misses time with other adults. It's exhausting with two kids, apparently. We need to think about that. But maybe it's just a question of being organized.'

I thumbnailed a piece of discoloured paint on the doorframe and nodded.

'I should go then,' he said. 'Have a nice day to yourself and sorry again for being unsupportive yesterday. New day and all?'

'Should we at least talk more about yesterday? You know, if you think I'm doing too much charity stuff, or even the wrong kind of stuff. I was thinking of cutting back—'

'Nope, it's fine. Let's chalk it up to stress.'

I left the room, and less than five minutes later, he and Mia were gone.

For a while I paced the rooms. Too tired to clean and too twitchy to sleep. Unable to concentrate on reading, or watching TV.

Then I saw Mia's medicine on the mantelpiece, scooped up my coat and left the house.

I was surprised to find them still in the park despite what Dave had said about their busy lunch schedule. He seemed to have all the time in the world as he chatted to Jane and alternated between pushing Mia and one of Jane's boys on the swings.

It wasn't until I was through the gate that they noticed me. They looked up simultaneously, a flash of something in each of their faces that was so ugly my mind wouldn't let me see it for a moment.

Disappointment.

'Great to see you.' A broad smile broke across Jane's face as she pulled me into an embrace – one that, from the outside, would have looked like we were good friends, but that felt twiggy and cold, draughts between the gaps where she stopped our bodies from fully touching. We pulled away and regarded each other. She stood in a cloud of orchid-scent and her own orderliness: no stray flaps or folds of clothing. No escaped hairs or messy eyebrows or wrinkles at the knee where denim and calf-length leather boot met. She didn't look the kind of tired Dave had implied she felt. She looked well, in fact, her skin shining and taut with health and sleep. She smiled.

We all smiled.

'So lovely to see you,' I said, because someone had to say something. I had never known her well enough for it to be truly lovely, but it was better than saying: *Fine enough to see you*. We'd never talked about anything other than the people we knew in common. I wasn't that interested in what she had to say and she probably felt the same about me.

'I brought Mia's meds.' I handed Dave the cool pack and he nodded. 'Kids look gorgeous,' I said. They did – all white-blond hair and huge blue eyes. 'Dave says it's pretty knackering with two.'

'It's fine, actually,' she said, still smiling. 'They give me the run-around but it's a happy chaos. I wouldn't have it any other way.'

'Oh, good. And how's Pete? Away a lot?'

'Yes, he travels quite a bit, but it's great for all of us. He loves it. It gives him a chance to see the world, you know? Although I'm never sure how much he actually sees, locked in a conference room all day. And it gives me some space, which I don't get a lot of nowadays. It works very well for all of us.' Her laugh was too loud, directed like a jet hose at her children hopping over stones. 'And how's your stuff? Thinking about going back to work? What is Mia now? Six months?'

'Yes, almost. But she still feels far too young for me to leave her.'

'Tell me about it. I still haven't left! Something nobody tells you. Everything, and I mean everything changes when babies come along.'

I balled my fists and smiled politely because there were no words. Her change was not the same as my change and . . . 'Anyway. I'll take the full year. I hope. Have a think about what's next.'

'Hmm, yes. Take stock.' She looked thoughtful. 'I can imagine an experience like yours makes you think about what's important in life. Such a tough thing for you all. I do hope the shock of it all is settling? A bit?'

The shock of it all? I heard Dave's words in her mouth.

'Oh you know, getting my head round it all gradually.'

'I think you're amazing. All those medications, all that physio.'

'Any parent would do the same.'

'You'd hope!' She laughed, again. 'You never know until you're faced with it. I'd be rubbish. I'm so disorganized.' She was wearing weather-appropriate clothes and her children wore colours that coordinated with each other and the scarlet red of the swings. I looked towards the park gate and planned my exit. 'And some people are too damn selfish to stand up to a challenge like that.' She threw back her head and her hair rippled in time with her laugh. 'A bit like that girl at your office, Dave. She could learn some humility.' Jane turned from me to Dave. 'Everything's always about her!' She laughed again.

'What girl at work?' I smiled, trying to hold my own.

'Oh, just an admin assistant called Gemma,' said Dave, gazing wistfully at the plane trees – as if the facts of it all were as unimportant and inevitable as the change in seasons. 'She's ambitious. You know, a heel-biter. Wants to run when she can't walk, is all. Boring office politics.'

'She sounds like a pain in the arse,' I said.

'She so is,' said Jane.

No one said anything more about Gemma.

'But look, we should go,' said Jane. 'We've got a reservation at that new pizza place on the high street. Gets so busy on a Sunday.'

'I've been wanting to go there for ages.' But we never seemed to get round to it.

'You should, you should . . . Archie!' She called to one of her boys. 'You should come with us, if you like? Archie, come here, we have to go now.'

Dave turned his back to gather Mia from the swings and I wondered when he was going to verify Jane's invitation and ask me along too.

But he didn't and perhaps he didn't hear so I said, 'You don't want to miss your reservation. And fitting other people in if they're busy is . . . Anyway. Have a good time.' As if they needed my blessing.

I raised my hand and said goodbye again as they gathered and organized their children.

Back home I watched them from the bathroom window as they walked up from the park at a leisurely pace: Mia strapped to Dave's chest, her arms and legs kicking joyfully, and Jane, pushing her neat beige double-buggy. They were engrossed in each other. I could tell by the way their heads turned at awkward angles so they could pay more attention to each other's words. She was waving a hand in the air and he was laughing as his hands grasped Mia's kicking feet.

Together, they looked like a family.

I stepped back as they passed under the house and in the opposite direction to the pizza place. They were taking the long way round, the same way Dave and I used to take before Mia came along, when we wanted to talk about something to each other. When we hadn't wanted the energy between us to be broken by a change in scene.

I tried to remember the last time Dave and I had chosen to go for a walk together, and couldn't. Unless I counted the muted outings in the days after diagnosis when we walked, but we didn't ever talk. Not unless it was about the heat or the good butcher that was closed on a Monday or the now-felled oak tree that used to shade the toddlers from the sun.

Moments before they disappeared from view, I noticed Dave was wearing a pair of trainers I had never seen before; amber with a flash of green at their sides. He never bought new trainers and if he did they always replaced the same brand in the same colour: navy blue and white, high around the sides so he could wear them like upturned collars at the base of his jeans.

Those amber-green trainers reminded me of a traffic light saying: *It's nearly safe to go.*

I sat at the window and watched, and waited, for Dave to return.

The clock measured an hour, and then two, until finally he emerged at the corner again, a sleeping Mia at his chest. Checking his phone. Alone.

I was standing on the stairs as he came in. 'Did you have a nice time?'

'I did actually.' He didn't look up, still engrossed in his phone.

I took Mia from him and perched on the steps with her in my arms, getting ready to feed her. 'My radio interview got pulled from the schedules by some bigger news item.' I gave the explanation in case he asked what had happened. I knew he wouldn't but that didn't stop me from hoping.

'Oh yes?' he said disinterestedly. Still looking at his phone.

'There will only be a few more charity events now . . . perhaps only one.'

'Fine,' he said.

'Or two. I'm not sure what I want to do.'

But he didn't look up so I couldn't see whether Jane's image was still burnt on to his pupils.

I watched him as he continued to read his phone, standing in the hall in his socks like that.

'Would you mind if I went away for the weekend at the end of the month?' I said.

And before I had a chance to justify it or to tell him it's what I needed, he said, 'Sure. I'm going to jump in the shower.'

Chapter 17

'You're going to Manchester?' I sat on the bottom step – coat buttoned, keys digging into my palm – and craned my head towards the clatter and chaos in the bathroom.

Dave opened and closed the medicine cabinet. 'Where's my razor? Have you been using it for your . . . there it is.' An avalanche of nail files and cardboard pill boxes landed in the sink. I nudged my carefully packed suitcase towards the front door as if it was still going somewhere.

'Sunny Manchester,' he said, delighted by his own disbelief. 'But there won't be any fun. It'll all be work.' He crammed things back in the medicine cabinet but objects escaped his grasp and tumbled back into the sink. 'This cupboard is a mess.' He looked up. 'I'm sorry, I expect you were looking forward to your weekend away.' At another time he would have known I was looking forward to a weekend away. 'Clinic starts at ten. They want you there on time because all the kids with the nasty superbugs come in at eleven so you need to avoid them. There'll be an assessment of how her antibiotics are going.'

He examined a razor blade. 'I thought about not going

up north and Skyping them instead, you know? But then I thought: there's nothing better than putting a face to the name.' Always good to put a face to a name. 'Particularly if you want someone to write you a massive cheque. New investment . . . that would be a result.'

I pulled a thread from the hem of my coat and watched it unravel in a jolting zig-zag.

'But it's such short notice,' he continued. A negative statement, delivered with such delight and hope. 'We'll spend the entire train journey prepping for the meeting. Can you chuck me my headphones?'

I balled tangled wires into my palm and held them there. 'Why do you need your headphones if you're going to be prepping on the journey?'

He zipped his wash bag closed and walked to the threshold of the bathroom. 'I've still got the tube journey to Euston. Since when do you care when I listen to my music?'

'Why did you pack that aftershave? You never wear aftershave.'

'If I never wear aftershave, why did you buy it for me as a birthday present?'

Because the smell of aftershave on Richard made me want him.

'Because I've bought you every football annual on Amazon. I just don't understand why you're taking that aftershave with you now. You've never worn it with me.'

'First time for everything. Especially in Manchester!'

He walked down the stairs carefully and stepped over me into the hallway. 'Are you feeling all right? Apart from missing out on your weekend? Look, I did try. Mum's got a stinking cold so that rules her out, and Caroline's already got plans, and even if somebody was around Mia still needs a parent with her at clinic. So it's Mummy all the way!'

I looked down at his shoes, shiny and tapered like mussel shells. 'Why are you wearing your wedding shoes?'

He raised his eyebrows. 'Because I can't wear trainers at the kind of restaurants we have bookings for.'

'Are you eating out with the investors both nights? Aren't you going to do something fun, for at least one evening?' Then, when he didn't bother answering, 'Is this some kind of punishment? Is it a way of getting back at me because I've been away so much?' I couldn't keep the childish petty foot-stamping hurt out of my voice.

He bent down to look at me. 'God, no. I wouldn't do that. I'm working—'

'With who, though?' I thought of Jane and the woman he'd called 'heel-biter' in the park the other day. I thought of the woman with the asymmetric fringe and ice-blue eyes who worked in the coffee shop round the corner and another woman I couldn't put a face or a name to – who I may never be able to put a face or a name to. I clenched Dave's headphones in my fists and resisted the urge to throw them at the wall.

He leaned down and looked at me like he was checking

exactly who was sitting on his steps. 'I'm working. I'm with colleagues. My God, do you think I'm lying? You think I'm lying.'

I pressed at his face with the pads of my fingers, examining the clean shave, gently pulling at skin round his glass green eyes.

'What are you looking for?'

The look in his eyes that used to blunt every sharp corner in me.

'I'm not looking for anything.' My hands fell by my sides. 'I'm disappointed and . . .' I swallowed back something. 'I hate taking Mia to the hospital for clinics. I hate that hospital.'

He held my hand in his and spoke with the same heartfelt sincerity he always did when talking about Mia. 'I know you do, I know you hate the hospital, but it's only an assessment. Nothing to worry about. She's shaking that cough. You'll be in and out in an hour.' He took his hand away and looked at his packing and his arrangements, his voice vaporizing as he spoke about me. 'You could get on the train straight after clinic? Take Mia with you on your weekend away? Then it really would be a girls' trip.'

'I can't take Mia on a girls' weekend away. What would I do with her at the restaurant in the evening? Carting round a nappy bag and stopping every ten minutes is hardly the same as having some time out with friends.'

'Call them and explain the situation. If you gave them

a chance to help, they would. They all know what they're doing.'

I unbuttoned my coat and let it fall off my shoulders.

'Go on,' he said. 'Call them.'

'I will.'

'Do it now. Then, if it works, we can pack Mia's stuff together, I'll order you a cab to clinic and you can go straight on to the train station. Go on. Find out.'

I bristled. 'No, I . . .'

'Come on, there isn't much time. This is a good idea.'

I held up my hand, the joints of my fingers locking. 'Stop, Dave. Just stop. I don't want to. I don't want to take her with me.'

He turned away from me to arrange something in his wallet because he needed to get on now, no more time for this conversation. His jeans were dark indigo and pressed flat because they were still so new, untouched by hot washes and spins.

I stood up and climbed the stairs two at a time. 'I should pack Mia's bag for clinic.'

At the top of the house I closed the door firmly behind me. Sat on the edge of a once jet-black sofa – now greying and threadbare, the first Dave and I had bought together – and dialled.

Richard answered immediately. 'Everything all right? I'm leaving now.'

I pulled at a loose thread on the sofa. 'I can't come. Dave's going to Manchester for the weekend on work.'

'But the taxi's in the driveway.'

'I'm sorry, it was landed on him, and me, last minute.'

Mia sent desperate cries up through the house, Dave shouted my name and I felt a drumming ache under my arms and in my kneecaps, like I was holding on to the rafters while my feet were pulled back through the rooms beneath.

On the rack.

'But I've got a bottle of special vintage champagne.' Richard continued talking in a joyful tone, as if I hadn't disappointed him at all. 'It has this amazing blue glass, like one of those old apothecary bottles. And I found a kind of cross between a blow-up mattress and feather duvet that you'll love . . . When does he leave? Put the baby to bed and I'll come round with it all. We can make a camp in the living room and eat marshmallows under a blanket. It'll be fun.'

'Of course we can't do that. You can't come anywhere near my house, you know that. The cross-infection risk . . .' I didn't finish the sentence because he knew although he never seemed to actually *know*. 'Anyway, I've got to take her to clinic.'

'What's wrong?' he said, though it wasn't clear who or what he was asking about.

'Nothing. It's a check-up. That's all.'

I looked out at a soft dirty scrub of clouds and missed the sun.

'A simple check-up,' he said wistfully, as if he were

remembering the last sun he'd felt on *his* skin. 'You . . . how lucky you are.' The line was distorting, his words crumpling into nonsense. '. . . How long . . . your clinic be? Twenty minutes?' His words made sounds like bending metal.

'Can you move to another room in the house? The reception is terrible.'

'I'm in the shed and it's tipping down outside.'

'Go into the house?'

'I can't go into the house.' But before I had a chance to ask him why he said, 'I'm not drinking that champagne alone. I'll drop it off.'

'I already told you, you can't come over.'

'You can drink it alone.'

A silence, again, which could have been him, could have been the bad phone line. 'Please don't be like that,' I said. 'This whole situation is unavoidable.'

'I really wanted to talk to you about something.' A barely discernible whine laced his words.

'I can't cancel clinic.' Aggravated, now, that he wasn't listening.

'Did you know?' His voice louder, demanding that I listen to him. 'Did you know that the last clinic we had went on for nearly a day?' He paused, as if searching for the right words and the right tone. 'Rachel has NTM,' he said.

But there is no right tone when there are, simply, the facts of it. The gut-punching, air-thieving, life-changing facts of it.

'Do you know what that is? It's Non-Tuberculosis Mycobacteria,' he said.

I stood on legs that quivered with the need to crumble under me. Held my hand over the phone, my stomach lurching through my lungs, smashing out air and life, retching up something it had long since held.

'I know what it is.' My voice shredded and tripped and did not sound like my own.

I had done my reading.

NTM was virulent and clever: the Father, the Son and the Holy Ghost of all bacteria.

All the skittish concerns I'd had about Dave and affairs and Richard and weekends away were blown into the air around me, smashed into particulates as the vortex spun its tar-black circles at my feet, pulling me further and further towards its axis.

'It could colonize my sinuses,' I said, reciting the scripture I'd learned by heart, 'and though it would never affect me, I could transfer them back into the atmosphere with a sneeze or a discarded used tissue, and infect Mia.'

I was outside my body, watching myself – face white, eyes dead, arm hanging limp by my side – churning out the observed facts like the survivor of a terrible accident, standing at the side of the road, smashed through to the core with shock.

'It's not great,' he said.

'NTM molecules stay in the air for up to an hour and on clothes and surfaces for up to two weeks. NTM causes irreversible lung damage. It's more virulent and more dangerous to the CF lung than any other bacteria. All the research backs up that statement. I've read it.'

'Yes,' he said quietly – chastened, perhaps, by my recitations or shocked all over again at hearing them reflected back in all their life-stealing violence.

And the silence that followed was not the bad phone line.

Just confirmation of facts that needed no adjustment or excuse or downplaying.

'I know what it is and what it does, Cath.'

'It's not even sensitive to normal antibacterial cleaners. So every time I've been with you, all the precautions I've taken washing my skin. Every time I've been with you . . . pointless—'

'It's a dangerous, horrible thing. But it is my daughter that is colonized with it. Not yours, and not you. I'm sure of it.'

'But when did you find out?'

'I don't know, a few weeks ago. Three, maybe. It's been getting harder to—'

I wiped something from the edges of my mouth. Spittle, bile and mucus. Rubbed it off in an angry streak on my jeans. 'But I've seen you at least three times since then. Why didn't you tell me?'

'Because it didn't come up and besides, they think she's had it a while so any damage that might have been done . . . They picked it up while they were conducting advanced tests to see if her pseudomonas was behaving.'

'What do you mean *a while*? Exactly how long has she had it?'

'Does it fucking matter?'

'Yes, it fucking matters. My daughter has been coughing for weeks and she isn't subject to the kind of advanced tests your daughter has . . . *I* could have passed NTM on to her without knowing. You should have told me.'

My stomach moved, retched, bubbled with bile again. I hated the presumption in him.

In that moment, I felt blind, killing hatred for him and for me.

Vomit out the blame, you stupid woman, you awful mother. Vomit it out and all that you will be left with is yourself.

'I just told you my daughter is colonized with a bacteria that is resistant to all known antibiotics, you've cancelled our trip away for a twenty-minute check-up for your mostly healthy daughter, and you're worrying about an infection that she is unlikely to have . . .'

It wasn't unlikely, it wasn't unlikely at all.

I picked up a vase. Terracotta. Shaped like a woman's body. Threw it against the wall. It landed in clean pieces.

Silence. A calm.

'Your daughter is fine,' he said. 'Mine is not.'

He was speaking the facts of it. Was he?

'I'm sorry,' I said, needing to end the call. 'I'm genuinely sorry for your news.' I regretted saying it in a way that sounded as if I was saying *I'm sorry for your loss* but I couldn't ground my words or even find the right ones because there was no time and I needed to get Mia to her clinic. Needed to get her to a safe place. 'This is a lot to take in,' I said. 'Why don't I get Mia sorted out and call you later? It must be terrible for you all. And I'm sorry about camping. I have to go now. Speak later.'

There was a rustle behind me at the door and Dave stood, his fingers folded around the frame. 'Mia needs a feed. Don't mind me. Friends disappointed?' he said. 'I bet they are. Who wouldn't want to spend time with a woman like you?'

Then he turned without an answer.

Chapter 18

The consultant untangled a vibrant purple lanyard from around her neck and looked up, smiling. 'And how is Mia?'

'I don't know, yes, I . . . she seems well enough in herself, I think, but I know that *seeming* well is not the same as *being* well.' The consultant smiled kindly. 'I guess that's why they call CF an *invisible illness*,' I said.

She nodded and swept away a fringe that was beginning to grow out. She looked healthy and calm, her skin tone a shade darker than the last time we'd seen her. A holiday, perhaps. She was *well in herself*. Diet, exercise, choice of life partner – all working for her whatever the weather. Not that I really knew about the weather in her life, whereas she, and the rest of the medical staff, knew exactly what happened to my appearance when the storms came calling. *Are you eating?* the nurse asked me, a week after diagnosis, like a good friend might, and for a moment I had been struck by how nice it was to be asked, before I realized that they needed assurance I was eating properly because I needed to produce enough breastmilk for Mia, because breastfeeding was good for her immunity. Weight gain was essential for Mia. The facts of it were that my wellbeing was connected to her wellbeing and if Mia was their patient then I might be her medicine. One of many.

When tears ran down my cheeks at her early appointments they wanted to know I was seeking the appropriate support from family and friends – because for their patient to be given the best chance, I needed to be *well in myself*.

'You look well,' the consultant said, still smiling.

'Thank you. I feel well.' My jeans weren't sagging at the bum like they had done a few months before. 'Helps that she's sleeping better.' I nodded towards a snoozing Mia, bundled in the pram, cheeks sheened with pink since we'd entered the heat of the hospital. 'This is only a check-up, right?'

'Standard clinic, yes, no new tests. Does Mia still have that cough?'

'It comes and goes, but yes.'

The consultant scrawled something in Mia's file and closed it. 'That looks sore.' Her face rumpled in concern at the bandage around my wrist. Her arms were folded neatly over each other, and over my daughter's medical file.

'I fell.'

'Poor you. Must have hurt.'

'Yes,' I said, holding it up as if it still felt swollen.

'But it's fine. I tripped on the pavement. Just lucky I didn't have Mia with me. If she'd been in a sling or something . . .'

I thought of Richard asking me, *Are you all right?* Then I thought of how he'd withheld the results of Rachel's NTM infection.

'Could have been a lot worse,' I said.

The consultant opened out Mia's file again like the wings of a butterfly, and found a page with enough room to write. She paused then wrote something else, in a scrawl I couldn't read.

'But it's all fine,' I added quickly. I didn't want a written record of the story I'd told her, not when a story was all it was. Not when I had been with him, amassing an army of silent killers on my skin. 'I can still breastfeed. I can still hold her. I can still give her medicines. My wrist still works.' I laughed. 'I don't think it's relevant for the records.'

'Good,' she said, continuing to write.

'I tripped over someone else's foot on Oxford Street. Outside TopShop. I was buying jeans. First new pair since getting pregnant.'

She smiled benignly, looking up. 'Oxford Street. Hell of a place. I tend to avoid it.' Her fingers pressed into a typed page on the desk as if to hold it in place. She glanced down at it, not wanting to lose her place. There were numbers and the black outlined diagram of a pair of lungs. She wasn't recording my tale of jeans buying on Oxford Street. She was writing numbers in a margin. I sat back in my chair.

My wrist hadn't been relevant. Mia was her patient.

'Do we think those new antibiotics have done the job?' she said.

'It's hard to tell. All her cough swab tests have been negative. They haven't shown any sign of bacterial infection. Do you still think it's a virus?'

'There's a lot going round.' Her head dipped to her notes again.

Mia opened her eyes and whimpered softly. I scooped her out of the pram and held her up on my knee, bleary-eyed and warm.

'She's sitting up now,' I said, as Mia turned to me, to check my expression, to see what I was saying. She raised a hand to my face and pressed it to my cheek, hooked her fingers into my mouth and drew them away. She let her body go soft and gave a gentle kick, my cue to sit her down on the floor. 'She loves showing off her new skill.'

'I can see,' laughed the consultant as Mia tipped sideways, then on to her stomach, kicking legs and hands in the air. I bent down and smothered her hands in antibacterial gel. 'I never know how much to track her with the antibac. Never know whether I should be there all the time, standing in the shadows.'

I righted Mia and positioned her at my feet.

'It's all a judgement call. Balancing the threats in favour of a normal life. For you and your child.' She smiled as

255

I found her answer lacking, as I found myself on the roller-rink again. Balancing. I snapped the lid of the gel shut and held the bottle in my grasp, ready to use at a moment's notice.

'Could this cough be teething? She's definitely teething. I've read online that teething can cause coughs? Open wide?' I smiled at Mia and she obliged. 'We've got two already and a third on the way. Look at those red cheeks.' Mia held up her arms to be collected. I scooped her up and she cried in protest, ramming her legs towards the floor again.

She stood in scarlet ballet pumps, my hands clenched round her torso, her hands stuck hotly to my legs for balance. She smiled at me. I kissed her and put a rice cake in her hand. She gummed it and dropped it, wiped damp and crumby hands gleefully on my jeans and fell on to her bottom.

For a moment both the consultant and I watched her. I wiped at her hands with antibacterial gel – once, twice maybe. They cleaned hospitals well nowadays, but all it would take was for them to miss a hair's breadth with the mop and for Mia to mop up the danger instead.

Mia's chest heaved, her little face changing to rich raspberry as a guttural, claggy cough caught the back of her throat and sent shock waves through her body.

'How many times has she coughed like that?' said the consultant, still calm. 'That kind of wet, productive cough, I mean.'

My stomach rolled. 'I don't know. It's been a dry cough. Mostly, I think. But like that? The first time was maybe yesterday? I gave her some mashed parsnips and she got a bit stuck, like she was choking on it. I thought it was that. Or the teething. It could be the teething, couldn't it? The swab was negative only a week ago. Is that on your notes?'

The consultant turned pages in the file and ran a finger along a chart. 'Mia's been on oral antibiotics for over seven weeks now.' Her soft, kind, conversational tone had gone, stiffening into something more formal. She referred to more pages in Mia's notes. 'You understand our need to take defensive action if a cough has been going on for too long.'

'Yes, of course.'

Too long. It had to stop.

I vowed to myself I would stop.

'But what would you be taking defensive action against?' I asked.

'We won't know precisely until we carry out a bronchoscopy. That way, we can take some samples from the bronchial secretions in the lungs and send them off to the lab where they check for rarer forms of bacteria. The kind that standard tests alone wouldn't flag.'

The wave in me rose.

'A bronchoscopy? Does that mean there could be something down in her lungs that normal tests haven't picked up?'

'A bronchoscopy is the only way of getting truly accurate samples at this age. It gets easier once they can produce sputum for us.'

'And you want to do one on her?'

'At this stage I think it might be best. We'll put a camera into the lungs to see what's going on. Take some samples there. Do a CT scan and blood draws. She'll be under general anaesthetic all the time so she won't be aware of any of it and won't be in pain. It should all be over within an hour. Then we'll keep her on the ward for two weeks of intravenous antibiotics.'

'CT scan and general anaesthetic? And two weeks in hospital? Will she . . . will we be home for Christmas?'

Information on your child's illness. Symptoms. Progression. End-stage.

Information on hospital stays.

An intravenous line to her heart.

Only last week I'd found the leaflets we'd been given after diagnosis in the back of a kitchen drawer. But I didn't file them away. I read them, line by line, then threw them in the bin because Richard's voice had been singing loud and clear in my mind that we would be the lucky ones.

Everything will be fine. You will be saved.

'It can sound intimidating,' said the consultant, 'and it's a lot to take in, even if you've read around it. But we especially want to keep Mia healthy through her first three years when a lot of lung structures are forming.

We're aggressive about treatment but only because we believe that it'll put her in the best position to benefit from new treatments in the future.'

'That the NHS won't pay for.'

'A lot can change, including governments. And drug prices can come down. There's going to be competition in the market soon.'

'Soon enough for Mia?'

'I'd hope so.'

'It's never just a plain "yes", is it?'

I looked down at Mia, a fist jammed into her mouth.

'Mia, no,' I shouted, pulling her hand out of her mouth, grabbing her by the waist, too hard perhaps, pulling her up into the air and away from the invisible bacteria of the hospital floor where she was learning to crawl. I thought of an eagle holding its eaglet in her beak, tearing her away from danger and reaching its wingspan wide before flying off into the clouds. I smothered Mia's palms in antibacterial gel, staring at them, examining them for an enemy I couldn't see.

'Exactly how effective are those antibacterial gels?' I said, scrabbling in my bag for a tissue amidst the nappies and wipes and medication. 'And antibacterial household cleaner? I've read that they don't work on all bacteria. Is that true?'

'There are some bacteria that aren't responsive to those products. Is there something you want to discuss, Cath? I'm here to answer your questions as well.'

Parts of me were shutting down; my stomach turning, a pain somewhere, everywhere perhaps, my breath shortening, a flood of something – acid where blood should be. 'Why are you doing a CT scan? They did one for my dad. They found something . . .'

'A CT scan will tell us if there is any lung damage.'

'I feel like I clean everything so much that if she's picked something up it must be one of the really bad ones. One of the ones that normal alcohol gel doesn't kill.'

Mia sat upright on my knee, her back straight, legs dangling in front of her, looking at where the gel was sinking into her hands. She trailed a line on her palm with a finger. A palm reader's heart line: the one that determined length of life.

'Let's not jump to conclusions. Infection can cause lung damage but I can't tell you any more until we do the tests and work out what's causing this exacerbation. I understand that this is very hard. Hospital admission is an upheaval. Particularly the first time.'

There will be others, but here is where you start.

'Is your husband available?' she asked.

'I, er . . . No. He's away.'

She tapped at her computer. 'Because ideally I'd like to admit her tomorrow. We can make space for a bronchoscopy in the afternoon and we'll find a bed for her on the ward after that. If we don't grab this slot it could be another six weeks. In the meantime, please go home and get some rest,' she said. 'Pack for ten to fourteen days. I'll get one of the nurses to talk you through the arrangements; where to store her normal medicines, where you'll be sleeping, that kind of thing.'

'Where I'll be sleeping?'

'A parent or guardian will need to be with Mia throughout.'

'Why is this happening so quickly? Is it because this is serious?'

'I've reserved the slot for a bronc now. I don't think we should wait. If there's anything going on we can nip it in the bud early.'

In the bud.

Like Mia was growing roses in her lungs.

The consultant had a sheaf of forms in front of her to fill out for this new stage, this *admission*.

Her admission.

For what?

You know. Of course you know. You brought it back from your lover's skin and then you breathed it into her as you kissed her, and now she'll cough until her lungs are bleeding wreckage. This is the price.

'Could she have picked up something in the last few weeks?' My breath was short and laboured. I wanted to hold on tight to Mia but I also wanted to put her away – somewhere she was safer than with me – and so I collected her up and strapped her into the pram. She took a deep breath and let out a howl, crying and kicking, kicking and crying at her incarceration. 'Is it possible that something bad could have been transmitted from clothing, or skin, to her?' I shouted over her cries.

'There are a thousand sources of bacteria in our environment. She could have picked up anything from anywhere.'

'I know, but, other bugs, bad bugs? Like, antibiotic-resistant bugs? She could have picked them up from somewhere?'

'Has she been in contact with that kind of bug? To the best of your knowledge?'

Admit before you are admitted.

'Yes, but not exactly, no. Not directly, at least.'

'Then it's unlikely. Not beyond the bounds of reason, but unlikely.'

'But she could have got unlucky, right? If she'd been in a place where a nasty, antibiotic-resistant bug was transferred from skin, or the surface of something, on to her? Isn't that why you have all the kids with the difficult infections come in after everyone else for clinic? In case of the infectious air they breathe in the lift, in case they lean against a wall or a chair and transfer it?'

She put her hand on my arm to steady me. 'That kind of cross infection is possible. But there's no point in beating yourself up. The chances are you'll never know where the infection came from. The first step is the bronchoscopy. Then IVs while we wait for the cultures. Then let's see where we are.'

I had been so careful after the first time.

And then, less careful.

Everything will be fine. You'll see.

'If it's something I've done, I'm sorry.' I drew my arms round myself and began to cry.

'You mustn't blame yourself. You take plenty of precautions with your child, that's clear to me.' She nodded at the antibacterial gel. 'When you fall and sprain your wrist your first comment is about how you can still feed and hold and medicate your child. You are a good mother.'

A good mother?

That was not the truth.

'We'll do our best to support you through this. This kind of thing,' she added sombrely, '. . . an opportunistic infection that jumps on top of a virus and beds down in thick CF mucus? This kind of thing is the nature of the illness.' Her voice was soft now. A professionalism, tempered.

Cries calmed, Mia was gazing up from the hood of her pram making cooing sounds.

What was the point in any of it? So many meals, so many nappies, a million stories to read and for what? Building her body up for what kind of future? Brutishly short. Stunted and painful.

None of your ambitions will be in your reach.

Kinder to lay our heads together on the railway line.

'Cath?'

'Yes. I'll go home and pack our bags.'
'The nurses will call you to go over everything again.'
'Thank you.'

Chapter 19

Mia's favourite stuffed animal was a koala. There was something about the size of its head, I think, or the way it was smothered and fringed with brown fur, that meant she could nestle into it at night, nose to nose, her fat arm flung over its soft body.

At the entrance to the hospital she held the stuffed animal to her face, one arm looped around my neck, legs hooked around my waist as if she, too, were a koala clinging to its favourite eucalyptus. But I'd taken her out of her natural habitat – standing at the entrance to a set of revolving doors that were moving too quickly, looking up at the big, blue monster of a hospital made of glass and steel, wire and life, machines and death.

She kicked her legs in excitement as if we were about to do something wonderful and fun together. I drew a deep breath of West London air that was so chilled it felt like it was burning my lung's membranes. But I let it burn. What I had caused . . . if I breathed harder, faster, perhaps I would combust. An easier punishment than guilt.

I hadn't called Dave right away. I had packed and fed

and medicated and settled Mia before calling him late. He'd been in a restaurant, barely able to hear me against the music and chatter. I managed to say *Get home whenever you can – tomorrow, no rush, whenever you like.* He wasn't having any of that but I told him not to spoil his evening.

Not when this was something I had caused and needed to fix. But I didn't tell him that bit.

I sang softly into her ear: *I will not leave your side now that we are here.* However stifling, painful or exhausting. *I will stay right by your side.* Whoever came to visit, I promised myself – even if it was Dave telling me to take a break, get coffee and read a magazine – I would say: *No, thank you for the offer, but this is where I need to stay.* Keeping vigil. Checking that the nurse sanitizes her hands properly before touching my daughter. Watching that the hospital janitor covers every square inch of the linoleum floor with disinfectant. Watching. Protecting. Leaving nothing to chance, ever again.

A text message from Richard, the fifth since yesterday: *Where are you? Please don't be angry with me.*

I replied: *Hospital admission. Suspected infection. Please don't call.*

I squeezed Mia's legs and held her trunk tightly – as if we were about to jump over a fast-moving body of water, one that we must clear – and inside the vents blew hot air. A line of chairs in A & E, mostly empty but for a teenage boy on an iPhone, his hand on ice. A man, age indeterminate, grimed and swaying, his blood sunk through dirty denim.

In a parallel life I might have been sitting two places down from them, because of an accident. Something small. A snap. A twist. A jolt. A sprain. Perhaps I had singed my arm on the barbecue trying to turn a steak, or snapped a tendon playing rounders on a green and sunny field. Slashed my palm with a broken bottle as I tried to open it, drunk, on a beach. In a parallel life this kind of hurt would seem big at the time because it would temporarily disable a hand or foot.

In a parallel life, I was childless but didn't know how lucky I was.

In a parallel life, I left Dave early on and my children, with another man, now ran through sand dunes, their young bodies like immortals, and me trailing behind them, afraid of nothing.

In a parallel life, I dropped a pound coin into a fund-raiser's bucket and wondered briefly at how ugly the words *cystic fibrosis* were, and then forgot the words forever.

Another text from him: *I am sorry . . . this won't be what you think, I . . .*

The rest went unread by me.

My spine crackled with the weight of Mia and our bag, full of the toothbrushes and pyjamas we would need for our stay. I shifted her position round my waist as she curled into my neck and held me tighter.

She wriggled to be let down but I held her firmly,

looking to the floor, seeing what filthy, invisible prints were left by the swaying man and bleeding boy. No mistakes. Ever again. I held her tighter.

Tighter still.

Never let her go.

But her body bent away from me, a flower craning towards a sun I couldn't see. She jabbed her finger in the general direction of a place that sold sweets to fortify visitors whose strength was waning, and banana milk to placate children, chocolates to celebrate birth, something sugary for shock, a newspaper to take your mind off it, something to punctuate the hours and hours of waiting.

By the rows of purple and orange and red shining chocolate wrappers a mother bent down and spoke to her teenage daughter in a wheelchair. The girl – run dry of colour, hair drawn back, hands in her lap – and a drip, dripping down from a tall metal frame into a thin, thin body. Perhaps they weren't mother and daughter but the way the older woman leaned in like that – speaking softly, wanting to hear what the teenager said in case it helped her understand better how to help the pain. A mother. By blood, or not. I wondered what her mistakes had been and what they were yet to be.

Rolo or Twix today? the mother, or woman, seemed to say, as if it were a wonderful thing. As if the two of them had come to live like that; one, long hospital day punctuated by a visit to the newsagent in A & E. As if they had been there for weeks, months even.

'Can I help you?' said a woman in blue-grey with a bright orange *Helper* badge. She looked at me like she had seen me before.

'I have a letter,' I said, holding out papers like documents at border control.

She glanced at them. 'Yes, you need inpatients. Lift ten. Round the corner.' She pointed to a corridor lined with glass. She paused, something occurring with a smile. 'Come this way,' she said. 'I can take you there.'

'Thank you, but I'm early. I think I'll wait here,' I said, still standing, holding up the weights of daughter and bag. The helper nodded and left. I would wait a little longer so I could hold my daughter tight and whisper a thousand *sorrys* directly into her ear. So that I could delay the moment when the only way I could talk to her would be leaning over a bed or gurney, and I could delay the moment when the hospital claimed her for its own.

I had been responsible for her birth, the progression and the damage, and sooner than I knew I would be leaning over a wheelchair asking: *Rolos or Twix today?*

I glanced back towards the revolving doors and considered leaving, thought about taking her to the park round the corner from our house. She was enjoying sitting upright in the baby swings. Then for hot chocolate. Then home to bed, wrapped in her own duvet, protected by the wooden bars of her own cot and her mother sleeping a broken sleep on the bed next to her.

I want you, Cath. I want to fuck you. I want to make you happy.

I couldn't afford to make another mistake.

'It's OK, darling. Only one more vial to go.' The nurse held Mia's forearm so tight, red thumbprints appeared on her skin. But the nurse gripped harder, trying to keep the needle from slipping as it moved into Mia's veins. Mia cried and flailed in my arms, struggling painfully with the process of being plugged into the building. 'I'm sorry, darling,' said the nurse.

I'm sorry, darling.

So many sorrys.

I wanted to cry, of course I did, what mother wouldn't – but I swallowed back every jagged, sharp-edged feeling I had.

It will be all right, I whispered into her ear.

The same words Richard had whispered into my ear to soothe me.

He and I, liars both.

Mia's mouth widened in agony; her face, scarlet, as if flayed. Beaded with sweat. The wails peaked as the needle was removed and wadding placed quickly down on her skin to swab the area clean and cover the damage made. I swallowed harder at the thought of speeding round the roller-rink, of walking drunkenly on a beach, of the hotel rooms and strolling through museums. Of a hundred embraces. A thousand kisses.

Transported to the moon, at an astronomical cost.

I swallowed and felt something like a cut in my wind-pipe. I swallowed and felt the sting and slice of it again as if something within me was being re-sculpted.

'Here you are!' Dave arrived in the room, a nurse flanking him. 'Why didn't you answer your phone? I've been looking for you everywhere.'

'Sorry.' I looked up, surprised, somehow, to see him. 'I haven't been able to put her down. Haven't been able to look at my phone. Thank you for coming back.'

'I would have been here sooner . . . I don't understand why you didn't call me straight after clinic . . .' Not the right place for this conversation. 'Then there weren't any parking spaces. I had to take it to a . . .' No one cared about the car. 'Oh God, are you OK?' he said, and I looked up, blinked, felt the slight breath and breeze as he passed me and swept up Mia into his neck. Cuddling her tight.

'Bloods. They've done her bloods,' I said, ticking things off a list in my head. 'They said they could check for infection that way, too. And how strong her—'

'Was that hard? I bet it was hard.' Dave's gaze followed the cardboard tray of vials as the nurse departed the room. 'You should have told me where you were. I could have done the blood tests with her.'

'The car,' I said.

'Yes, the car. Somebody had to park the car.'

'Besides. It should be me, here. I'm her mum.'

'And I'm her dad.' He smiled thinly, lines reaching out

in triangles at the corners of tired eyes. 'Here, I got you this,' he said, pulling a bar of chocolate from his coat pocket.

Chocolate for shock. *Twix or Rolo?*

Here already.

Cells dividing.

Genes given.

Mistakes made.

Chocolate for shock.

'You need to eat,' he said, as if I'd spoken.

'No. No, I really don't.'

We were looking at each other, blankly, tiredly, for some time – I don't know how long – when the consultant arrived.

'Hello, and how are we all today?' she said.

Nobody wants a negative answer when they ask a question like that.

I smiled, Dave smiled. Happy family group-smiling.

I took Mia from Dave and she closed her eyes as I held her face to my chest, her legs encircling me.

'So Mia is scheduled to have the CT scan and bronchoscopy,' said the consultant. 'The general anaesthetic will be administered next to the CT scanner so we can scan her as soon as she loses consciousness. Then we'll get to the bronchoscopy. One parent will be allowed into the room to help put Mia to sleep. You'll need to decide who.'

'I'll go,' I said quickly. 'Of course it should be me.'

'We'll discuss it,' said Dave abruptly.

The consultant's eyes dipped to her notes. 'Any family history of high blood pressure or stroke?'

'No,' Dave said.

'Have either of you had a negative response to general anaesthetic?'

'My dad—' I said.

'Neither of us has ever had a general anaesthetic,' said Dave.

'Why do you need to know all this?' I swung Mia on to my other hip.

The consultant looked up. 'We're looking for indications of how Mia might respond. Responses to GA can be hereditary.'

'My dad,' I said, clawing at an itch on my palm. 'He had a CT scan. And then he had a general anaesthetic.'

Dave scratched his forehead. 'That was for emergency surgery. Invasive, dangerous surgery.'

'But he died because . . .' My blood was heating to a temperature I couldn't stand. I handed Mia to Dave so that I had more space, more strength and more room to breathe. I thumbed the hem of my shirt back and forth, like a string of rosary beads. 'My dad went to the GP with stomach pain. He hadn't been to the loo for five days. Only wanted constipation medicine because it was making him feel queasy.'

Dave sighed and put his hand on my arm. 'He'd been getting thin. He looked ill.'

I pushed his hand away. 'But no one knew he was *that* fucking ill.'

I took a breath and continued. 'The doctor listened to his stomach and an hour later he was in hospital. Less than twenty-four hours after that he was at the doors of the operating theatre, prepped for surgery. The results of his X-ray, CT scan and blood tests showed a tumour obstructing his bowel. He had the surgery but haemorrhaged soon after. Died.' My hands were on my hips, as if that would make me stronger: as if somehow that would change the facts of it. 'He popped to his GP for constipation medicine and two days later he was dead.'

The consultant passed me a tissue from a box on the windowsill. 'That sounds very distressing. I am sorry.'

I searched the consultant's eyes for danger signs, like I always took my lead from the flight attendant's expression during turbulence: the best way to determine the difference between normal bumpy flight and impending crash.

But the consultant's eyes only narrowed.

'Is that OK?' I said, when too much time had passed. 'I mean, of course it's not OK. He died,' I said, blinking back more tears. 'But does it make the possibility of something awful happening to Mia under general anaesthetic more likely?'

'Probably not,' said the consultant.

'What does that mean?'

'Cath,' said Dave, 'you need to—'

'No, I won't calm down. Is there a greater chance Mia could die under GA because of my dad?'

'It sounds like your father died of post-operative complications,' said the consultant.

'But it was made worse by him being put under general. It's stressful for the body, to be shut down like that. Right? They said his blood pressure dipped because of the general and it didn't ever return to normal. They said the low blood pressure contributed to the haemorrhage. What if the same thing happens with Mia? What if the general anaesthetic messes with her blood pressure, what if—'

'What your father went through sounds traumatic. There are, sometimes, complications after an operation, and bowel-obstruction surgery is a particularly complicated and high-risk procedure. His response to the GA may have contributed to those complications, but they may well have happened anyway. I can't give you an accurate answer. What you need to bear in mind is that Mia is having a bronchoscopy and the risk of complication is low. It's very unlikely that Mia will react in an adverse—'

'*Very unlikely*,' I said. 'That's not the same as *it won't happen*. I mean, if you're not entirely sure, maybe we should cancel.'

Dave turned to me. 'You need to calm down. I know this is . . .' His voice lowered. 'I know this is upsetting . . .'

I looked down at my palm, lined with red scratches.

'I understand your anxiety,' said the consultant. Her

voice dipped as if she were calming a child. 'But we need to carry out these procedures so we can treat Mia properly. The risks of this infection getting out of control are higher than either the risks of the procedure, or a general anaesthetic under other circumstances. Please, take a moment, discuss this with your husband, and I will come back in a few minutes. I'll leave the paperwork here.'

The door swung shut and I took Mia from Dave. I sat on one of the plastic chairs and held Mia in my arms as she looked down at the printed teddies and fire engines on her hospital gown.

Dave knelt down beside us, leaning over and addressing me like I was the drained teenager in the sweet shop. 'Cath.'

'No,' I said quietly. 'What if she's inherited a gene from me that I inherited from Dad; the same gene that makes a general anaesthetic a real risk for her? Or of post-operative complications? It's possible, it's all possible.'

'A gene? She wasn't really saying that.'

'She said that reactions can be hereditary. That's a gene. If I'd had cause for a general anaesthetic in my life I might have died already. Unlikely doesn't mean anything to me any more. What if she dies?'

He put his arm round me. Kissed my head gently, tentatively, as if testing the ground again. 'You're scared. This is a stressful time. You need to be strong. Mia needs this procedure. The alternative is far worse. To see an infection they can't identify take hold? To lessen the time they have to treat it?' I collapsed into tears. 'Come on. You know this is the right thing to do.'

A nurse peered round the door. 'Time to go, little one,' she said to the back of Mia's head. 'Who's taking you in, darling?'

'Where do we sign?' said Dave.

The nurse pointed to a dotted line on the consent form and Dave signed with the biro the consultant had left.

Then he stepped forward and closed his grip around Mia's waist.

Mia let out a wail and held on to me tighter and tighter still. I stood up and took a step towards the door.

'What are you doing?' Dave said, all the softness and warmth now gone from his voice.

'I'm taking her into the general.'

'But you're in no state. She needs calm.'

'I'm her mum,' I said.

'And I'm her dad.'

'And I caused this.'

But the door had closed and the nurse was leading Mia and I through the ward before Dave had time to say anything more than: *Why? I don't understand.*

All the way to the scanning room, I sang a nursery rhyme about the moon and the stars. Astronomy. Astronomical costs. She held on to me, the coarse cotton of the hospital gown pressed to her skin where I held on to her.

'Look, it's a space rocket,' I said quietly into her ear as we beheld the enormous shining white of the MRI scanner. Her fingers dug into my shoulder, holding me like she would never let me go. But soon she would have to. Soon they would ask me to leave and she would be launched on the rocket without me.

The anaesthetist held out a mask attached to tubes.

'Look, it's an octopus,' I said to Mia. I held it to her face. 'It's all right. Everything is going to be all right,' I lied. She needed to hear it as much as I had needed to believe it. 'You'll have a nice sleep.'

I was a good mother to soothe her, a bad mother to be the cause of her distress.

A good mother to provide her food and clothes, a bad mother to provide her broken genes.

A good mother to bring her into a family, a bad mother to break that family.

A good mother to medicate her illness, a bad mother to pass on a deadly infection from a man who made that mother feel better.

Mia struggled free of the mask and turned to face me, sensing something was wrong but not understanding what. Not understanding me, or what was to become of her. Forehead furrowing, eyes filling with black panic.

'It's all right, I'm here,' I said.

'Mrs Freeland, we need to start the general when you're ready,' said the consultant from the gallery.

This was how I imagined death row to be. A place where I didn't die, but my baby did.

I took the mask and placed it over her face.

'It's OK,' said the anaesthetist. 'Keep going. You're doing so well.'

Mia struggled and kicked, as if she couldn't breathe. I took the mask away from her face so she could breathe again. Swallowed, and the tiny cuts continued their work inside me, taking what I was and slicing the arteries that had given that person life.

It wasn't going to be all right.

I looked to the anaesthetist, who nodded a *Keep going, try again* kind of nod, and so I put the mask back on.

Mia cried, wailed and kicked her legs as I pressed the mask to her face.

I sang. Something about mocking birds and moons.

This was the right thing to do, of course it was.

And then with a final kick, her limbs fell – drained and lifeless.

'Is she OK?' I said, breath clotting in me. 'She's gone limp. It's like there's nothing in her, like she's dead. Is she still alive? Is she breathing?'

'Yes, she is fine, Mrs Freeland.' The anaesthetist checked a dial and smiled. 'Please lay her down on the gurney at the scanner.'

'Can I stay?' My tears fell and fell. 'Please, let me stay with her?'

I couldn't leave her. As long as I was with her she would be safe. Every time I left I made it worse.

'I'm sorry, Mrs Freeland, but you need to leave now. We'll take good care of her.'

I held Mia's lifeless hand and squeezed it tight.

Laid her down and kissed her forehead as if I was saying goodbye.

The cutting pain in me worsened.

The knife, twisted.

Life, finally, haemorrhaging out of me.

The punishment for everything I had caused.

A death within me.

I found Dave reading a newspaper back in the room.

He looked up as the door swung shut behind me. 'You all right, love? How was it?'

'It was OK,' I said. 'It was OK. She was great.'

I turned my back on him and the hospital and faced London from four floors up, through a window whose glass was strong enough to withstand wind and rain and bomb explosions. Century old rooftops, the spire of a grand church. Bankers' wives coming back to their smart homes. Sunlight shone through my skin and flesh and I saw my life-blood pumping through blue veins that twisted and curled round fine finger bones. And I prayed that her heart would pump and her blood would speed and her lungs would inflate for decades after I died.

I kissed her head, pale and waxen under the strip light of the recovery ward. 'Mia,' I said softly. 'My darling one.'

She twitched but did not wake.

I turned to the nurse. 'Is she OK?'

'She's fine.' She smiled. 'She woke briefly, cried and went back to sleep. She's fine.'

Someone, something had looked kindly upon us.

'She was stable throughout. She's just coming round. Could be groggy but she'll be fine. She'll want a feed soon, I imagine. It's horrible keeping them hungry.'

'Thank you, thank you so much.' I looked up at the nurse, tears tracking my cheeks.

'That's OK,' she said. 'All in a day's work.'

Back in the room I sat on one side of the bed – my hand covering Mia's at the point where the cannula had broken the skin and pressed itself through the vein. My hand hovered gently, defiantly, over the entry point and I imagined my veins soldering themselves to hers, all my life energy flowing through her.

'You're strong,' said Dave. I looked up and saw his tears. 'The consultant said you were great with her in the anaesthetic. What you did must have been . . .' And then the words fell back into his mouth like a printer crumpling and suffocating on its own paper. His eyes were wide with desperation. 'Do you think she's going to be all right?'

'I hope so,' I said. Because that was all the truth I had in me.

'I don't understand, you see,' he said with such assurance – as if that was the simple and powerful sum total of all I should have ever known about him. 'I don't understand how we came to be here. With our precious baby drinking antibiotics every day and a team of doctors dedicated to keeping her alive. And now this – her, all tangled up in wires and something bad hanging over her head, like, like an axe.' I went to him and kissed his forehead as he cried. 'Sometimes I feel like, if I look at it – in the face, you know? Like truly face the facts of it. The fact is that her life . . . She's not like other babies . . . If I faced the possibility of her . . . Sometimes I feel that, if I start thinking that way? I might never stop.'

This. Yes, this. Holding him. Telling each other the truth.

I knew we could be This.

'Remember when we went sailing that time in Ireland off that little harbour? Where was it?' he said.

'Cobh.' I smiled, remembering a holiday of lochs and lakes and oysters a year after we met.

'That was it.' He smiled, remembering too. 'The wind got up. The speed of it. Happened so fast.'

'We were miles from the mainland. If we'd kept going at that pace we'd have reached America.' We could laugh about it now. 'Never seen you look so scared.' Which was true. Up to that point I had never seen him scared.

'You calmed me down. Took the tiller. Got us back to shore.' He looked at me and swallowed. 'I couldn't control the boat. I was scared, with the waves and the angle and the speed . . . I thought, you know, I thought well *this is it* and I think, I think . . .' He looked up at the marked foam tiles in the ceiling, his eyes filling with tears. 'I feel like that now.'

'Except there is no tiller at all this time.'

Then the door opened and I knew something bad was coming and I didn't want that moment with my husband to end because we'd lost too much already. I tried to hold on to him, took his hand and felt it in mine.

The consultant cradled a sheaf of notes. 'Mia remained stable throughout. But.'

I let go of his hand and stood straight to face the consultant.

'We found a lot of congestion and significant signs of infection.'

I saw Dave go, travelling away from me, too fast to ever get him back. Or perhaps it was me that went.

'We've taken samples that we'll have tested, the results of which will determine her treatment plan. Meantime a nurse will administer the first line intravenous antibiotics tonight. We'll need to watch and wait.'

We both nodded and there was one more silence, enough time to allow our heads to re-emerge at the surface of the water.

'I have to tell you that the CT scan shows there has been some damage, perhaps from whatever infection she's harbouring. We will do all we can to arrest it and minimize that damage, but this is something we need to get on top of. It's good that she's here.'

Oh God, you have not looked on me kindly. You are burning me slowly instead of shooting me dead.

Once the consultant had left we stood in stunned silence, until I turned to Dave. 'It's late, you should go.'

The water was rising fast around me once again and soon I would drown.

'If she wakes, I'll be here. You should rest. Go home,' I said.

'But—' Dave's eyes remained softened with his earlier tears. 'I can stay with you both . . .'

'No, no, you don't need to do that. Use the time. Go for a drink with Darren. Talk to him.'

He was lost and he wanted me to put my arms around him as I had done earlier but instead I said, 'Please. Just go.'

If I can't find myself out there then how can I find you?

'If that's what you want?' He paused. 'I guess I'll be back first thing in the morning. Cath?' he said, as if he were trying something out. 'What you said about causing this? Did you mean the genes? Because that was both of us. Nothing could have stopped it. You mustn't blame yourself.'

'I hope you get some sleep.'

His eyes stilled and froze over, and his spirit retreated – as it had learnt to on so many occasions.

Then he left.

On my phone, another text: *Where is your room? If*

you are at the front of the hospital and you look out,
you will see me.

I walked to the window and looked out at the city
first.

And then down, at Richard, sitting on the concrete
bench by the ambulances. Richard – looking around.
Craning his head. Occasionally glancing at a newspaper
opened out next to him. I put my hand to the glass,
covered him, took my hand away and he was still there.
I rested my head against the glass for a while, giving my
breath life as mist.

Watching the mist evaporate as I leaned away. Just like
his reassurances.

Dave walked quickly across the forecourt. For a
moment it looked as if he were walking towards Richard
but then he veered off in the direction of the car park.
Both of them now facing opposite ways.

I looked away from Richard and up at the empty sky.
Keep her safe. Please don't let anything happen to her.
I've learnt my lesson.
Never again shall I worship a false god.
I deleted his text messages.
Deleted his number.
Deleted him.
I looked at Mia, still asleep and breathing softly.
Her life in exchange for two deaths.
I sat down on the stiff plastic of the hospital chair,
closed my eyes and fell deeply asleep.

Chapter 20

I told one of the doctors on his ward rounds that Mia's infection was NTM. *Non-Tuberculosis Bacterium*, I said, to make it sound like I'd done my reading – in case he thought I was impressionable and hysterical and overtired like lots of people who got caught in hospital.

I said I knew the bacteria had been transported on skin and clothes and that there was a lot of it, probably, because of how much Richard had touched me.

I put my hand on the sleeve of the doctor's coat and said, *Richard is the father, you see, of a girl with CF chronically colonized with NTM.* He listened patiently and stopped me when I started crying and said, *We slept together . . .*

He said he understood my concern but that at this stage they couldn't treat conjecture.

No cure for conjecture.

You had to know what you were dealing with. Face it head on . . . only then.

The doctor said they needed an accurate read on the type of bacteria Mia was culturing and even with the most advanced processes, that could take at least a week: and any definitive results for NTM, longer still.

A week, possibly several, watching the fast-moving and potentially fatal and antibiotic-resistant bacteria bed down further into Mia's lungs.

I thought I would die, watching my daughter die because of me.

But soon the hours turned into a night and then another day and soon enough those days took on a rhythm I found as comforting as a swaying cot. A nurse administered all Mia's usual medicines, taking the syringes away with her to be washed and sterilized in a place I didn't need to know about. Nurses performed physiotherapy, the shock waves of every pat and beat rippling through their arms and not mine. They delivered the antibiotics through a drip in Mia's hand while she played during the day and slept at night. And then there were the meal orders and mealtimes as regular as clock-work and the hourly observations for temperature and heart rate.

Beep beep, beep beep.

Sway, sway.

I knew what levels to look out for. I knew what was high and what was low.

But better than that, the nurses were only steps away and they knew better than I . . .

Sway, sway.

Cocooned.

There was safety in the rhythm. Safety in the routine. Safety in the proximity of doctors.

At night I rested on a pull-out bed by hers, my sleep bombed with horrifying images I could never remember, until finally I would crawl on to the mattress beside her, flinging my arms over her, her arms flung over her koala. Together, a family. I would cuddle her until the dreams came for me again and I was dragged through bodies of water – mouthfuls of the stuff threatening to dam the screams in me.

All those dreams with the beep beep, levels up, levels down, hammering out their tune in the background, telling me that the doctors and nurses and machines were keeping us safe.

Other than Dave, who visited every day – relaying news I didn't understand or care about – I kept the outside world away. My email and phone were logged with requests to visit, ideas for toys and promises of juices and salads and magazines for me.

No, I said to all of them. *Thank you anyway but we'll be out soon. You're all so kind.*

It would be treacherous to encourage the outside world to support and give me gifts when they knew nothing of the mistakes I had made.

They would never forgive me if they found out.

But the broken sleep and anxieties roiling in my head took their toll and one night I needed to talk so desperately. Despite it all, I wanted to hear Richard's voice and his promises because what else did I have to get me through. What else . . .

Ring ring ring, beep beep, ring ring ring in the middle of the night.

'Hello. Hello, Cath.'

'Dave? I'm frightened.' I whispered, the midnight hour allowing through the words I'd never permit in the day. 'I mean, what I mean is, what if she gets, I don't know . . . even worse. And then her lungs . . .' I couldn't bear to say it, not really, but he deserved a clear picture of the truth and the possibilities. 'What if, what if her lungs are so badly damaged by all this that it's impossible for her to even have a lung transplant. What if—'

'Cath, stop.'

Would you forgive me?

'I wish you'd let me do some of the nights,' he said with a sigh. 'You're tired, anxious. This is all too much.'

'That's not the point.' A flash of impatience that he couldn't . . . 'What I'm saying is . . . What if none of this works? What then?'

'We're not there yet. Let the doctors do their jobs first.'

'You don't know . . .'

'Of course I don't know. None of us knows a thing.'

No.

'But, Dave . . .'

'You need some sleep. You'll feel better for some sleep. I'll come and visit you both tomorrow. I'll bring proper coffee and some cake. Meantime, why don't you

289

get out of that room? Just for a bit? Maybe a walk, or something.'

And so we did.

The next day – her in a sling, the two of us wrapped in a shawl with my coat buttoned round her, a clean muslin draped over her mouth so she couldn't breathe in the sick air around her – I walked us through the corridors of the hospital in between mealtimes and medication. We took the lift to the ground floor and the hospital newsagent.

'These walls are grey,' I whispered to Mia, kissing her cheek and feeling her face turn to me. 'These walls are lined with metal shelves that hold reported news from the outside world.' I walked to one shelf and laid my palm on the cover of a magazine. 'Look at these photographs,' I said to her, turning my body so she could see an athlete in shining Lycra holding up her gold medal. 'She has run very fast and won something. Look,' I said again, pointing to the front of a newspaper. 'There is a war on the other side of the world. This is rubble where a bomb has fallen. And while we were sleeping we got a new prime minister. She is a woman. And here, a child has been taken from an estate in the north of England.'

I looked at Mia looking at the four walls and the news that had happened already and that was being delivered to us as we stood there in the middle of that grey room.

'Let's go for a different walk,' I said. 'See some of the outside world and live dangerously,' I said, kissing the top of her head and feeling the jolt beneath my chin as she kicked her legs. And we stepped out into the cold streets, past small children clasping their nannies' hands as chores were done, past shopgirls on their break and tourists tacking from one landmark to another.

Oh, the heart-warming relief of temporarily escaping a place where normal lives were suspended, into the outside world. To a place where the air was cold and unconditioned, where people stopped and walked and spoke and mostly got on with their lives.

Something lodged in me then. Something more than hope. Belief, perhaps, that we too might be granted the chance of getting on with life again. That we could be strong, survive and adapt like human beings do.

'You will go to school one day,' I found myself saying. And I laughed to myself because it was such a . . . *motherly* thing to say: neither truth, nor lies, just a fragile piece of belief. 'When this is over, life will start again.' I kissed her warm brow and squeezed the ribcage that mirrored itself against mine. She giggled, gurgled vowels and kicked her legs and I knew these things meant she was happy.

I nodded to a nurse striding out on to the street. To a doctor in a white coat with his clipboard and his pens and his pocket watch. 'Those are the people that look after us.'

And we continued to walk until we found a small tarmac-floored playground made of candy-coloured steel and rope wires, hemmed to the back of an estate.

I swung her in a swing made for children of her age, took photographs.

Then to a café where we drank expensive hot chocolate and Mia giggled at the foam and wanted more. Where she stabbed a jammy finger on to a leaflet printed with cows. Where she giggled and I laughed. 'Cow,' I said. 'Yes, that's a cow.'

And then we walked further and further still, away from the hospital, over the road and to the library. 'Come on,' I said brightly, as if I were a normal mother chivvying her child on the street before lunch at home. 'Let's find a picture of a sheep this time. I'll find you more pictures. A pig. A goat, maybe.' I kissed her head and touched her cheeks where I felt a smile form.

It was love.

Or something greater than love, if that were possible.

Inside the library, with its tiny yellow chairs and tables and its grey nylon carpets, was a lady dressed in check. She read, slowly and deliberately, to a circle of mothers; babies resting in the nests of their laps. The check lady pointed to a farm on the pages of a picture book.

'Here, look, Mia, it's our lucky day. More animals,' I said, as I took her to the periphery of the circle. Mia cast her gaze around and kicked her legs.

I stepped back, seeing the streaming nose of one child and hearing the cough of another. I couldn't risk it. More infection on top of the infection she already had would be damage and more damage still.

Mia kicked her legs harder when I didn't move. Then I felt her cries as if they came from my own throat. Felt the sadness in her at being on the borders of something. Felt how much happier she would be if she was part of things again.

What a shame. How sad. Someone's words echoed in me and I wanted to banish them with the volume of my screams.

So I knelt down outside the circle.

And Mia's cries subsided.

She strained forward, so I unbuttoned my coat and took her from the sling, still holding her close to me, my arms a rope around her – a poor substitute for the cord that had once joined our bloodstreams and kept us both so safe.

Two mothers opened a gap in the circle and there it was.

A break in the border.

Mia laid her warm palms on the backs of my hands as I balanced her on my knee. She gazed at the picture book and around at the circle of mothers and babies and giggled, as if to show how happy she was at having arrived in a place where she belonged.

A few seconds later she reached out her bandaged hand to a little boy in a red wool cardigan. She put her hand on his leg, leaning over so much I tipped to catch her. Mia smiled at the boy as if he was her friend and leaned further.

The boy swiped at his nose with the back of his hand and left a smear of green snot on his top lip.

'Mia, come here,' I snapped, whipping her away but regretting my tone as the mother flinched and so did Mia.

But Mia continued to lean in and look at him, giggles bubbling from a generous and fearless smile that reminded me so much of Dave. I thought of the morning after I'd come home from Richard, and found Mia being sick, and how I had lain in bed and listened to Mia's giggles and Dave's roars through the walls and floors as they played in the kitchen. A neighbour listening to that would have thought what a happy family and would never know that the mother was two floors up, listening to the same joy with such envy. I had been *envious* of Dave taking such uncomplicated joy in our baby, despite the dark cloud that hung over us, and wondered if my jealousy at not being able to do the same had put the ceilings and walls between us. Had I alone been responsible for their building?

But in the library that afternoon I saw the baby girl we had made together and the person that was emerging so brightly from her genes and her experiences, her nature and her nurture, her labels and her layers. There were no limits to her joy despite all the limits imposed on her, and I admired her for it.

Dave, too, perhaps.

'I love you,' I whispered, squeezing both her hands. 'But we should get back,' I said, louder that time. 'It's nearly time for your next dose.' And still she reached out for the boy's hand because it made her happy.

I had reached out for a hand once because it had made me happy, and I softened.

'A moment more,' I said.

The place where she had lived inside me had been so safe, a place where the outside world could never touch her. But she needed to reach out of there to feel someone's hand. To have a chance at living.

I looked at my watch. Her next antibiotic was due in ten minutes. 'Come on, it's time.' And I adjusted her on my knee in preparation for going. She wriggled and cried because she didn't want to leave. Or she didn't want to go back to where I was taking her. Or both. I understood. I had felt the same.

And so I kissed the soft hair on her head. 'You are wonderful and I understand,' I said. 'I do. Let's go together. As long as we're together. Me and you. You and me. We'll be all right.'

That night, Mia slept well. And so did I.

Beep, beep.

Sway, sway.

Beep, beep, beep, beep.

Rock, rock.

A panicked minor chord.

A level in the background that wasn't right.

I opened my eyes to see the nurse bent over Mia taking

her temperature. Once, twice, three times. She left the room and a moment later two more people had entered.

'Is everything OK?' I said, climbing out of the fold-up bed.

'We tried to do the first of the day's observations without waking her,' said the nurse. 'But Mia's temperature is very high. We'll need to wake her.'

'How high?'

'Higher than it should be.'

I shook myself free of the images in my sleep where Richard had been, in a place where I had stood and he had put his arms around me. 'But she was fine yesterday afternoon. She was playing. She even made a friend.' I watched my baby wake groggily, her skin the colour of strawberry milkshake, a sheen of sweat, her brow furrowed with a single wrinkle. Beep beep beep beep. I looked up at the nurse.

'Her heart rate is elevated so we've paged the consultant.'

Heart rate?

The soundtrack to her life; the pace mirroring her joy and distress.

A quickening, a slowing, a cease.

'When will she be here?' I said. 'Have you told her to hurry?'

'She'll be here as soon as she's able. We'll put Mia on a heart-rate monitor in the meantime.'

Beep, beep. Quicker and quicker. Distress coming, something bad.

Be with you just as soon as I can.

I'd had a heart-rate monitor strapped to me little more than six months before, monitoring Mia while she was still curled inside my womb. The beeps increasing as the contractions became more frequent and more intense. *Soon it will be over*, I'd thought. But looking back at how the beeps tripped over each other, my own heart rate chasing hers – it had only just begun.

'Try to sit down and rest, Mrs Freeland. We're doing all we can here.'

I turned to the window and called Dave.

Ring, ring, ring, ring, ring.

Beep, beep. Beep, beep.

Pick up, Dave. Ring, ring.

No answer.

Anxiety reeling, spiralling out in streamers.

I went to my baby, put my hand on her warm head. 'Come on, Mia,' I said, then rested my hand on her little rising chest, feeling her heart; *thaboom thaboom*.

Her heart.

My heart.

So many hearts.

The consultant arrived and joined us all at Mia's bedside. There were five of us in that room if you included Mia and I.

She turned to me. 'The increased temperature and heart rate could be signs of the infection not responding to the antibiotic. We still don't have the full bronchoscopy results so we'll need to change antibiotics again and hope they have an effect.'

'Hope? *Hope*? What good is hope? Don't you *know*?' My voice rising, my panic bubbling over. 'I keep saying to you all . . . Why won't you listen to me when I tell you she is culturing Non Tuberculosis Mycobacterium,' I spat out. 'NTM. Please, I'm telling you that's what she's got. Treat her for that. Please, please treat her for that. Make her better. Make it better—'

'Mrs Freeland, the treatment for NTM is complicated and potentially dangerous in itself. I don't want to start that until we know for sure.'

'But *I* know for sure. I know because I gave it to her.'

'Mrs Freeland.' The consultant gathered herself with a swallow and an adjustment of her white coat. 'This is a very difficult and stressful time. I do understand. Perhaps it would be good for you to take a brief break. We will switch antibiotics, monitor her regularly, and take stock in twenty-four hours. As soon as we have the results we can look at further treatment.'

'Please, listen to me,' I said as the tears rose up and overflowed, tipping over the level, my voice rising higher and higher, my heart rate escalating. Beep, beep. Beep, beep. 'Please, before it's too late.'

A nurse came to me then and with an understanding glance shared by the consultant, she took charge of me. Held my arm. Sat me down on a chair and gave me sugary tea. Sat with me wordlessly as I watched for snatches of my daughter through white coats and shifting limbs. As I watched doctors whose names I didn't catch busying themselves with tubes and vials.

Plastic snapped. A packet opened. Something sterile removed with care.

Such a lot of stuff for a baby as new and small as mine.

I watched and I cried because nobody was listening.

Unable to bear it any more, I reached for my phone and walked out into the corridor, heart hammering in my chest. Needing something as I felt cast adrift from the safety of the doctors, as their doubt became my own. Needing something before I overflowed. Needing. Wanting.

Dialling the dead number I thought I could still remember. 07968, No, 079769, No . . .

Ring.

'Cath.'

I hung up on him.

'Cath.'

My sister. Saving me from myself, again.

I turned to face her with tears smudging my vision. Threw my arms around her, hid my face in her hair and thanked God for sending her.

She took me by the arms and looked at me, my tears making her cry.

Pains.

Genes.

Shared.

An enduring blueprint for life.

She held me to her. 'Nurse let me in,' she said, while I tried to find the words through my tears. 'I got lucky with a shift change. Come on, it's OK. Oh dear.' And still she held on to me.

'It was getting offensive,' she said, as my tears calmed. 'Not being asked for a visit. Thought I'd take the bull by the horns.'

A relief more profound than anything. If only for a few moments, my sister would be my shield from a time and place where I was accountable and brimming with the possibility of irreversible mistakes.

'It's not good, Caroline. It's not working,' I said. 'She's in trouble.'

The nurse came out to get us then, and my sister held my hand like she'd held my hand when we were younger. Like a mother holds the hand of her toddler. In hers, almost covered. As close as it is possible to get without the skin being joined at its seams. A grip that tells of all things, a grip that tells a child so much about the love that is directed toward them in that moment.

A love that is fierce and strong and possesses a jaw that will tear apart anything that threatens it.

A lion's love for her cub.

Together we went back into the room, still holding hands. The nurses were adjusting Mia's position as they fixed a heart-rate monitor and a tube that fed new liquids into her blood. As the grip on my own heart tightened and we waited and waited until finally there was nothing else to do but sit and watch my baby sleep.

And so the minutes turned to an hour, and another hour, and we sat without words, as the blue-black of an early winter's morning disappeared and the city turned to sodium.

Without words as the light poured in and the sun rose golden in the sky.

My sister and I. Opposite each other. Dozing on chairs. Propped on elbows, necks bent and aching. Twitching and falling and sleeping and waking and realizing.

At once our gazes joined over the mountain range of blanket and I asked, 'How are the boys?'

'But how are you?'

'Please,' I said. 'Tell me something normal. Tell me news from the outside world. How are they?'

'The boys are the boys. They are fine. Excited about Christmas.' She looked to the ceiling. 'What else? The neighbour is threatening to sue over the bent apple tree and her precious brick wall. And I don't fit into that red dress I bought in the summer, which I'm choosing to ignore. I need my roots doing and I'm depressed that I can't find anything I like watching on Netflix because the winter evenings feel too long nowadays.' She paused. 'Having a company car isn't all it's cracked up to be because they still break down and Rory is being difficult. About most things – including but not limited to doing absolutely bloody nothing to contribute to Christmas. So, in summary, same as it ever was. Now tell me. How are you?'

'Terrible.' I laughed.

And we both laughed.

I looked down at my hands. 'All this reminds me of Dad,' I said. 'Of him lying in the hospital bed after the operation. Of me sitting next to him finishing *The Times* crossword he had started while waiting to see that GP. How pale he was by the time I'd returned with coffee and then his words. They were slurred and I couldn't understand what he was saying. And then the alarm went off. It was so loud. Like a newborn screaming . . .'

Caroline came over to my side of the bed and kissed me on the forehead as my sentence splintered.

'I don't know how long I sat there with him after they called it,' I said.

After the doctors called it what it was.

'I needed the loo and all I could think was, I can't leave him. I can't leave him.' My voice was choked and broken with saliva and tears. 'I thought, something will happen to him if I leave him. How silly is that? He was dead. He was bloody dead! What more could have happened to him? But I sat there like he needed me.' I looked at Mia dozing so peacefully. 'And I waited, for someone to take over so I could go to the loo and you all took your time.'

'Cath, come on—'

'Mum thought she'd finish her parish visit despite her husband being dead. Nothing worse than a task half done.'

'Be fair. She'd turned her mobile off. She didn't get the message.'

'This,' I waved my hand in the direction of the heart-rate monitor and beeping drips as if they were to blame for my coarse criticisms. 'This. How, how . . . ?'

'This, Cath . . .' Caroline made me look at her by tilting her head to find my gaze. 'This is cystic fibrosis. I know this is hard, but this . . . This.'

I stared at her. Something needling my insides. 'Don't patronize me, Caroline. I know what CF is.'

Beep, beep . . .

Silence.

Beep, beep . . .

'God,' I said. 'You were the first person I called when Dad died, and even you took your time.'

She blinked – tripped up by the jagged, crumbling paths of my thoughts. 'I needed to find childcare. I came as soon as I could . . .'

'You only stayed an hour. And then you left me to look after Mum.'

'My God, sometimes Cath . . .' Caroline's words were so sharp and loud that I looked up to face her. 'You really don't get it, do you? All that time I spent with her in the days after Dad died? Do you know what we talked about? Not Dad. Not how sad she felt. We talked about you. Always you, you and you. She was worried about you and how you were coping. Like everyone was always worried about you, Cath, because you were always more "fragile" than the rest of us.' Her voice grew harder, louder again – a mother's reprimand. 'But not so fragile you couldn't take all the oxygen in the room. You left nothing for the rest of us. She wanted to know how to mother you because Dad had always been the one who knew how to deal with you.'

I wiped tears from my cheeks.

'You're not always an easy person to help.' Caroline looked around her. 'This place should be full of toys for Mia and magazines for you, but I know what you've said to people. You've told them all to go away.'

'That's because no one understands—'

'Stop it. Stop making assumptions about people. Just because they don't say the right things, it doesn't mean they aren't hurting or feeling. It doesn't mean they aren't trying to work out what to do or how to say it. You don't give anyone credit for trying,' she said. 'You just resent them for not giving you what you need. Well, the truth is nobody can give you what you need. It's not going to happen like that. It doesn't happen that way for anyone. So grow up.'

I wiped tears from my cheeks and we looked at each other in silence. Like the staring games we played as children. This time, I would blink first. This time, I would lose. And that was as it should be.

My phone beeped a message.

The monitor beeped a heart rate.

'You can check it,' said Caroline.

I wanted to. I was desperate to, because I saw Richard's words flash up on the screen.

It will be OK

'No.' I turned it over.

'Is it the guy we met at the gene conference? Come on,' she said off my look. 'I'd give anything for a man to look at me like that again. It's been years since Rory . . .'

I held Mia's hand in mine and blinked again.

'It is him, isn't it? Look, no judgement. You know . . . Rory and I nearly separated a few years ago. I got as far as packing a bag and working out what to say to the children.'

'You never told me that. But maybe I was sucking all the oxygen out of the air.'

Caroline smiled. 'Perhaps. But the point is, we got through it . . .'

The phone rang and Caroline's eyes darted in its direction. 'Take the call if you need to.' It rang and rang. 'I just think . . . whatever you do, remember that Dave is a good man who is struggling as well. When Mia stabilizes—'

'*If* she stabilizes.'

'*When* they stabilize her let me come and babysit one night. For a few hours? Or if you don't want to leave her in the hospital, how about when you come to ours for Christmas Day? I can mind her while the two of you go for a walk. Get away from it all and talk. Or don't talk. Just . . . don't give up on it yet.' She paused, studied the ceiling. 'Rory's still an annoying bastard but I'm glad I didn't go. Not sure I've got the strength to internet date now anyway.'

A nurse knocked and entered the room. 'Time for obs, OK?'

Caroline's hand reached over Mia to take mine.

Beep, beep, and I held my breath.

Beep, beep, as the nurse looked up at me. 'Temp's down. It looks as though those antibiotics are working their magic.'

'That's great.' I smiled. 'That's so great.' And the breath rushed in, lowering the levels.

'Let's see how she gets on in the next twelve hours. Hopefully we're on the home straight.'

Caroline turned to me. 'As soon as Mia is back home then. I'll babysit?'

'Maybe. It's hard with her medication.' Caroline raised her eyebrows at me. 'But perhaps I could teach you,' I said.

Caroline stood and slung a bag over her shoulder. Looped a toggle on her coat. 'Come back to your family.' She laid a palm on Mia's rising chest. 'We need you. We love you. We're here to help you through all this, even though you're bloody difficult.'

'Thank you.' I hugged Caroline and then I kissed Mia.

As soon as I got out of hospital I promised myself I would end it with Richard.

I would find a way to atone.

Chapter 21

In the days after Mia was released from hospital Dave and I were thrown, exhausted and hollow, into the Christmas festivities. No time for posting Christmas cards and barely enough time to buy one size fits all presents: candles, socks, chocolate.

On Christmas Day itself Dave and I exchanged a hug, a set of green enamel teaspoons and perfume for me, a tie and a bobble hat for him. After lunch at Caroline's I found myself in the kitchen scraping burnt turkey grease out of the oven, while Dave sat, silent, on an armchair in the living room. On the periphery of a circle of family as they caught up, drinking Baileys, plucking chocolate-covered biscuits out of a tin, an animated film singing in the background.

The truth was that we were tired, quiet, still quaking from the shock of our child lying in a hospital bed. Then there was the wait for NTM test results which Dave dismissed as an impossibility and the doctors unlikely. All the signs showed that Mia's treatment had been effective. And yet.

We had defied statistical probability before. I would always believe we could do it again. And until we were sure, I wasn't prepared to leave Mia, wasn't prepared to take Caroline's offer to mind her on Christmas Day while Dave and I went for *that walk*.

Come Christmas Day evening we left Caroline's warm, tinselled, roast-meat smelling house with both reticence and relief. Our house was cold, colourless and silent but at least we didn't have to speak there. To each other. To anyone.

But as New Year approached, Mia regained her strength, and so did I. Her raspberry cheeks returned gradually, as if she were slowly being delivered from the white waxen vernix of illness to full health.

Only then did I resume contact with Richard. A text, to prepare the ground for what I had to do.

Happy New Year. We are out of the hospital.

He wanted to meet, and talk, and meet, and talk. It was a flood of wants.

But I held off because the test results had not arrived. And I needed to be sure.

In the meantime, talking and texting was fine because Mia and I would be protected by satellite waves and distance.

Until we could meet and I could end it properly.

What better time to break old habits than the New Year?

Very occasionally I would forget to turn off the volume

on my phone and leave it somewhere. Then Dave would stride into whatever room I was sitting in, aggravation leaking from every pore, saying: *Your thing, your phone in there, it's been beeping and vibrating. Who wants to speak to you so much?* I'd feel nervous, for a moment, thinking he was calling my bluff, though all he'd have seen on the screen was:

Unknown (7 missed calls)

Then I'd feel anger that Dave thought there was no one in the world who could want to speak to me so desperately.

And that feeling, that anger, was the closest I came to telling him the truth.

But instead I told him the floodgates were open now that we were back from hospital and friends and family getting in touch: *How are you? What an ordeal. Hope you're hitting the bottle? Getting some rest. That's the kind of thing they're saying, Dave. They're only being supportive.*

By the first week of January we were back at the hospital for a check-up and they said Mia was doing very well. I asked them when we could expect the NTM test results and they said; *Oh they are fine.* Like they were answering a question as insignificant as, *So how is your aunt that lives in Canada?* Like they might never have told me had I not asked.

Less than half an hour had passed before I made my

excuses in the hospital cafeteria and said I should call the family to let them know the good news.

Outside the revolving doors I called Richard.

We can meet now.

Soon, Dave and Mia stepped out to meet me where the ambulances lined up and patients smoked and I said to Dave, 'I'd like to go for a walk.'

'A walk?' he said, shifting Mia on to his other side. 'Don't you want to come home? Get a pizza and some beer and draw a line under this whole chapter?'

I tried to sound bright. 'There's nothing I'd like more but . . . I need some air, some . . .'

'Space?' His brow furrowed. 'With one of those many friends who keep calling you?' And his eyes bored into me as if to give me a chance to say: *There's something I need to tell you.*

But I smiled as if I had not seen the doubt in him and said, 'No. Space is all it is.' Space is all, space is everything. And I prayed he wouldn't ask me anything further, even if he did suspect just the smallest amount, because there would be no point.

I would see Richard and I would *draw a line under that whole chapter*.

But Dave continued looking at me through half-closed eyes and I was afraid of what he might say so I said:

'I had a lot of time to think in hospital and I've decided that I want us to start trying for another baby. I feel ready.'

'Oh, OK, great . . .' His eyes brightened, and my shoulders dropped.

'I've been so worried these last months about how we would deal with a newborn alongside stressful times like hospital admission, or something as bad as NTM. And now we know the results are negative I feel like having been through that . . . Well, the important thing is that we got through it. Whatever doesn't kill you makes you . . . Anyway, new year, new plans? All I'm saying is, maybe we could have that other baby. That would be exciting. Right?'

'Yes,' he said. 'Right.' His smile wasn't as wide and warm as I expected. But it was still a smile.

'I need to clear my head. Is that OK?'

He nodded. Took the brake off the pram. 'Yes, of course it is.'

And so I walked along the River Thames, the wind filling my lungs in cold bursts, and I promised myself on another occasion when things were easier, I would walk all the way to Battersea. But this time I came to a stop on Waterloo Bridge. Watched each dark crest of water churn and surge and catch the moonlight before disappearing to the other side.

I had been expecting him and yet the strong grip on my shoulder felt like it belonged to a stranger. When his hand slipped down my arm and traced the line of my ribcage as if it housed the rarest bird I knew that, when it was gone for good, I would miss that sense of being wanted. So I did not turn immediately, wanting to hold close the moment before it tipped and fell away into the waves.

When I did turn to face him, I was relieved to find the man I had known and perhaps, loved. Even in the dark I could see something darker still roil within him; a dread, an anger, a sadness and a love that was smothering him or goading him. All of those feelings – stirred and broken and soldered in parts – all reflected back in their war-torn glory, were both frightening and exciting to me.

That he could stand for so much in only one look, delayed me from saying right then and there:

Stop. We must stop.

I stepped closer and took his hand in mine.

No good reason for anger now. There was no NTM. Dave and the doctors had been right. Impossible. Unlikely. Time had drained me of my anger and I was left with him and what I needed to do: to end it, to break it. To risk no more and continue with my life as it was given to me.

My daughter was safe.

And so I kissed him.

Just because it was the last time.

He was the one to step away, pain appearing in the lines of his face. 'Where does he think you are?' His words were quiet and low, as if heaving themselves up from the viscous mud of the seabed.

'Walking. Getting some air. It's all right.'

He turned away from me to look at the water. 'The NTM results were negative then?'

I shoved my hands into my coat pockets to warm them. 'Turns out they were treating a pathogen called haemophilus influenzae.'

'Good.' The corner of a frail smile. 'Always good to put a name to a face,' he said. 'So it's thanks to that pathetic, cowardly haemophilus influenzae that you're here with me. If it had been NTM, I'd never have seen you again.'

The wind was up and stealing volume from me. 'I'm here because I thought it was time . . .'

'Ah. I might have guessed from the silence,' he said, and his face turned a further inch away from me to track an orange lifeboat tipping and bowing through the water. I thought I heard something else in the twist of his mouth.

'Are you angry with me?' I said.

He shrugged. 'When I told you how ill Rachel was, you dropped me like I was radioactive. I would never have treated you like that. It was so obvious that you didn't care about me.'

I took his arm and tried to make him face me. 'I did care about you. I do care about you . . .' A silence passed between us. 'If anyone's angry, it should be me. You lied to me. You should have told me weeks before that your daughter had NTM. It was dangerous to see you. You put my child at risk.'

'No,' he said firmly. '*You* put your child at risk.'

I stepped back. 'But you misled me.'

'I wanted to keep seeing you . . .' He grabbed hold of me urgently. 'And *you* wanted to keep seeing me.'

I stepped back. 'You selfish man.' I bit my lip but no distracting pain held back how much I wanted to cry. 'You lied to me.'

'I told you—'

'No. You told me that Mia was always going to be all right. And yet there she was in a hospital bed, heart rate through the roof, coughing up her lungs, and I had good reason to think it was because of an infection we gave her. I believed you when you said that she would be one of the lucky ones. I am angry with you for not telling me the truth about how wrong things can go with this illness.'

I was shouting because I could not allow the wind to steal what I was about to say.

'You're a liar,' I said. 'What you did . . . it was like telling a child the needle isn't going to hurt when it goes into her arm. Of course the needle fucking hurts. Once when the skin is broken and again when she realizes she was lied to.'

He turned to me then, eyes shining with rage. 'Then you are that child. I was never responsible for telling you the truth about the realities of CF. You were wrong for giving me that responsibility. Child.'

Child?

'Two years ago Rachel was in hospital for *four* months,' he said, hands out of his pockets, flashing white as they sliced through the air in front of him. 'The year before she had an operation on her bowels that nearly killed her, but you didn't know those things because you didn't ask about how life had been.'

I didn't look away, couldn't, wouldn't.

'You want the truth?' he said. 'Nothing and no one can change the fact that part of our daughters simply doesn't work.' His words were short and static and book-ended with a furious mess of feeling. He was talking to me. He was talking to himself. He was shouting at the wind as if it were warring with him. 'Is that what you wanted to hear?'

The chill in my bone marrow. Ice words in my mouth. Colder and colder the closer his words came to my heart.

Part of her doesn't work.

Part of me doesn't work.

Part of him doesn't work.

We are the same in our brokenness.

I turned away from him. And he turned away from me so that for a moment we stood, together, side by side on that bridge – him looking toward the sky and my eyes fixed on the water beneath us.

I wanted to stretch out my hand and for him to find it. To feel his fingers close around mine and for it to be as simple as me wanting him and him wanting me. For those tarred and painful words to be un-said.

315

'I – I didn't pursue those subjects,' I said. 'Because I am a coward. I didn't want to know how bad . . .'

He reached out for my hand, holding it tight, and I held his hand like I might die if I let go.

For a moment we were both adults that had only ever had as much courage as children. Children who still needed their mothers in the dark of night.

I led him to a bench, no longer wanting to be in the path of the wind, and I asked, 'How is she? How is Rachel?' Because I wanted to show him I could be better than a coward. 'Tell me.'

He turned to me, relief flooding his eyes. 'You're the only person I've wanted to speak to. There have been so many times . . .' He pulled me to him.

'I'm sorry,' I said into his chest. 'I'm sorry for not being there. But I'm here now.' I moved closer. 'You can talk to me.'

'They're on top of the NTM infection. I mean, they are fairly sure it's gone. It's been a lucky escape.'

'But I thought it was resistant . . .'

'It's miraculous. That's not to say she has escaped unharmed. She hasn't. Her lung function has declined. Significantly. Things are kind of bad with my marriage. I've been living in the shed for the past few nights. I wouldn't mind the cold but most of all I miss Rachel. I want to help her with treatments, and spend time with her. Reading, talking, whatever . . .'

I felt his shoulders narrow and shudder.

'You can tell me,' I said. 'You're such a good dad. You try so hard.' I shouldn't have been that close to him, all the time knowing I was there to end it, but he needed to know that someone had seen how hard he tried. He had once seen that in me and I had needed that gift.

'Here,' I said, 'Warm your hands on me,' and I opened my coat.

He was the one that laid his hands under my top, but I did not stop him, feeling how they moved around my ribcage for the back of me, pulling me to him.

'Her lungs are so damaged . . .' His words stumbled.

I wanted him to stop but to deny him his chance to talk was to continue denying the existence of those waters. And yet. Watching his fear grasp so greedily, so hungrily at him? I was looking in a mirror. Myself in eighteen years. I wanted to run.

'I want to forget. I need to forget,' he said. He kissed me then, so tenderly. It seemed simple. One last time, together, so that he would know there was something else he could feel other than pain.

He pulled me to my feet and then we ran against the wind, faster and faster, between lines of commuters. He was pulling me along so fast I almost fell, until he stopped suddenly at the top of wet concrete steps. He lifted me into his arms and carried me down the steps, deeper and deeper towards an unlit arch beneath the bridge. The tide was out, the dark rocks and weed exposed. Holding me close to him all the while, kissing my face.

317

And under that bridge we stood on a muddied shore-line, feet turned sideways by pebble and soaked driftwood, as the water slipped away beyond us. He pushed me against the damp flagstones of the wall and if he hadn't needed me as much as he did I would have bucked under his hands, hating that they pinned me there. He held on to me too tight and he kissed me so hard on the mouth that my lips felt like the blood was pressed out of them.

'Stop,' I said. 'You've got me. You don't need to . . . I'm here.'

And I made him look at me, before I kissed him gently again, to bring him back to the way we had been.

Then he was inside me and fucking me, all my clothes still on or pulled up around me, people walking on the concrete above us, the water dripping off the side of the bridge. Holding on to me too tight, again. And although I kept trying to look at him, to bring him back, he fucked me harder – not like it had been before – as if he was trying to find something or break something or run from something. And if it had been Dave or another man I would have said stop. But it was him, so I didn't and so he kept going, kept excavating and all I could think was:

You can't find what you need.

I can't give you what you're looking for.

I'm not giving you enough.

Not giving you what you once gave me.

He came, and quickly fell quiet, and I said, 'Everything's going to be all right.'

He wouldn't look at me, his face to the flagstones. He began quivering as waves of something travelled through him. Tears, then, and without warning his legs buckled, and so we fell together.

I pushed myself up, palms pressing down on sharp flint and gritted mud, and held him up – his upper body, all I could manage – and in my lap I gave him a place where he could sob until he was spent, draining into silence.

A boat's horn in the background.

I turned to see it speeding into the distance, through those wide-reaching and dark waters, to a dock I couldn't see.

Full of pity and remorse and disgust and love, I held him in my arms and it felt like holding a death.

'Help me,' he said.

Chapter 22

January went on, punctuated with a few newsworthy storms – walls of water battering cliff faces and the fishing ports of the Cornish coast. One morning I heard siren overlapping siren and felt the cold sense of something close and wrong. Reports soon emerged that high winds had blown a hoarding off the local supermarket and that the high street was blocked by the emergency services as they tried to rescue a man in a critical condition.

Meanwhile, my list of resolutions remained untouched.

Richard and I continued to see each other.

He'd calmed down since the bridge. Sometimes we were almost as happy as we had been in those hotel rooms when we first met.

I wanted him. I cut spaces in my life to accommodate him. After a while I even stopped telling myself that I would break it off soon, and instead let my skin grow over the secret. The lies I told grew easier.

But I still needed a life plan because the end of maternity leave was only a few months away.

Had to get to grips.

One bitterly cold morning towards the end of the month I told myself I had to start somewhere otherwise I'd never start at all. I'd start small, with the house. I was listing all the things in need of some care and attention – the arthritically stiff letterbox, the crumbling window frames and the redundant cat flap – when the doorbell rang.

That bell would be the first on my list. It clacked rather than rang, a dull machine-gun stutter instead of bright tones. 'Time to mend and seal up and lock out this winter,' I said to Mia, scooping her into my arms.

Time to say goodbye to the old and usher in the new.

'But lunch first,' I sang into my daughter's ear as I walked towards the door, her soft face pressed to mine. 'We'll be eating soup until you're seven at this rate.'

That morning I had made a lake of the stuff, far more than we needed. Thick enough for her to eat like the purees we started her on. Dave always seemed to have eaten by the time he got home. I wondered about it sometimes – whether he was eating a kebab around the corner rather than sit across a table from me, standing out there in the cold with a can of Coke until there wasn't much left of the evening.

I opened the door to a pretty young woman.

'Can I help you?'

The woman tugged lightly at a lanyard under her scarf then wriggled a gloved finger in Mia's direction. 'Hello, little one.'

She looked at me expectantly and shivered under her oversized mohair coat.

'I'm here to go through some new breathing games and exercises for physio? We haven't met before. I'm new.' She dipped her head and cleared her throat. 'Did you not get a letter?'

'No. I mean . . .' I glanced round at the can of WD40 that was bookending an uneven stack of lacquered menus, paper envelopes and taxi company cards on our hall table. 'It's probably in that pile. I haven't been through it since before she went into hospital. Sorry, it's been, I've been . . .'

'Don't worry! Hospital stays are so hard on normal life.' She dotted Mia's nose with her gloved finger. 'I don't know why they don't email over the info to people. Luddites!' She smiled. 'Why don't I come back another time?'

Mia reached out a hand towards the woman.

'Oh, aren't you a poppet!' she said, smiling widely.

'Come in,' I said. 'It's freezing outside.' I shifted Mia on my hip. 'She's so energetic now. Crawling any day soon. I could do with some new exercises to keep physio interesting. Come in. As long as you don't mind the chaos of lunch.'

The woman stepped in and held up her hands. 'Where's your nearest sink? I should wash my hands.' She bent her head and coughed into a cupped hand. 'Tail end of a virus. Nothing contagious, obviously,' she said, and I nodded in agreement – because her tone had insisted on it.

'Can I take your coat?'

'No, thank you,' she said firmly, turning enough to keep me from touching her coat. 'I feel the cold. I'll need a few minutes.' She took off her shoes – the first advice we were given by the consultant to keep our house safe from outdoor bacteria.

'Our heating's not the best either. Draughts everywhere.'

The woman pushed back her tortoiseshell glasses, revealing a charcoal smudge of shadow underneath her eyes. She was beautiful, with pale skin and sharply defined cheekbones. Probably spent every free hour in the gym. Typical physio. Half of them seemed to play sport for England in their free time.

I led her through to the kitchen and motioned to the sink.

The woman stifled something – a catch, an irritation – at the back of her throat as she scrubbed at her hands.

'How do you know when a cough's not contagious any more? I've always wanted to know,' I said. Asking her to reassess her situation.

'I'm here to make things better, not worse.'

It wasn't really what I was getting at. I might have insulted her, questioning her judgement. I suddenly wished I had told her, *Yes, another time would be better* because the truth was I didn't quite feel ready for her, for this or anything like it.

'Are you married?'

'Is Dave not listed on the records?'

'I'm only trying to make conversation. Sorry. When did you meet?'

'We've been together ages.'

'Is he a good dad?'

'Yes. He tries.'

'My mum's the one in my life who's always looked after me. She's unbelievably strong.'

I looked at her again. She was young, underneath that make-up. Maybe she was still living at home. The city was so expensive now. How long would Mia be with us, in that room? How many times would we redecorate it for her?

I swung Mia off my hip and held her over the high chair covered in spittle and a muddle of breadsticks.

'Let me help,' the physio said, extending both arms and slotting them under Mia like a fork-lift truck, before I could lower her into the chair. 'I can hold her while you do what you need to do.'

'Thanks.'

The woman brought Mia close, ruffling her hair and holding up a long loose thread on her jacket as a plaything. Mia smiled and babbled at this woman who possessed a knack for children. I still felt like I was learning a foreign language.

'I've just been trying and failing to get this horrible medicine into her.' I took Mia back and sat her in the high chair, kissed her forehead and waved a plastic casing full of electric pink medicine lightly in the air as if it was as much fun as a Firework Night glo-stick. As I held it forward, Mia clamped her mouth down on the syringe but she didn't swallow and the medicine dribbled in vampiric lines from the corners of her mouth.

'Mia!'

Mia jumped at the force of my words, her face rumpling into tears, and I was so sorry for shouting.

'Shit. Sorry. I'm such . . .'

'I can help you with that,' the woman said. 'I've got a load of tricks. They're easy at this age. Wait until she hits her teens. Then it'll be virtually impossible to give her anything. Have you got any honey?'

'I'm not supposed to give her that until she's twelve months, am I?'

'It's fine. That's just the doctors being over-careful. Honey is the best way to give a difficult medicine. Trust me, I've done it a hundred times.'

I handed her the honey jar, a spoon, some medicine.

'Try this,' she sang to Mia, dotting her nose as she had done at the doorway, and spooning the honey into her mouth. She followed quickly with the syringe of medicine and Mia was so busy smiling at her that she swallowed. 'It's a trick. A honey-trap.' She laughed.

The woman continued looking at me as the corners of her smile began to settle in a straight line, scanning my face like she was identifying places on a map she had heard about. There was something in her tone like the tap-tapping of a drawing pin lodged in a rubber shoe tread.

'Look at me wasting your time with all this,' I said. 'We should get on with that physio so I can let you go.'

But the woman had turned her attention back to Mia. 'Doesn't she look like you?' She spoke so quietly I strained to hear. 'I've got my dad's nose; so bloody thin and weak-looking, like it would break if you slapped it.'

'I think you look very pretty.' She looked so young and suddenly so vulnerable too.

Mia turned and held her arms up to the woman in supplication. The source of the honey. Suddenly the woman lifted Mia from the chair, took two steps away from me and shifted my baby to her hip. Then they were turning around and around together, faces bent in close like the new bud of a flower, dancing a waltz so quick I felt a breeze each time they passed. My mouth turned in a smile but it ached to keep it there as I watched the white flash of flesh beneath the rips and tears of the woman's denim jeans, and the Minnie Mouse faces on the pink cotton of her socks as she balanced on the balls of her feet.

I tried hard to keep smiling because I knew these moments were the ones I needed to live in, not the past traumas or the future anxieties. And yet. My thoughts crackled with a doubtful energy that would not be grounded as I watched that woman hold a girl she had only known for a few minutes with the joy of a mother and delight of a gangling teenage sister.

'When did you say you joined the hospital team?'

'I'm very new,' she said, and before I had time to say anything else she had slotted Mia back into her high chair. 'Time for lunch, beautiful girl.'

The woman pressed a palm to her chest and leaned against the back of Mia's high chair for support. 'I must get fit again,' she said, chasing her breath like she'd been running a race.

She was struggling. That short dance had drained colour from her already-pale face and it was then that I saw more than good cheekbones. I saw prominent brow bones and the determined jut of her jaw – all the low and high hanging outcrops of a skull.

She coughed, much harder this time, twisting her body to direct it away from Mia. Her whole body shook and she used an arm to brace herself against the table as if she might fall over without it. The cough sounded like it was from deep in her chest. It sounded thick and junky and like it might never stop.

I pulled Mia's high chair in the opposite direction across the kitchen, at least twelve feet, and pushed open the kitchen window as far as its rusting hinges would allow. 'Please don't take this the wrong way,' I said. 'But it doesn't sound like your cough has gone. Maybe we should delay this appointment?'

'It's something caught at the back of my throat.'

'You said you'd had a virus.'

'Whatever. A dry throat, something's aggravating it.'

'Let's do this another time.'

'No,' she said firmly. 'I'm busy. I've got other things to be doing and other people I need to see. I don't have time to come back.'

She reached into her handbag on the table and took out a cough swab stick sealed in plastic and printed hospital paper. 'Let's at least do a cough swab. Test her for any nasties she may have picked up since leaving hospital.'

She crossed the room and collected Mia into her arms once more – wrist bones jutting, her long and fine fingers curling around my daughter's waist.

I stepped forward to take Mia back but she held up her hand, straight and rigid, like a lollipop lady.

'I don't think I caught your name.' I reached for Mia again and the woman pushed me away with a palm at my chest, holding me at arm's length from my own child. I lurched toward Mia again and the woman pushed me back again, harder that time. I wanted to scream in anger that she had what was mine.

'Who are you?' I shouted, to hide the fear that made my legs unsteady and my mouth dry. 'Give me my daughter before I call the police.'

As the woman shifted Mia from one arm to the next the folds of her heavy coat opened. In the gape of her shirt I saw an object beneath her collarbone, pushing up under the skin like it was trying to escape her body.

A portacath, surgically implanted, for the ease of giving regular IV drugs.

'Tell me what you want, Rachel,' I said.

'I think that's fairly obvious, isn't it?' Her voice, as cold as the wind rattling the letterbox.

'Please give me back my baby.'

'No. Stand there. You've been fucking my dad.'

'I don't know what—'

'Oh don't even. He likes all the flashy Apple stuff but he hardly knows how it works. A message from you to his phone popped straight up on the iPad I've borrowed off him. So I know. You don't say much, do you? But what you do say, well, it's clear to me you like fucking him.'

'Please, stop saying that.'

'Why?' she shouted. 'It's the truth. You're fucking him,' Rachel shouted. 'You're fucking me. Fucking my family. Really fucking my family so there's nothing left. You don't get to steal someone else's family because yours isn't working. I want my family back.'

Mia began crying, reaching for me and dipping forward on air that would not support her.

'I won't go anywhere near him again,' I said, reaching out to grab Mia's leg. 'I swear to God I won't. Give her back and leave.'

But Rachel pulled Mia away and held up her hand again. 'No you don't. Not yet.'

My heart was jittering, my feet prickling with sweat as I watched her, and tried to work out what to do.

I wondered if I could kill her.

'Your dad loves you,' I said, because it was true and simple and maybe what she wanted to hear. 'He loves you so much. He loves his Sunday family dinners with you and helping you with physio and reading to you. He told me about your holiday to Spain and that he wanted to learn how to ski with you . . . He thinks about you all the time. Everything he does is for you.'

'What are you talking about? He doesn't do any of that stuff . . .' Her pale eyes filled with disbelief and tears, blurring the lines of her pupils. 'What holiday to Spain? I haven't been able to travel for a year now, and I couldn't ski even if I wanted to . . .' Her eyes narrowed. 'Did he not tell you that I've been listed for the past six months?'

'The transplant list?'

Rachel laughed as she cried. 'Oh bless you, you make it sound like a guest list for the first trip to Mars . . . And yet you look so *sad*. So he didn't tell you much about me, did he? All my news . . .'

Every single time he'd looked at me, touched me, spoken to me, for the six months we'd known each other – he'd known that his daughter was dying, waiting for someone else's lungs to save her.

Perhaps only days had passed between Rachel being listed and him meeting me. Hours, even . . .

Felling, turning, twisting sentences back on themselves.

'I didn't know,' I said, a pressure building in my head. 'I've been colonized with pseudomonas since I was eight. I've had NTM for the last few years. My lung function's shit. Even if I get a donor, I'm high-risk because of my bugs. I'm mostly doing it for them. For my mum.'

'But he told me those infections were gone?' I heard my voice, a silly voice, raised at the ends like a child's, challenging it all like I could convince her otherwise.

But she raised her eyebrows, and I don't know why but something about the smile and sadness in her eyes told me that soon enough I would be spinning into orbit surrounded by the detonated pieces of my life.

But still I tried. 'He told me that you'd got pseudomonas recently and that it was sensitive to only one antibiotic.'

Tell me anything.

Please tell me that you're lying to me.

Her face unchanged.

'He told me they were on top of the NTM,' I said.

Pity.

That's what the sadness and the smiles were.

Bang.

I cried out: a haunting, animal sound issuing from my mouth, like wind whistling high and loud through a chimney breast.

On top of, Richard had said the doctors were *on top of* the NTM. But just because you're on top of the murderer doesn't mean you've slashed his throat . . .

'You stupid bitch,' Rachel said bitterly. 'Do you only ever hear what you want to hear? What a fucking joke.' Then she held her head away from Mia as she continued to cough. Her face was stained with shades of colour. The bruised navy of purple, the bright blood of red, the grey death of blue when the cells are starved of oxygen and drowning is close.

She clung to my child and I wanted to run at her with everything I had.

But if she coughed in Mia's face . . . that was the knife she was holding to my child's throat. We both knew it.

'Please give me Mia,' I said. 'Give me my daughter. I won't see your dad for as long as I live.'

There was a pot, on the counter, holding rolling pins and wooden spoons like an arrangement of long-stem roses. A wooden block next to it that held sharp blades for cutting bird flesh and tough skins. I calculated how many steps it would take to get round her.

'Must be hard, parenting a child with CF,' she said at last, still struggling for breath, spitting out the words as if they were reluctant to leave her. 'Your job is to protect and save and you can't even do that. You're fighting against something stronger than you.'

'I need some water,' I breathed. 'I think I'm going to faint.'

I walked to the sink behind her, and ran the tap into one of Mia's plastic sippy-cups that had been sitting on the draining board. With my other hand I felt for the rolling pin handle, her back still turned.

'What happens next, Rachel?' I said.

'I decide that,' she said. 'I decide how you pay for what you've done to my family.'

I turned slowly, then whipped the rolling pin hard on to Rachel's head. If she'd held Mia closer I couldn't have done it. The wooden pin caught her a solid blow. As she fell, stunned, I grabbed Mia.

I moved to the far side of the room holding Mia close to my chest.

I realized I had wet myself. My legs, my feet.

Rachel twitched on the floor, blood flecking around her nose, her cough rumbling out of her, a sea at storm in her chest. She rolled over and pushed as though to raise herself up, then began to weep.

I left the house, Mia and a nappy bag bundled into my arms.

Hammered on the neighbour's door. Hammered again.

Marian opened the door, squinting and smiling.

I almost pushed Mia into her comforting, cardigan-clad arms. 'Please, Marian. Could you take her? I won't be more than an hour. Please?'

Please keep her safe.

She looked down at my sockless feet – dead white and damp on the mossy concrete.

There wasn't a part of me that didn't quiver and ripple with the cold, the fear and the adrenalin. 'Please, it's an emergency.'

'Yes, sweetie. Yes, of course,' she said, recovering quickly, as if she'd never have said anything else.

And I loved that near-stranger for kissing Mia's head as if she were her own grandchild, and for not asking anything of me.

'Thank you. Thank you,' I said as I turned and ran back to the house, Mia crying for me in the background. But I knew she would be safe: it was decades, perhaps, since Marian had been a mother to a baby but the lessons learnt are quick and deep and ones you never forget.

Back in the kitchen I found Rachel propped against the cupboards; eyes glazed, a trickle of dark blood trailing the side of her face. Helping her to her feet I took her outside.

Put a rug in the back seat of the car and made her lie down on it.

She did what I told her – the fight gone, semi-concussed. A beaten child.

The drive was silent but for her coughs, and every time she wasn't coughing I worried that she had lost consciousness. I was so worried that it was a relief when she began crying again. I glanced in the back mirror, saw her snot mixing with blood as she coughed and cried.

I stopped the car in a layby near Richard's house and helped Rachel to climb out of the car. I leaned in after her and took the blanket out, threw it behind a tree. Let the council deal with it.

She leaned against the closed car door.

'I won't see him again. Not ever,' I said, stepping

towards her. 'And I'm sorry for hurting you like that. I didn't mean to make you bleed . . . But I didn't know what else to do.' We stood for a moment and I considered the possibility of Rachel not having fallen in the way that she did. The possibility of her continuing to struggle and to keep Mia from me . . .

I would have done what any lion in the jungle needed to do to save her cub from danger.

Yes, that. A hundred times over.

But Mia was safe and Rachel was bloodied and bruised and crying and dying and I wanted to hold her, comfort her, dry her tears and bury her face in my neck. Tell her she would be fine and that all this would pass because nothing ever lasts forever, not really. I wanted to offer her all the comforting truths and lies a mother might offer a frightened child.

Because lies were necessary sometimes.

Lies could sustain a life that might otherwise have shuddered to a standstill.

Despite it all, could I thank him for that?

I wanted to reach out to her but she would push me away.

'What I said about him loving you? It's true,' I said. 'He sounded so proud of you.'

She looked up at me then, and stopped crying, residue still draining from rims in a slow trail. 'He does the charity and his business but he avoids me, mostly. Sitting in that shed of his at treatment times and mealtimes. He sometimes sleeps there. When I'm angry about it all I think he's avoiding me because he's competitive and selfish and I remind him that he's lost this one. But at other times I think he avoids me because I remind him of the fact he's going to lose a child. Which is a kind of love, I suppose.'

I winced inside again, my soul turning in on itself, feeling stupid and ashamed at not having seen his delusions.

At not wanting to see his delusions.

Rachel dipped her head as if the pain was bearing down on top of her, crushing the spaces between her vertebrae. 'He was my hero when I was little.' She tipped forward and now I did catch her and hold her as she began to cry again. 'He taught me how to ride a bike and play the drums. Then it all stopped.'

I could smell her hair, which smelt like flowers and oil.

And I listened.

'Despite all that . . . my mum doesn't work without him. They're still a family and they will need each other when I am gone. And I'm going. Don't let him tell you otherwise.'

'I'm sorry, Rachel,' I said.

I was crying for her and I was crying because as she spoke about the concerts and holidays I remembered Our List. How the zoo visits, the dinners and trips to the beach, all those ways we'd thought of spending time together and getting to know each other, were crumbling to dust and soon my child would be crying too unless I tried harder to solder together the family.

Rachel looked up at me, blinked, and started coughing again, missing breaths, crushing breaths, losing breaths.

'Maybe you need to talk to him. Tell him what you feel,' I said.

'Don't you think I've tried that?' She shook her head slowly. 'It's like I'm already dead.'

Those words crawled into my heart before she pushed me away and began walking towards her home.

Back home I took Mia's high chair from the kitchen and laid it in the garden, in air that smelt of dead leaves and the ghost of a bonfire. Swabbed it with bleach.

Everything had to be scrubbed clean and I did what I could before I heard Mia's cries next door and knew I couldn't leave her any longer.

Marian handed her over with a smile.

No more a near-stranger.

I took Mia back out into the garden. Strapped her into her high chair and wrapped her in a woollen shawl so I could continue with the cleaning.

'Breathe out. Breathe out,' I said urgently, speaking close to her face, as if she would ever understand me. 'Breathe out like you are blowing bubbles. No, breathe out like you are expelling something.'

The bacteria that had lived and evolved inside another pair of human lungs. A dislocated, malicious soul inside her.

The dybukk inside her.

Needed to be exorcised.
Everything had to be exorcised.
Everything had to be scrubbed clean.
Clothes boiled, furniture bleached.
The whole world.

Chapter 23

'Your arms look sore,' Dave said. 'They look so red and sore.'

'It's a rash or something.'

'You should get it checked by the doctor.'

'It's fine. I've been cleaning, is all. Making the house look all pretty again.'

Decorating the carpets with the clean stripes of a vacuum cleaner.

Scrubbing the windows with paper and vinegar until they shine.

Cleaning the floors and tabletops, and skin, with bleach.

Ignoring his calls.

Ignoring all pain.

'What shall we do for Easter this year? It's only a few months away.'

'I'm not bothered about Easter,' he said.

'But I am.'

And we looked at each other. Dropped the subject otherwise round and round we would go.

'While I was making the dinner I came up with an

idea,' I said. 'We should always make time to eat together, at least once a week. Otherwise things get so busy that we won't see each other. Let's say every Sunday night?'

The family that eats together stays together.

'It's a nice idea but I can't this Sunday,' he said. 'I've got to work. Speaking of which, I should get on. I'll eat at my desk, as long as you don't mind?'

The sun rose, and set, rose and set and every day I cleaned the carpet with the stripes of a vacuum cleaner and tickled Mia and jumped with her and threw her up and down. And prayed.

'Look at this,' I said, jabbing at my laptop screen. 'It's a special deal in the paper for a long weekend in Rome. I think we should go before Easter. All three of us. We could walk Mia around, eat ice cream, see the sights. But we'd need to book now.'

'Mia's far too young to be going on a European city break.'

'For next year, or the year after, then. Let's book it now or we never will and then time will go, and we'll still be here.'

Then I imagined us still sitting in that kitchen a year on, having the same conversations we were having now: broken and monochrome and what else?

Dave was looking at me like he'd been looking at me a lot recently.

Politely.

'Have you been cleaning again today?' he said.

Decorating the carpets with the clean stripes of a vacuum cleaner.

Scrubbing the windows until they shine.

Cleaning the floors and tabletops, and skin, with bleach.

Ignoring, deleting.

'That rash looks infected,' he said.

'Does it?'

'Did you clean all day?'

'And thought of holidays for us. And made a stew. How was your day?'

And the sun set.

The skin on my arms got so infected that I went into the surgery to have them bandaged. Then Mia and I made a day of it and went to Caroline's house in the afternoon. Such a soothing and memorable day with the fresh white bandages, the boys doing a jigsaw on the living room carpet after school, heating on full tilt, TV in the background, more toys, more talk and a pudding with custard.

At dinner, over sausages and mash and onion gravy, Caroline had said that Mia and I should think about coming to stay for a few days, like a mini holiday. She had a travel cot and a high chair. As I drove back that night I thought about her offer, about the soft carpets and bleach white towels, pearly white soap that dispensed from glass bottles in all the bathrooms and how her house was always warm and smelling of fresh laundry.

I was planning the next time that Mia and I could go back, at the weekend perhaps, when I saw Richard's car – black and low and distinctive with its wide silver bumper.

It was parked outside my house. A jolt, an electric charge to my cells, a sight so unexpected after two weeks of ignoring him and the calls tailing off into texts . . . so unexpected I was nearly sick.

It was too dark to see his face but his silhouette was set by the streetlight – the length of his neck, the curve of his head. I would forever know that outline.

I drove past him and around the neighbourhood and then past the house a few times more until I was sure he was gone and when I stepped through the door Dave said, 'Why did you keep driving round the block? I don't know how many times I saw you do it.'

'Mia was asleep in her car seat and I didn't want to wake her.'

'Oh.' It made sense. 'Did you see that twat in that showy-looking car? He kept looking at our house. I was about to call the police.'

'I don't know,' I said, taking off my coat. 'I didn't see anything.'

He looked at me and I thought he was going to say something more.

Later that night I put Mia to bed then propped myself against a bank of pillows next to her. Settled down with my computer, the night-light elephant glowing pink in the corner and the streetlights thrumming orange outside.

Clicks here and there. Photos, news, photos, Facebook, news, photos.

I hesitated mid-newsfeed-scroll and then did what I'd always intended on doing: I googled Rachel's name and found a blog, all pink and grey and orange lines, timeline unfurling down one side and below its masthead – *Love and Peas* – painted in black on a white flag, I read these words:

This is Rachel's mother, Nancy.

And I knew.

And before I read further, because I knew what was coming, I looked to my daughter to check she was still there, her chest rising and falling, evenly and soundly.

I kissed her warm cheeks and her temples and put my ear to her nose to hear the warm sounds of her life. The clarity of her breathing. No infection, no blockage. I kissed her.

This is Rachel's mother, Nancy.

I held the side of Mia's cot bars and then slid my hand through to hold hers.

At 7.09 a.m. on 10 February Rachel lost her battle with cystic fibrosis, waiting for the new lungs she so desperately needed.

I will always remember Rachel as a fighter.

She was someone who fought for and against everything, all the time.

At school she fought for her fellow pupils when the governors threatened to take away the snack stand at school – Lucy Munroe, I know you will never forget the banner you painted together and how it was too big to fit inside the school's entrance so you hung it on the flagpole outside. What a result.

And the battle she fought every day wasn't against cystic fibrosis. It was for normality. She fought for the chance to do everything her friends did despite CF laying down barriers every day, sometimes every hour.

She went away too soon. Too soon for her to accomplish all she wanted. Too soon for us all to have loved her longer and better.

We have run out of chances to make new memories with her but she will live in our hearts forever. Our darling daughter, Rachel. Rest In Peace now.

I left Mia sleeping and found Dave in the living room eating a casserole I had made, straight out of the pot.

I went to him and cried and he held on to me.

'It's OK,' he said, stroking my hair. 'What's happened? Tell me, what's happened?'

I was crying so much I couldn't get the words out. I held on to him tight and spoke into his neck. 'A girl. A teenage girl with CF has died.'

'I'm sorry.' He held me back to wipe my tears away and to look at me. 'Did you know her through the charity?'

'No,' I sobbed. 'I read about it and it caught me by surprise.'

'Are you OK?' he said eventually, gently. 'Is there anything else wrong?'

'No, just the girl.'

'Are you sure? I wondered because there isn't a surface in this house that hasn't been cleaned more than a hundred times in the past few weeks.'

'I know.' I sniffed, coughed. 'But I'm fine.'

After a few moments, he said, 'Let's have a drink, shall we?' And it was such an odd thing for him to say when usually he would suggest I sleep, that I wiped my damp cheeks with a sleeve and watched him.

He opened a cupboard at the bottom of the dresser and reached into it.

Laid a heavy-bottomed blue glass bottle in the vacant space before me. 'Champagne?' he said. 'I'd prefer a beer but there's nothing else in the house.'

I looked at him, and then back at the bottle.

Champagne. Vintage. In a very special, apothecary blue bottle. Chosen and touched and sent by Richard at another time.

And so this was how it would be done.

'Want some?' he said indifferently, making the bottle look impossibly light as he picked it up and waved it in the air with one hand. 'Champagne shouldn't only be a good-news drink. It should be a memorable-news drink. A when-JFK-was-shot kind of drink.' He placed two glasses on the table.

'It'll be warm.'

'Not in this house it won't. Come on, sit down.'

He poured and allowed the bubbles to overflow, pooling sparkles around the base of the glass. I sat down, glanced up to see his mouth set and his eyes cast toward his own empty glass.

'Where did it come from?' I said.

He ignored the question.

'Came while you were in hospital,' he said. 'I think it's for you.'

'How do you know that? How did it get here? Post? How?'

'I don't know, I can't remember. It was delivered by someone. A courier, I think. Kept meaning to tell you. No label or anything but it must be for you. Could have been for the neighbours but I say we drink it. I've opened it now.'

'Perhaps it was from your new investors?'

He looked up. 'We didn't get the investment so there are no new investors. I told you that.'

'Did you?' I tugged at the bandages on my arms. 'I'm sorry, I forgot about the investors. Dave, please can we do this another day?'

'You need to leave those bandages alone.'

'I don't want a drink. I want a bath.' I needed to sit

346

in silence, then to be delivered into a numb and dreamless sleep.

His chest rose and fell. 'You ask me how my day was but you never listen to the answer.' His anger was unexpected. 'You're silent one day, crying the next. And you never tell me why.'

I pushed the glass away from me.

'Other people have asked me about the investors,' he continued. 'And about my life in general.' He scratched his head. 'What other things about my life, you ask? Let's see. I've been getting headaches. I don't think it's any big deal but they've sent me for some scans. I've had the blood tests. They came back clear.'

'You didn't say anything.'

'You. Didn't. Ask.'

'But why would I? Why would I ask about your health like that?'

'I'm thinking about taking on a new business partner. And I've lost half a stone. And my mum's thinking about retiring so she can spend more time with Mia.'

'Is she?'

'I've told you all those things in the past weeks. Darren knows more about my life than you do. He knows because he asks questions. And then – this is the crucial bit, Cath, so do remember this – he listens when I tell him stuff.' He looked up, spoke words into the ceiling. 'Sometime before Christmas, before Mia was admitted to hospital, me and him were having a pint at The Crown and he

347

said he was thinking about proposing to that new girl-friend of his, because she was lovely and kind and understanding. And you know what I thought? I thought fuck, yes, mate, doesn't that sound nice?'

I wanted to cry, I did, because there was a force behind his words. And it was something more than hate.

But I didn't cry because it felt important to not have my vision blurred with tears. I couldn't protect myself if I couldn't see what was coming for me.

I pulled one of the bandages off my arm and scratched at the raw wound until it stung and blood started to come through.

'I cook and I clean and I ask you how your day was.' My words feather-light and dilute in their conviction.

'You don't *care* how my day was.' His tone mirrored mine. But it was mocking, too.

I stood up and paced the length of the kitchen, adjusted a picture frame.

'I think you should sit down, Cath.' Harsher, louder now. In case I walked out.

'Why?'

Make sure your husband is with you . . .

I went back to the table and took my seat and waited for the moment of impact.

'So I got back from seeing Darren,' Dave continued. 'I think it was a night you were out at a charity thing? I sat here and drank half a bottle of vodka. And I thought . . . I don't know if I can have another baby like this.'

'I don't understand. What do you mean?'

He looked down at the table as he spoke. 'Don't get me wrong: I want a whole rugby team of children. I love kids. But I don't want more with you. I'm sorry, but that's the truth.'

He didn't want any more children with me.

Was that the same as not wanting any more of me?

For a moment, it was only us and the sounds of our house. The tinny echo of a hot water pipe expanding. The airy rumble of the tumble dryer going round and around.

He looked up briefly. Green eyes. Mean, green eyes now because he was starting to break something, really starting to smash us up.

'I don't understand,' I said again, buying moments for myself as I combusted with a silent scream – tissues inside my skeleton inflaming, pushing against my skull and my ribcage.

'I mean,' Dave said coolly, 'that I don't think we should be together any more. You asked what we would do at Easter and, well, I'm happy to take Mia with me, but I don't think I'll be here.'

He was lying, that was all.

Lying, to get a reaction. Lying to get me to change.

'Don't you understand?' I said, giving in to the tears and reaching out for his hand. Trying to take hold but not finding a grip. 'Things have been difficult. A lot of couples don't survive this kind of thing, a diagnosis like CF, you read about that online all the time. But the ones that do? They get stronger for it. I can change things, I can mend things. I can, I know I can.'

He watched the floor and then the shadow I cast across the table as I leaned further towards him.

'I can, Dave. I can change.' He can't have heard me through the crying and the spit so I shouted louder. 'I can change. I know you think I've got Obsessive Compulsive Disorder. I can see why you'd think that. I know what it looks like when you walk in here. But that's not the truth of it. I mean, that's the lie of it . . .' Tripping, tangling words. 'That's a lie. I'm not putting the cleaning before her. I'm not. I'm looking after her. Really I am. I'm keeping her safe.'

You have no idea.

A gasp issued from my throat. There was so much he would never know.

'I've made some stupid decisions because of wanting to feel differently, and honestly needing to feel differently, but . . .' He had such a still, intransigent, inflexible face. 'Dave.' Screamed for him to change. 'Why don't you believe me?'

But he wouldn't look up.

'You're breaking our family,' I spat. 'I will not let you do that. Dave, look at me.' I grasped at him, pulling at the skin on his arms, raking it red, and though he winced with pain he still didn't look at me.

I held his chin hard, between my fingers, pulled his face to meet me.

He pushed me away, I held, he pushed.

'Look at me,' I screamed. 'Please look at me.'

Tears welled again, the concentration of salt water stinging my eyes. 'Please don't do this, Dave. Please, please let me try?' I said quietly, my legs buckling, crumpling me to the floor.

I looked up at him. 'I can try to make my pain smaller. I'll see someone. Like you always wanted me to. I'll make an appointment and go tomorrow. Then we can see?' My words were louder then. 'I need to make the pain a smaller part of every day, I know that . . . If I can do that I'll be all right, we'll be all right. Please don't go. Don't leave me on my own to deal with this. Please, please, don't leave me on my own.'

'And that's the biggest reason you want me to stay . . .' He looked at me, finally. Down on the floor like that. 'Not because you love me. Because you can't bear to be alone with *this*.'

And there was a moment, a lapse in time that I could have filled with words and counter-arguments about how it was him and always him, and how it would always and forever more be him and him and more *him*.

But I didn't.

The words stuck, damming something in me, like the walls of water I often dreamed of.

'I deserve more than that, Cath,' he said. 'I want to be with someone who cares about my work and health and welfare . . . Someone who wants to be with *me*.'

The water I dreamed of that dammed the screams, that filled my lungs and ended the breath.

He knelt on the cold tiles in front of me.

We grasped each other's hands so tightly that the skin stretched in white and pink stripes on both our knuckles.

'Why are you leaving me? Why now?' I said.

Tell me it's because I have hurt you.

Tell me it's because of something I can atone for.

'I'm leaving you,' he said, 'because we don't love each other any more.'

Both of us to blame, and yet neither of us to blame.

Round and round no more.

Chapter 24

Some time passed, I don't know how long: enough for him to pack things into a bag for an unspecified period. He returned wearing a winter coat – kissed me once, kissed his daughter twice, said he'd take the bus. When he said he'd leave the car for us I almost unravelled: partly because he was being generous at a difficult time but mostly because I wondered how generous he'd be when it came to splitting a double bed, a chest of drawers and a child.

He didn't say where he was going: he no longer needed to tell me and I no longer felt I had the right to ask. Perhaps his mum's. Perhaps to Jane's house for too much whisky, a shoulder to cry on and for one thing to lead to another.

I wouldn't have blamed him. People do things under pressure. Things they'd never otherwise consider.

But early the next morning I had a call from his mum to say that he was there and still in bed and could I please *verify* the info she'd been given, which was that her son's marriage to me was over.

She didn't shout at me or blame me, or him, for anything. But then she had always been good and fair like that. After a while she cried a bit and said: *I suppose it takes two to tango.* I chewed at my thumbnail and tried to stop my voice from cracking when I said I hoped we could still stay in touch. She said: *So is that it? Is there really no hope? Couples seem to give up so easily these days.* And I thought, *That might be what it looks like from the outside.*

There's a lot of hard work goes into making something look easy.

Later, in the darkness, when Mia was asleep and dreaming, the words jumped out of their green text bubble.

Can we meet? Tonight? Now? I'll go anywhere you want.

I shut the curtains to make it darker for us both, and I tried to sleep.

Something bad has happened. Please call.

Three more days passed and the news travelled along the social networks that there'd been a severance.

Caroline said she'd been told we were on a break.

If by break you mean broken, then yes.

Every time I walked down the hall with Mia in my arms I noticed his trainers, unmoved from where he had left them. His spare change in a pile on the mantel and his umbrella open like a flower on the floor. I kept expecting the key in the lock.

I wondered, Is this how Nancy is living her days? *Where are you? Your phone still rings. I know you're screening my calls.*

Family and friends visited, offering tea and cake and their obvious solutions and while they talked I thought, There are events in people's lives that leave them suffering the results of trauma.

Moving house.

Diagnosis of a life-threatening illness.

Separation from a significant other.

Death of a child.

I was racking them up.

When one of my work colleagues found out that Dave had moved out, she sent me a chocolate-chip muffin basket. It was the same one she sent me when Mia was born.

Answer your fucking phone. Please.

I was so sorry for his loss.

I cried at the fridge door, at the sink, and at Mia's bedside as she slept.

Cried for all the waste.

But every time he tried to get in touch, I thought: Please go away and let me do my job avoiding you. Together we blew up my life. Let's not blow up yours.

Think of the children.

Isn't that what they say?

We should have thought of the children.

*   *   *

One afternoon I came back from Sainsbury's to find gaps on the shoe rack and the stencil of dust on a plug socket where his phone charger used to live. He'd collected all his stuff, but left the things we'd bought together, the things we'd shared.

I didn't think I'd ever stop crying.

But as winter came to an end and spring made its first shy attempts with purple crocus and green life breaking through dry branches, Mia and I spent time together. We did things together until the most fun activities, the nicest times, bent and linked themselves together into a routine. Porridge made with cream and brown sugar, for breakfast. Feeding and physio and soft play. A nap together, and then a job search for me because there were logistics to consider: a mortgage and bills, a proper income, a life plan. The list of issues to address and resolve was long, but then it always would be.

In between, there was the zoo or the beach with Caroline and the boys.

I pushed the kitchen table against the wall so that two places didn't seem too few in a space that had been designed to hold *the rugby team*. I threw out rusting cans of shaving gel and the toothpaste Dave used on his sensitive teeth.

This is it, I thought, as I pushed our bed – the bed, my bed – up against the wall and banked pillows, cushions and teddies in the space where he used to lie, making

a space where Mia could sleep on the nights she didn't
want to sleep in her cot.

This is it.

Where are you, please where are you where are you
where are you where are you.

Chapter 25

Spring was turning out to be a good one with more crisp blue sunny days than not.

It was one of those days. Birdsong and the scent of flowers in the air.

And yet not one of those days. A special day, a marked day. Three months to the day. A good period of time to have waited and decided whether my plan was viable. And so that morning, details noted from the Facebook page, I left Mia with Mum, and drove.

Three months to the day since her death and the flowers on Rachel's grave were still being tended well: someone weeding out the wilted and faded, replacing blooms, changing the water and position regularly. No use leaving them all in the shadow of the headstone. But it was their colours that caught the eye: the rich purples and paint-pot yellows in a graveyard otherwise scattered with colour-faded, frost-bitten, wind-dried flower stems held together reluctantly by twine.

Purple and yellow, the colours of spring and a new start.

The colours of a life arrested in its first season.

The only blooms left untouched were those that filled each letter of the name, 'Rachel'. A word laid across the back of the hearse and then on the coffin. Now laid at the foot of her grave – capitalized and rounded like the childish letters that decorated school exercise book covers – blooms now decomposed and nearly gone.

All the well-wishing cards, carefully propped up against the flowers now – curled edges, ink splashed with rain, biro faded by sun – inscribed with messages written and rewritten because it was hard to find the final words:

> *Always and forever.*
> *Gone too soon.*
> *Rach. Our angel in heaven.*
> *The brightest light.*
> *I love you, Rachel.*
> *I won't forget you.*
> *Wish you were here.*
> *You'll always be my baby – Dad xxxx*

And there I was, by her graveside, still gripping the flowers I had bought, without a card, and only one thing to tell her, uselessly, which was that I had kept my promise and would continue to keep it.

Is there relief in the end of suffering?

I knelt on the grass at the foot of her grave, cold damp

earth pressing at my kneecaps, and lay my flowers next to the letter 'L' of her name, like a full stop.

Poking out under the letter 'E' I saw a folded page, rippled with the effects of drying sun on rain-soaked paper. An order of service for Rachel Brightman: 17 March 1999–10 February 2017. A picture of her smiling face and someone's arm looped round her neck. Her mother, her friend – someone who loved her fiercely.

I held the order of service in open palms like I was holding a sick bird, pages like wings, and imagined myself in that church a few months back. Damp, mouldering hymnbook pages. Her coffin as light as a weekend suitcase. The knife-wound gasp at the back of a parent's throat.

'Jerusalem', they had sung. We'd played it at Dad's funeral service, too. Best sung with committed voices, one of his friends had said. I'd left it to him.

Eulogy. Read by Nancy Brightman.

No mention of her father.

No mention at all.

'What are you doing here?'

I looked up and saw Richard standing on the other side of the headstone – so pale, so frail. My nerves rippled cold, like I had seen something ghostly and uncanny.

I looked down at Rachel's grave. Got to my feet and turned to walk away, feeling the need to go quickly, as if her judgement, alive or dead, was still on me.

'Cath, tell me what you're doing here?' His voice faltered, clogged with something.

I turned and saw Rachel in him. The same coal-black hair, head tipped to the side in thought, long fingers and the nose she had complained about.

'I – I'm so sorry about Rachel.'

'I didn't think I'd see you again. Least of all here.'

Silence. A breeze, birdsong between us. Who knew where to begin.

So begin nowhere.

'I brought her some flowers. That's all.' I gestured uselessly to the bouquet I'd laid.

'I'm here a lot. So is my wife.' His voice trailed off. 'We bring our watering cans.' He held up a blue tin watering can, water sloshing over its sides. 'Today is the three-month annivers—'

'Yes.'

He knelt down and emptied a jam jar of yellowing water, then refilled it with fresh water from the can. He arranged something, pulled something else out of the ground, going about his business as if I wasn't there, as if stopping was dangerous.

'Sorry,' I said.

'I heard you the first time.'

He placed the watering can by the side of the grave and looked up.

I saw then in sharp relief how much of himself he had already lost to grief. His hair hung in strips and the lines on his face, once clear and singular, now seemed bent and multiplied. He was thinner and smaller, hunched into himself as if he were now decades younger and yet to grow into himself, an old man but one made in the outline of a boy who, knees grazed, still called for his mother.

'And how's life with you, Cath? Back at work yet?'

'I won't go back.' I stifled a cough, buying time perhaps. 'Going to start something new.'

'And how is your daughter?'

'She's fine, Richard.'

But I did not tell him that in two weekends' time we would have a party with cake and streamers to celebrate her first birthday.

'My daughter was dying. You didn't call. I called you every day for the month after she died.'

'I didn't think it was right for us to keep in touch. It was time for us to stop.'

'Why?'

Because he had put my daughter's life in danger.

Because his daughter's dying wish had been to have her family back.

'I stopped having feelings for you,' I said. 'I wanted it to be over.'

'I fucking *loved* you,' he said. He kicked a small mound of earth as if he were kicking down a door. A kind of stamping. 'I was prepared to give up everything for you and you disappeared, like a cunt.'

I realized then that he hated me. Or at least I was somewhere he might safely pour his anger. That was fine. I could live a life knowing that he hated me, knowing that the line had been drawn. It was not about me. It had never been about me. I was free. But I had to know.

'Why didn't you tell me how unwell she was?' I said.

He looked confused by the question, as if it had never occurred to him.

'From the way you talked about her, it sounded like she was doing quite well,' I continued.

'She was.' He turned away. 'Then things changed.' He started to cry and soon his shoulders rose and fell. 'You have no idea.'

'Hey.' A woman approached from behind Richard and laid her hand on his arm. 'I changed my mind,' she said quietly. 'Didn't want to be alone.'

I hadn't noticed her approaching, this middle-aged woman in a bright purple sweatshirt with pink and yellow go faster stripes down the arms, black tracksuit bottoms and oxblood Doc Martens boots.

'This is my wife, Nancy,' said Richard, blankly; news that, at another time, would have caused wide and panic-stricken eyes. 'I changed the water,' he said to her.

'My name is Cath.'

'She's the one I told you about,' said Richard. Like a pistol fired inside me, adrenalin. Released into the blood. Racing fast. Cold in my veins. Whispering *Get out of there*.

As she stepped around the headstone, I saw that Nancy was pregnant. She saw me see.

She held her bump proudly. 'Barely five months gone. When I was pregnant with Rachel I didn't show until I was six months. Do you remember that, Richard?'

Richard nodded.

'Congratulations.' Reedy words – wind blowing through the hollow of a tree.

'I had a seven-week viability scan done. That kind of thing didn't exist when I was pregnant with Rachel. Anyway, I took the result to her at the hospital a few days before she died. So she knew about her sibling. Just.' She swallowed and her eyes narrowed with the need to hold back tears. Something. 'I was pleased she knew. She looked so happy about it. Didn't she, Rich?'

Richard nodded again but I could not see the shapes his face made as it was looking elsewhere now.

'Did you . . .' I trailed off. You can't ask a stranger that kind of question.

'No, go on.'

'I wondered if the baby has . . . If you already know.'

'Will she have CF? Yes. We got tested at three months. It's positive. She'll be born with CF. Richard's told me all about you,' she said.

'Nancy, let's go home,' Richard said, like home was the ending.

I wiped at my brow as if I was sweating but I was shivering cold.

'I like your scarf,' she said to me. I felt for the green mohair scarf around my neck. 'Such a nice colour. You have one that colour, don't you Richard?' I felt it again and thought: Is it his? I thought it was mine. I panicked, couldn't think who it belonged to.

'I like your tracksuit top,' I said – to sidetrack or delay. I wondered if she could see what was new in me or whether she thought I was the kind of person who always looked twisted and fraught and guilty.

'It's my daughter's. I've been wearing her clothes since she died. They smell of her. Did you know my daughter?'

'No.'

'She was the loveliest kid. We were very close.'

I looked at Richard, who was looking at his feet.

'Cath has a daughter with CF,' said Richard.

'Diagnosis made me crazy,' said Nancy, every part of her focused on me again. 'You too, huh?'

I nodded.

'Let's go home.' Richard was stepping on the spot, agitated.

'I can't stop eating McDonald's cheeseburgers at the moment,' she said. 'But it's not a craving, it's not for the baby. It's what Rachel liked to eat. We wanted her to put on weight, so I used to buy them for her, four or five at a time.'

'I should go,' I said.

Richard looked at me, I looked at him and my eyes flicked to Nancy who was still looking at me.

'One thing before you go,' she said. She stepped over to me, brushed a stray hair behind my ear, and hit me as hard as she could with the back of a hand, fingers circled with diamond rings.

For a moment there wasn't any pain, so I thought I'd got away with not feeling anything. Then the stirring agony began – something split and cold and dripping at my cheek, blood welling between my teeth on one side of my face – and I realized I had not escaped it. That it was like everything: the real pain comes later.

'Leave us alone,' said Richard to the damp ground, his voice hoarse. 'For God's sake, leave our family in peace now. Nancy, let's go. I don't want you getting upset. You need to rest.'

Nancy turned away from me abruptly, linking her arm with her husband's, and led him away.

I wiped at my face with the back of my hand, felt the wet gape of a cut that was sticky with blood and would need stitches.

I think I held my breath until I was sure they had gone.

I would scar and that scar would remind me daily that I was still alive and that Mia was still alive.

And the sun shone and the birds sang, and summer was just around the corner.

EPILOGUE

She is the reason I am here.

Sitting in this white room on a rattan chair. A cream canvas sofa stretching out opposite, an unopened box of tissues patterned in peppermint green perching on its arm. The floorboards are painted white so that the grain and nails are visible and there are no rugs. There are no curtains at the windows but there is a skylight so I always know the weather.

Richard's child will have just celebrated her third birthday.

Early on, I heard from one of the fundraising managers at the charity that things had started rockily with Richard's child having part of her bowel removed soon after birth. Maybe things didn't get any less rocky because by the looks of his Facebook page, and I don't check it often, Richard lives in an ex-pat part of Portugal with a woman called Susanna. I hope he finds what he's looking for in the sun.

And as for Nancy, at home with her child? There isn't a day goes by when I don't want to call her and find out how she is and how it was with Rachel and a husband who removed himself. I like to think that, in another time and place, we might have been friends.

It has been two hours since I said goodbye to Mia as I dropped her at school for her second week of reception class.

I kissed her head, handed the teaching assistant a fresh water bottle and her day's medication. Then I kissed her again and picked her up, held her tight: *Stay safe*, I whispered in her ear and she giggled as she does every morning, because my words so close to her ear tickle her. Then she wriggled out of my arms and ran towards the classroom and her friends and the toy trucks and the sugar-paper and pens and the lessons about how to be in the world.

She is living her life and she has no idea how hard that can be.

Dave smiled at me this morning, as I dropped off Mia's overnight bag and medications. He takes her on Wednesdays, Saturdays and Sundays. Weekends are family times and I don't like to invade my friends who are busy with their children and their trips to the zoo and the seaside, so I've found new things to do with my time, like walking and watching films. I would never have known I had a passion for old screwball comedies had I not spent so much time watching TV. I like to look at the positive side.

I've thought about joining some clubs because sometimes forty-eight hours can pass without me talking to anyone other than a supermarket cashier and that's a different kind of loneliness to the one I felt at home with Dave. It's not something I had been expecting – that kind of airless, soundless state that is anaesthetizing and yet painful as hell.

Sometimes there is no positive, sometimes I just get through the day.

But Dave smiled at me this morning. It was a start, a thaw, after months and months of polite and muted exchanges. Even if the smile wasn't a forgiveness, it was still a smile. He asked me if I wanted to come in for coffee and I said yes but I couldn't stay long because it was my first day. Two years of training was over and now it was time.

Good for you, he said, and I could tell that he was proud.

Then I stepped into his apartment and before I'd made it to the kitchen he said that I should know, before I heard it from anyone else, that he had been on a few dates with a friend of Jane's. Ruth was her name. So I smiled, because he had been generous with me. *Good for you*, I said. I asked him if it was the same Ruth who owned a knitting shop and he said it was. And I said I knew who he meant because I'd met her at a few birthday parties with all his old college friends, all those years ago, and that she had always seemed nice.

She looks like me.

I turned to go and he said: *Good luck for today.* That it was so positive for something to be rising from the ashes. That maybe things will work out the way they were supposed to.

My mother is the reason I am here.

I went to her, a few months after what happened in the graveyard, and said that I needed to talk to her. She opened her mouth to speak but I stopped her.

'Please,' I said. 'I need you to listen to me. Not as your daughter, not as Dad's daughter or Caroline's sister. Not as a wife or a mother. I need you to listen to me as a person. Please, can you do that for me?'

She nodded, and so I sat down opposite her, in her living room. 'I need to confess,' I said.

She looked a bit shocked because she obviously didn't know what was coming and Mum doesn't do well with surprises. I could tell she was finding it hard not to say anything.

'I need to confess,' I said again. 'Which may come as a surprise. Because I've always been so dismissive of your religion.' I paused. 'You know I don't believe there's anyone or anything up there so I don't need God's forgiveness – or yours, for that matter. So I suppose what I mean is that I need to tell someone. You . . .'

I couldn't tell whether she was pleased or terrified so I carried on. Get it over with.

'I slept with another man,' I said. 'A man that wasn't

Dave. More than once, while we were still married.'

She looked at me and didn't say anything. But she didn't look surprised either.

When she still hadn't said anything after a few minutes I said, 'Mum, did you hear what I said? I was unfaithful. I was in shock. After diagnosis. It was terrible . . . I don't know, like I was trying to find my bearings after an explosion. There was a lot of blame. Like this huge atomic cloud of blame settled on us both, and it never went. It just kept getting thicker and thicker and harder to see each other.'

Mum nodded and said, 'Well.' Which was what she always said before telling me her opinion.

Don't tell me what I am. I know what I am.

'Before you say anything,' I said. 'I don't think it came out of thin air. Even before the other man, I wondered what life would have been like had Dave and I not married. And then later, sometimes I wondered what would have happened if I'd married a man with different genes.'

Mum intertwined her fingers and looked down. 'Wondering how things might have been, and regret . . . They are two different things.'

'Yes,' I said. 'And I love Mia. I wouldn't change her for anything.' I broke off. 'But those early months . . . Loving your daughter isn't always the same as knowing how to be with her.'

Mum looked up, and smiled gently. 'Go on,' she said.

'So in my shock and mess . . . I destroyed something

special and that wasn't mine. I . . . I . . .' Mum smiled again, gentler still. 'The damage I caused felt criminal.' She sat back then, her face pale as milk, and it was all she could do not to panic because the way I spoke made it sound like I had taken life.

I hadn't.

But I had.

'Not that, Mum . . .' I said. 'What I mean is that it feels as if my actions are as irreversible as murder.' I started to cry. 'I regret it all. I regret it in my bones.'

She held out her hand quickly, and I took it. Then she threw her arms around me, as if taking my hand would never have been enough, as if she were welcoming me back after a long time away.

'I wish I could have protected you from it all,' she said.

And I believed her.

I robbed a dying girl of her peace. I blighted the last of her days.

And how do you atone for that?

Rachel is the reason I am here.

In my white room I hear a clock tick and I can see a patch on the wall that the paintbrush missed. The paint fumes have rested like smog in me and I am nervous because I have never done this before.

The doorbell goes and even though I am expecting it, my heart jumps like it's going the wrong way. My heart has done the same thing for more than three years: like it's still vibrating from the shock waves of Rachel's visit.

I open the door and a woman nods a hello before walking across the floorboards to the sofa. She sits with her legs uncrossed, staring down at her shoes – and for a few moments we sit in silence.

When she looks up I see her skin is anaemic white and the shadows under her eyes are tinged dark green. She hasn't tried to hide any of it with make-up because she is living in an airless place deep inside herself and she could care less about anything on the surface. She has brushed back her thick hair into a ponytail and tied it with a childish scrunchie. Her eyes are puffy and it will be a few sessions before I know whether that's how her eyes are, or if it's because she has spent the night crying.

She smiles then because she thinks she has to. It does not matter to me whether I am put at my ease because this is about her, not me. I will get chance enough to talk through anything I find difficult with my clinical supervisor.

She tells me her name although it is already written on the first page of my notebook. And I ask her why she is here although I already know, because we have spoken on the phone. It's how things are done.

She lost her baby at full term. Her much-wanted girl died in her womb before she even had chance to breathe in the world.

I let the silence rest and then I tell her that she has taken a good step, a strong step, in coming here today.

She tells me she is here because she is afraid she can't carry on. And then her voice cracks and I have to breathe deeply, I have to breathe through these hard bits, like I have been taught. And as I breathe out, I let my fingers brush the trace of the faint scar only I know is there, high on my cheekbone, hidden by make-up.

I see where she is. I know the crude shape of its walls and borders.

It's all right, I tell her. We have time.

And there, in the white room, as clouds reshape and gather in the skylight, I can smell the flowers and oil of Rachel's dark head pressed into mine.

ACKNOWLEDGEMENTS

Thank you to everyone at HarperCollins and in particular my editor, Martha Ashby, whose editorial comments are so insightful they double-up as life advice and end up plastered to my study wall.

Thank you to my very brilliant agent Veronique Baxter and to Laura West, Alice Howe and everyone at David Higham Associates.

And to St John Donald at United Agents for his work on the film and TV side, and for his support over many years.

I continue to be inspired and awe-struck by friends and colleagues working in the NHS. My family have come to rely on their advice and support sometimes daily. Huge thanks to the consultants and care team at The Royal London Hospital in Whitechapel and in particular specialist CF nurses Jacqui Cowlard, Cath Lambert and Sarah Williams who have given their time and expertise so generously. Any inaccuracies are mine alone.

Thanks also to dear friends Sam Spedding, Catherine Cafferkey and Mariana Turner who have all shared their knowledge with such passion in the fields of psychology, oncology and general practice.

I've been lucky to work with several people at The Cystic Fibrosis Trust and I salute the dedication they bring to both their daily work and the crucial battles ahead to save thousands of lives.

Thank you to all those who gave such valuable feedback on early drafts: City University Novel Studio class of 2015/16 and tutors Kirsten Hawkins and Emily Midorikawa. Extra special thanks must go to Emma Claire Sweeney for her ongoing encouragement over many years, and to course director Emily Pedder whose notes pushed my thinking into another realm.

Heartfelt thanks to Mum and Dad and my sister Louise for their unerring encouragement, whose absolute belief kept me looking forwards in moments of darkness. And to Kate and John whose positivity and support I feel blessed to have in my life.

And to Melissa, lifelong best friend, without whom there would be no words on the page because anything worth writing about has always been discussed with her first over wine and tears and laughter.

And finally, love and thanks to my three boys. Tom, Jack and Griffin. You are everything to me.

Fern
Britton
Picks

Exclusively for
TESCO

EXCLUSIVE ADDITIONAL CONTENT
Includes an author Q&A and details
of how to get involved in *Fern's Picks*

Dear Readers,

Hannah Begbie's unputdownable debut novel, *Mother*, opens with a parent's worst nightmare: after twenty-five perfect days with their much-wanted baby, Cath and Dave's daughter is diagnosed with a deadly, life-limiting illness. The shock of this tears them apart – Dave wants to keep calm and carry on but Cath is determined to find a cure – but the path she pursues turns out to be more dangerous than she could have imagined. Although this book deals with such a heartbreaking, serious issue, Hannah's brilliant, sharp writing stops you from even thinking about putting it down. It's a pacy, page-turning thriller, a story about the lengths we go to in order to save the ones we love, and the many identities that women carry within themselves: daughter, sister, wife, mother, friend, lover…

When I first read this, I was gripped by Cath's story from the very first page and as I navigated the choppy waters of domestic tension and the highs and lows of motherly love, I can only hope you find this brilliant novel as thrilling and as emotional as I did.

with love
Fern x

Q&A with Hannah Begbie

What inspired you to write *Mother*?

My youngest son was diagnosed with cystic fibrosis when he was five weeks old. I felt both overwhelmed with the sheer amount of stuff we'd have to do to keep him halfway healthy, and also frightened of the risks to his health that I now saw in the world around me. I felt like my job as a mother, to sustain and nurture life, had been impossibly compromised. There was guilt and pain, but there was also a new baby that I loved wholeheartedly. My response to these complex feelings was to write: I began creating characters and situations that allowed me to explore some of the possibilities that lay before me. Really, I think I was trying to come to terms with how to love while living with an acute fear of loss.

I was also interested in how mothers of chronically ill children are often seen as 'saintly', seeming to put aside *all* of their own needs in favour of supporting their child – a kind of Platonic ideal of motherhood, where nothing but the child is central. But can this imperative to protect and nurture really trump all other considerations? What happens to these women's desires and dreams, their complexity, their rage, their doubt?

Mother **deals with some intensely raw emotional depths as Cath negotiates a life-changing illness which affects her new baby. With the bare bones of the medical plot based on your own personal experience, how did you find the process of writing this novel?**

Some of the medical plot was indeed drawn from our experience of having a child diagnosed with cystic fibrosis, but I reconstituted all of it through Cath's eyes. Her background and character created a very different set of responses to the situation than those that I had experienced. Writing the novel was a complicated and sometimes unsettling process. As I wrote I was both removing myself from the pain of my own reality by inhabiting a character and yet diving into other dark and painful places. So it was a bruising process but I feel like the upside was getting to a raw truthfulness in Cath.

Was *Mother* the first book you wrote? Have you always written?

From the age of eight, my parents gave me a diary to write in every year and it's the most valuable present I've ever had. Writing every day allowed me to access an inner voice that gave me the confidence to build other voices. But I approached writing fiction very gradually. I used to be an agent (representing comedians and screenwriters) and one thing I always told my clients was: don't send out work until it's ready, because you never get a second shot at that first impression. I had embarked on early drafts for other ideas, but *Mother* was the first time I felt compelled to see an idea through to completion. It was a story I urgently wanted to tell. I couldn't have put it aside.

Cath is a very layered character and, on the surface, she makes some choices that seem incomprehensible from an outsider's perspective. How did you find her motivation when writing and how did you balance the need to explain her actions? Do you think it was important to make her likeable at all or was it more important to show her from all angles?

I didn't worry about making Cath likeable. I wanted to explore her truth. For me, one of the absolute joys of writing a character in the first person is that you get to explore your character's beliefs, their background, their thought processes and delusions – and the process of doing that naturally creates empathy, even when your character is thinking or doing things that you might recoil from. Cath is making decisions from a place of real pain, exhaustion and grief. I tried to fully inhabit those feelings and to suspend any judgement I might have felt for her.

The television rights for *Mother* have been bought by the multi-award winning production company, Clerkenwell Films. Will you be involved in its adaptation to screen? And is there anyone you've pictured in the roles for Cath, Dave and Richard?

My husband is an experienced screenwriter and he will be adapting *Mother* for television. I'm sure we'll discuss the issues over tea and gin at home, and I might even be at the odd meeting, but when it comes to television adaptations, he is the expert. I can't wait to see what he comes up with.

As for the casting, I've lived with those characters in my head for so long that I find it almost impossible to imagine them in another form. There are so many great actors working at the moment that I'd be thrilled to be a part of the audience, watching someone give their take on who Cath or Richard or Dave is beneath the surface.

What do you want readers to take away from *Mother*?

My greatest hope is that the book might inspire a conversation about how complex our entwining identities as mothers and fathers, partners, friends and lovers are. I think sometimes we are unforgiving of our failures, and of the failures we perceive in others. So I hope that the book generates a little more empathy. Some of my most-treasured moments as a reader have been when a story made me feel that I'm not alone in my questions. I'd love it if something I have written offered a reader that same comfort.

What are you working on next?

My next novel places another female protagonist in the heart of a terrible dilemma, one that forces her to consider the limits of what we owe strangers, and also how the small, personal moral choices that we make can sometimes profoundly shape the wider society we live in. I'm very excited about it.

Questions for your book club

- What do you think you would have done in Cath's place? How do you think you would have reacted to such terrible news?

- Cath says 'I was her mother. I had given her life. I was her mother. I had given her a death sentence.' What do you think of the way Cath takes on the guilt and responsibility for Mia's illness?

- One of the strongest themes in this book is identity and specifically, the identities that women carry with them: daughter, sister, woman, wife, mother, lover... Do you think one identity should take precedence over the others? Why?

- How does the novel deal with the idea of illness and psychological trauma?

- Do you judge Cath for the decisions she makes?

- What role do you feel Dave plays in the novel? Do you think he is to blame for anything that unfolds? Do you judge Dave or Cath more?

- This novels looks closely at the lengths a person would go to to save their loved ones. Can you think of anything you wouldn't do in a similar situation?

- The issue of parents making decisions on behalf of their children is very much discussed in the current climate. Where do you think the law should draw the line?

- Is Richard accountable for what happens over the course of the novel? What was your opinion of him by the end of the book?

- What do you think the future holds for Cath, Dave, Richard and Mia?

Our next
book club title

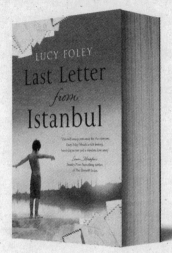

ISTANBUL, 1921

Before the Occupation, Nur's city was a tapestry of treasures:
the Grand Bazaar alive with colour, trinkets and spices;
beautiful saffron sunsets and the sweet fragrance of the
fig trees dancing on the summer breeze . . .

Now the shadow of war hangs over the city, and Nur lives for
the protection of a young boy with a terrible secret. As she
weaves through the streets, carrying the embroideries that
have become her livelihood, she avoids the gazes of the
Allied soldiers. Survival is everything.

When Nur chances upon George Monroe, a medical
officer in the British Army, it is easy to hate him. Yet the
lines between enemy and friend grow fainter.

She and the boy would both be at risk. Nur knows that she
cannot afford to fall – impossibly and dangerously – in love . . .